M000158790

Praise for the ~~~~~ ~~ ~~~~

The Apple Diary

Hill has always been known for captivating storylines and well-developed characters, so it should surprise no one that *The Apple Diary* is an enchanting, heartwarming story that will leave one wanting more. Readers will appreciate her intriguing storyline and immersive story world.

-Women Using Words

Hunter's Revenge

Hill brings it all together for Tori in book five of this series in ways only a skilled storyteller can. Readers will no doubt appreciate the depth she brings to Hunter's story. *Hunter's Revenge* is a first-rate piece of storytelling and I guarantee Hunter fans will not be disappointed.

-Women Using Words

As always, Hill does a fantastic job of weaving the reader through a multi-layered path into a beautiful meadow of a perfectly told story.

-Denise J., *NetGalley*

Such a great ending to one of this genre's most beloved series.

-Patricia B., *NetGalley*

I could wax on and on about this novel, but I won't. If you've yet to read this series, crack on with it now. It is brilliant.

-Natalie T., *NetGalley*

Timber Falls

Gerri Hill is the only lesfic writer I can think of who can write absolutely any genre, and consistently produce top-quality work. Romance, mystery, paranormal…Timber Falls is no exception.

-Karen C., *NetGalley*

I would say this is a typical Hill novel but only if you understand 'typical' to mean an outstanding story, intriguing characters, beautiful settings, and unparalleled writing.

-Della B., *NetGalley*

This book may well be the best book Gerri Hill has written in years. It has everything needed to keep her readers reading into the wee hours of the morning…

-Abbott F., *NetGalley*

The Great Charade

One of the big loves I had for this book, among other things, was it is so full of rich dialogue.

-Carol C., *NetGalley*

The Great Charade really is a heartwarming, romantic holiday book that I'm really glad I was able to read this season.

-Betty H., *NetGalley*

…this was a perfect Christmas book. Not only does it nail the Christmas theme, but the premise is also engaging from the very first page… I absolutely adored this Christmas novel and it's definitely one of my favourites from Gerri Hill.

-Natalie T., *NetGalley*

Red Tide at Heron Bay

Ms. Hill has certainly done it again. I was hooked from the beginning to the end. This is a murder, mystery, romance with loveable main characters who are fully developed and has great chemistry... You can actually picture yourself in the setting watching the story unfold. This is now one of my favorite books.

-Bonnie A., *NetGalley*

This is exactly why Gerri Hill is a master in suspense and crime and romance books! Sooo good! This book was a brilliant slow burn in both ways, the romance and the crime.

-Stephanie D., *NetGalley*

Another brilliant gripping crime thriller from Gerri Hill, couldn't put it down and read in one sitting!

-Claire E., *NetGalley*

Gerri Hill writes wonderful mysteries, and this is no exception. I know I'm reading something special when I can't put a book down.

-*The Lesbian Review*

The Stars at Night

The Stars at Night is a beautiful mountain romance that will transport you to a paradise. It's a story of self-discovery, family, and rural living. This romance was a budding romance that snuck-up and on two unsuspecting women who found themselves falling in love under the stars...It's a feel-good slow-burn romance that will make your heart melt.

-*Les Rêveur*

Hill is such a strong writer. She's able to move the plot along through the characters' dialogue and actions like a true boss. It's a masterclass in showing, not telling. The story unfolds at a languid pace which mirrors life in a small, mountain town, and her descriptions of the environment bring the world of the book alive.

-*The Lesbian Review*

Gillette Park

…is a phenomenal book! I wish I could give this more than five stars. Yes, there is a paranormal element, and a love story, and conflict, and danger. And it's all worth it. Thank you, Gerri Hill, for writing a brilliant masterpiece!

-Carolyn M., *NetGalley*

This book was just what I was hoping for and wickedly entertaining…
If you are a Hill fan, grab this.

-*Lex Kent's Reviews*

Gerri Hill has written another action-packed thriller. The writing is excellent and the characters engaging. Wow!

-Jenna F., *NetGalley*

JONES

GERRI HILL

Other Bella Books by Gerri Hill

About the Author

Gerri Hill has forty-four published works, including the 2022 GCLS winner *The Great Charade* and the 2021 GCLS winner *Gillette Park*, the 2020 GCLS winner *After the Summer Rain*, the 2019 winner *The Neighbor*, the 2017 GCLS winner *Paradox Valley*, 2014 GCLS winner *The Midnight Moon*, 2011, 2012 and 2013 winners *Devil's Rock*, *Hell's Highway* and *Snow Falls*, as well as the 2013 Lambda finalist *At Seventeen*. Gerri lives in south-central Texas, only a few hours from the Gulf Coast, a place that has inspired many of her books. With her partner, Diane, they share their life with two Australian shepherds—Rylee and Mason—and a couple of furry felines. For more, visit her website at gerrihill.com.

Copyright © 2024 by Gerri Hill

Bella Books, Inc.
P.O. Box 10543
Tallahassee, FL 32302

All rights reserved. No part of this book may be reproduced or transmitted in any form or by any means, electronic or mechanical, including photocopying, without permission in writing from the publisher.

This is a work of fiction. Names, characters, businesses, places, events and incidents are either the products of the author's imagination or used in a fictitious manner. Any resemblance to actual persons, living or dead, or actual events is purely coincidental. The publisher does not have any control over and does not assume any responsibility for author or third-party websites or their content.

First Edition - 2024

Editor: Medora MacDougall
Cover Designer: Kayla Mancuso

ISBN: 978-1-64247-598-2

PUBLISHER'S NOTE

The scanning, uploading, and distribution of this book via the Internet or via any other means without the permission of the publisher is illegal and punishable by law. Please purchase only authorized print or electronic editions, and do not participate in or encourage electronic piracy of copyrighted materials.Your support of the author's rights is appreciated.

JONES

GERRI HILL

BELLA BOOKS

2024

CHAPTER ONE

"Remember that time we stole your dad's Suburban and drove it all the way to Galveston to meet up with Ricky and the guys?"

Laughter filled the room and glasses clanked together in celebration. This was the third tequila shot, if she was counting correctly. "How could I forget? I got grounded for two months," Nina said before knocking back the shot.

Amy laughed nearly hysterically. "And you were the only one who didn't like boys and you were scared to tell us!"

"Like we didn't already know," Jones teased. "Your infatuation with Misty Greller gave it away."

They were sitting on the floor in her hotel room. Some were leaning against the bed, others against the lone sofa. Smiles lit every face and Nina looked at each of them, these lifelong friends of hers.

They'd all grown up in Sugar Land, back before it had been swallowed up by Houston. They'd gone through grade school, middle school, and high school—all still fast friends.

They'd made a pact when they'd graduated and before they went their separate ways for college. They'd get together for a long weekend each summer, just the girls. In the last fifteen years, they hadn't missed a single summer. Through marriages and childbirth, they still managed to find a weekend where they could all get together.

At first, they would make the rounds. Amy lived in Dallas, so they gathered there one summer. Jones used to live in Austin, and they'd gone there a couple of times. Now, though, since Jones had moved to the Corpus area too, Nina—the only one single and childless—made the plans and reservations and booked them at a beach hotel here on the island each summer.

"If we have any more tequila, I won't be able to stumble down for dinner," Beth warned.

"Me too. I promised Jeff I wouldn't drink too much this year. God, last year I was hung over for a week," Tammy complained.

"Don't be such lightweights," Jones said as she leaned over to pour more tequila into Beth's glass. "You should hang out with my friend Ingrid. She can knock back tequila like nobody's business."

"Who is Ingrid?" Tammy asked.

"Ingrid Cloudcroft." Jones smiled in a coy, yet silly grin. "She's very naughty. And very fun."

"Naughty?"

She laughed. "She does things even *I* wouldn't dare do."

"Wow! That's saying a lot," Beth teased her. She handed her shot glass back to Jones. "I can't drink this. Seriously, I'll fall down."

Nina watched in amazement as Jones knocked it back, then held her glass up in the air triumphantly. "To Ingrid! May I have as much fun as you tonight!"

Nina smiled back at her as did the others. Yeah, Jones appeared to be having fun. And whoever Ingrid Cloudcroft was, she apparently was the life of the party.

"Let's walk down the beach to Pelican's Bar and Grill," Amy suggested. "Do they still have that massive seafood platter like last year?"

Nina nodded. "I think so." She got to her feet, then helped Beth to hers. "Didn't we say last year that we weren't going to do tequila shots anymore?"

Jones held up the bottle and laughed. "I did not agree to that. This is my elixir, as you know."

Nina waited patiently as the other women all primped and reapplied lipstick until they deemed themselves presentable for dinner. Tequila giggles followed them into the elevator and, as usual, she felt like the mother hen as she tried to quiet them down when they hit the lobby.

Sheri, who now lived in Scottsdale, linked arms with her as they crossed the dunes on the boardwalk. "Why haven't you ever married? You're the best looking one out of all of us."

Nina rolled her eyes. No, *Sheri* was the best looking one and she knew it. "Just lucky I guess."

"What about that woman you'd been dating? Allison or something?"

Nina sighed. "That didn't work out. We broke up right after our girls' trip last year."

Jones came up beside her and took her other arm. "I think we need to set you up with someone. Someone wild and fun, like my Ingrid. Why don't we go to a bar after dinner?"

"Yes! Let's do!" Amy chimed in. "I haven't been dancing in ages."

"Last night didn't count?"

"Did we dance?" Amy asked and they all laughed.

Nina shook her head. Maybe she was getting too old for this. While she did enjoy seeing them each year, she didn't necessarily enjoy the wild partying that the others insisted on. Of course, they were all married with kids. This was their only time to shirk their responsibilities and let their hair down. It wasn't their fault that she seemed to be the only one who had outgrown these long weekends.

"Let's go to that disco place again," Tammy suggested. "That was fun last night."

"Okay. I'm game," Sheri said.

"Me, too," Amy and Jones said together.

Nina looked over at Beth. "Okay with you?"

"Sure. Even though you all know I have no rhythm and can't dance worth a damn!"

Nina kept the sigh that was threatening inside. She would rather be at her own house watching TV. Good god, when had she gotten to be so boring?

CHAPTER TWO

Quinn strummed her guitar, eyes closed. She liked to pretend that she knew how to play but the truth was, she pretty much sucked at it. She opened her eyes and smiled. Yeah. She was a lot of years removed from that young girl who thought she could sing and would someday become famous.

She reached for her drink—an herbal tea blend with a lime wedge—and sat back in the rocker. Her parents gave her piano lessons instead of guitar. Her piano teacher had been a big fan of the classics. To say she had not excelled was an understatement. After she begged her mother repeatedly to stop the lessons, her wish was granted three years later when her teacher—an old grump of a woman—finally retired.

She laid the guitar flat on her thighs and leaned her head back, resting against the back of the rocker. She could hear the surf. There was no moon, the clouds having obscured it earlier. Maybe they would get rain. God knew they needed it.

She felt Willie stir beside her, and she automatically dropped her hand into the dog's fur, rubbing lightly behind her ears. "Good girl," she whispered, getting a quick wag of the tail against the deck.

She was feeling reflective tonight, and she rocked slowly, letting in snippets of her life. She'd been a rather brash teenager, sneaking into bars with a fake ID. She couldn't believe she'd never been busted, especially since the police chief way back then had been friends with her dad.

She'd been a partier in college too—hitting the bars and picking up women. It had been too easy. She knew just how to play the game. It's a wonder she even graduated. College was one big party. And a lot of sex.

Then she blinked one day, and she was in her thirties—and alone. Time to settle down, her sisters had said. And that inner voice she rarely listened to was urging her to do the same. Slow down and settle down.

She stood up and went to the deck railing and leaned her elbows on it. Willie immediately got up and came beside her, resting against her leg. The Gulf breeze touched her face, and she tried to push her next thoughts away, the ones that normally followed when she was reflecting on her life. The ones that questioned everything about her past.

Christie. She'd settled down with Christie. She'd moved her into the small house she owned near the university campus in Corpus. She stopped going to the bars, stopped hanging out with her rowdy friends. She was going to try to make it work with Christie. Of course, she quickly found out that most of her friendships had been trivial and based solely on the bar atmosphere. Her friends said she was no longer fun. Her friends said she was a downer. Her friends disappeared.

Yeah, she'd had lousy friends back then. That didn't mean she didn't miss them. At first. But she had Christie. Christie loved her. Or so she said. Quinn had said the words back to her a couple of times, sure. Six months in, though, she knew the words rang hollow. She stuck it out for another five months, then realized she was making them both miserable. She called things off one night at dinner and suffered through Christie's tears while she packed some of her clothes. A week later, she came by with some friends to collect the rest of her things. Quinn hadn't known what to say to her, so she'd faded to the background as they packed. Christie left without a single word to her, and Quinn hadn't heard from her since.

Amazingly, most of her time with Christie was a blur, but that night she still remembered vividly. She had picked up a rotisserie chicken for their dinner and Christie had made scalloped potatoes from a box. She remembered they had added extra cheese to it because Christie had bought the wrong box of potato mix. And over dinner, while Christie was telling her about her day, Quinn hadn't listened to a word she was saying because she'd been trying to decide how to break the news to her. She'd simply blurted it right out, interrupting Christie. They'd stared at each other for the longest. "*Are you serious?*" Christie had asked. Quinn had taken a few seconds to contemplate the question. Before she could answer, tears had filled Christie's eyes and when she felt no emotion on seeing them, she knew she was sure of her answer. "*Yes.*"

She'd been thirty-five when Christie left, and she knew she was at a crossroads. She could go back to her old life and party a few more years away. But she wasn't happy in her personal life, and she was no longer happy with her career. She was in the proverbial rut, and she knew her only escape was to change things up. So, she sold her house near campus and bought this old beach house on Mustang Island. She quit her job in Corpus and transferred to the Port Aransas Police Department. She started hitting the gym—occasionally. She got a dog. And she made a few new friends, but really, most of her downtime was spent with her family. She had a large family with hordes of nieces and nephews. She was content. Actually, on most days, she'd say she was even happy.

She smiled and nodded into the darkness, recognizing the irony of that. Here it was, a Friday night—nearly midnight— and as usual, she was home alone. And, she reminded herself, she'd been going less and less to the gym. She couldn't even remember the last time she'd been. She went back to her chair and sat again, moving the guitar onto her lap once more. Willie came back to her side, and she smiled at the dog. Yeah, it was a Friday night, but no, she wasn't alone.

She'd just picked up her tea glass when her phone rang. She shifted on the chair and pulled it from her pocket.

"Yeah, Quinn here."

"Quinn, it's me, Fields. Got a situation on the beach."

She sat up straighter. "A situation?"

"Someone found a body."

Her eyes widened. "Like a *dead* body?"

"Yeah. Down the boardwalk from G.T.'s. Lots of blood, so not a drowning. I'm on my way there now."

She stood, hurrying into the house. "I'll be there in five minutes, Sarge."

CHAPTER THREE

"Where's Jones?" Amy shook her head and pointed to her ears, indicating she couldn't hear for the loud music. Nina leaned closer. "Jones? I haven't seen her in a while."

Amy waved her nearly empty margarita glass in the air. "She was dancing with some guy. Like three songs in a row."

Nina spotted Sheri and Beth leaning against a pillar, both of them holding margarita glasses as well. She went over and was engulfed in a tight hug from Sheri.

"You're the best, Nina. We can always count on you to get us back safely."

"Speaking of that. Where's Jones?"

"Jonesy?" Sheri hiccupped then laughed. "She's being naughty, I think."

Nina looked to Beth, hoping she wasn't quite as drunk. "Have you seen her?"

Beth pointed toward the entrance. "She left with some guy."

"Left?"

Beth shrugged. "She said she and Josh were having problems and she needed to get laid." Then she laughed. "Well, she actually said fucked, but I thought I'd clean it up for you."

That, of course, caused Sheri to double over in laughter. Nina pointed at them. "You two stay here. Amy is over there with Tammy."

"Where are you going?"

"To see if I can find Jones."

She didn't know why this responsibility always fell to her. Why was she the one who had to remain sober to take care of them? When had that started?

The place was crowded, and she practically had to shove her way out the door. A few couples stood outside talking, others walking to and from the parking lot. She looked for the mass of long blond hair that Jones was famous for. They were a little more than a block from the beach. Surely she wouldn't have gone out there with some guy she just met. No. Knowing Jones, she would have gone to his room instead. Or maybe hers. Wasn't it three summers ago that she'd ditched them for some guy? Poor Josh. He had no clue.

She was about to go back inside when her gaze was drawn down the dark street that ended at the dunes. With a sigh, she headed in that direction. *If she's there making out with some stranger, I'll kill her*, she thought.

The boardwalk to the dunes was lit only by a rather dim torch. Thankfully, the clouds seemed to have thinned, letting through a little moonlight. It was no longer pitch-black out there. The walkway dumped into the beach, and she stood still, a smile forming as she listened to the sound of the waves. She walked out a little way, then turned to the right. She hadn't taken ten or twelve steps when she heard a high-pitched scream down the beach behind her.

She turned, seeing two people standing at the edge of the dunes, pointing at something. She could see one of them fumbling with their phone. She ran in that direction, her heart beating nervously in her chest. She saw the spray of blond hair before she saw the body. She stopped up short, her eyes wide.

"Oh, dear god." She fell to her knees in the sand, reaching out a hand to touch her shoulder. "*Jones?*" Her breath lodged in her throat. "No. *No.*"

CHAPTER FOUR

Quinn trudged through the sand, still not believing that there was a dead body on the beach. Sure, when the population of the island swelled during the summer months, they had their share of assaults and drunken fights. And they had rape to deal with too on occasion. Especially during the Spring Break weeks. But murder? No. Not here on Mustang Island.

"Hey, Quinn…over here," Officer John Ramos called from behind the yellow crime scene tape that was draped along the dunes. "Shorts? Damn, maybe I should join Beach Patrol."

"Yeah, my job is pretty sweet."

She paused before ducking under the tape, seeing a crowd gathered up above the boardwalk. Yes, a murder was big news on the island. Of course, it was late May. Most of those gathered were probably tourists, not locals. She pulled the latex gloves from her shorts pocket and slipped them on. "What we got, John?"

"Victim is Sharon Downey, age thirty-two." He glanced at the small notepad he held. "From Corpus. Was staying here on the island for the weekend with some out-of-town friends."

Quinn squatted down, moving the long blond hair away from the victim's face. Blood covered her neck and torso. She appeared to have been stabbed multiple times. "Witnesses?"

"No. The guy who called it in, he and his wife were just taking a beach stroll. Found her right here."

The wound at the neck was violent, leaving a gaping hole in her throat. She flashed her light around the area where the body lay. Lots of blood. She was killed right there. Multiple footprints were in the sand, including hers. She glanced up and down the beach, noting the darkness in both directions. Easy for someone to have done this and disappeared into the night.

"The last time we had a murder, I wasn't even on the force yet," John said. "It was 2010 or something, I think. That businessman washed up on shore with a bullet hole in his head."

Yes. She knew the one. The infamous unsolved murder that they all still talked about.

"Of course, with you in Corpus, I'm sure you've worked your share."

"I have. And they're not much fun. Why do you think I joined Beach Patrol?"

"Oh, so it wasn't just because you can wear shorts to work and ogle pretty girls in bikinis?"

"That too." Quinn picked up the victim's hands, hoping to see evidence that she'd fought her attacker. There was none. "Got her last whereabouts?"

"Yeah. She was at G.T.'s up there. Left with some guy."

"Okay. Who else is here?"

"Probably the whole damn force. Silva is up at the boardwalk, trying to keep bystanders away. And Sergeant Fields is on his way."

"You talk to these friends of hers? Husband?"

"Girls' weekend only. No husbands with them. But yeah, I talked to one of them." He looked at his notepad. "Christina Evans. Pretty shook up. She saw the body."

She raised her eyebrows questioningly.

"She was out looking for her. Said the victim disappeared from the club. Silva took her back up with him."

She nodded. "Okay. I'll find her. What about the others in their group?"

"Yeah, I don't know," he said with a shrug. "I've been down here by the body."

She pulled her gloves off. "Okay. Let's see what we got."

She took the short trail through the dunes before it hit the boardwalk. The crowd gathered at the end of the street was subdued, most talking in quiet voices. She saw Silva holding his hands out, keeping them back. Beyond that, she could hear the pulsing music coming from the club—Good Time Disco. She could see the flashing lights on the neon sign. *G.T. Disco.* Those lights blended in perfectly with the lights of the four or five police cruisers that were parked along the curb. She spotted Sergeant Fields hurrying down the street and she motioned to him.

Officer Silva turned to her when she approached. "Quinn, where'd we run you from? Have a hot date?"

"Yeah, right," she murmured. "Me and my dog. Where is Christina Evans?"

"She's over there." He pointed. "That's the group that the victim was with." Then he addressed Fields as he walked up. "Hey, Sarge."

Fields nodded briskly at him but turned his attention to her. "Quinn? Is it true? Murdered?"

"Yes, sir. Multiple stab wounds."

"Dumped?"

"No, sir. She was killed there."

"Damn," he said as he rubbed a hand across the hair that he kept in a short crewcut. "Okay. The ME from Corpus should be here soon. Do we want to bring lights down there?"

"I think so. The area where she is, it's already been trampled, but we might get some shoe prints, either coming or going. Of course, after the ME and his guys get through, maybe not."

"Do we have a witness?"

"No. I'm about to speak to her friends. They were all at G.T.'s. And I'll pull their security footage too. See if we can ID this guy she walked out with it."

"Okay. Go ahead, Quinn. I'll wait for the ME."

She walked around the crowd to the side where five women were huddled together, arms around one another.

"I'm Detective Stewart," she said, holding up her shield. "Christina Evans?"

"Me."

A dark-haired woman stepped forward and the Gulf breeze blew the short strands around her face. She reached up to brush them away impatiently. The only light there was from the headlights of the police cruisers but even then, Quinn could see tears in her eyes.

"I'm sorry, Ms. Evans," she said automatically. "I understand you saw the victim."

"Yes."

"Did you happen to see who she left the club with?"

She shook her head. "No. But I think it was who she was dancing with. Amy? You saw him?"

"I…I don't know. I mean, he was just a guy. Kinda cute, I guess."

"He had sandy-blond hair," another one said. "I didn't really see his face though."

Another woman simply sunk down to the ground and covered her face with her hands. "Jonesy. I can't believe it. I mean…what the fuck just happened?" Loud sobs broke the night and one of the other women sat down beside her, rocking her in her arms.

Christina Evans stepped between her and the others. "They've been drinking," she said unnecessarily. "Most of the day. So…"

Quinn nodded. "Where are you staying?"

"We're at the Gilmore Hotel."

Quinn nodded again. It was only a few blocks away. "I'll have someone escort you back there. I need to interview you all. Maybe you could get some coffee in them. I'll come by after we're done here."

"Okay, of course."

"What about next of kin? Husband? Family?"

Ms. Evans shook her head. "No. I didn't know what to do. Jones and Beth were best friends. I thought it would be better for her to call Josh."

"Jones?"

"Sharon. We called her Jones."

"I see. And Josh is the husband?"

"Yes."

"And let me guess—Beth is the one sobbing on the ground?"

"Yes."

"Okay, Ms. Evans. Thank you. I'll be by in a few hours. We'll notify the husband. I should have a little more information for him shortly." She motioned to one of the officers standing nearby. "Let me get Officer Boyd to take you to your hotel."

Before she could turn away, a hand on her arm stopped her. "Is it necessary to tell Josh that…well, that she left with some guy? I mean—"

"I understand you want to protect your friend, but yes, her husband will get all the details, however condemning they may be. I'm sorry."

The woman nodded, then turned back to her friends. Quinn watched them for a moment, then walked over to where Boyd was waiting.

"Take them to their hotel, please. The Gilmore. I'll be over to interview them after we're done here."

"Sure, Quinn. You want me to hang out there?"

"I think so. Thanks."

She glanced at the women one more time, finding Christina Evans staring back at her. She gave a slight nod, then headed to the club, which was still blasting music. Seeing how many people were out on the street, she didn't imagine many were still inside dancing.

At the entrance, she held her shield up. "I'm Detective Stewart. I need to see your security footage. Is the manager around?"

"Oh, yes, ma'am. Let me call him."

"Thanks."

She was bumped from behind by two young women, both giggling uncontrollably. They gave her a quick glance, then continued on their way. She had a flashback to herself when she was that age. Barely eighteen—and armed with her fake ID—she made the rounds. In fact, she'd been here a time or two. Of course, back then it was called Surfside, and they claimed to have the coldest beer on the island. From what she remembered, that had been true.

CHAPTER FIVE

Nina wondered if they were all in shock or simply too drunk to comprehend what was happening. They had gathered in Beth and Jones's room. Beth had stopped crying, but she'd said next to nothing since her outburst on the street. She was on her bed now, lying face down. The other bed, the one Jones had used, was empty, as if they were all afraid to go near it. Amy and Sheri were on the sofa. Tammy was on the floor, leaning against Beth's bed. And she stood among them, seemingly the only one not drunk on her ass.

"You should…you should try to sober up. Take a shower or something. That detective said she'd be here in a couple of hours," she said quietly. "I'll order up some coffee."

Tammy looked up at her. "Who is going to call Josh?"

She wrapped her arms around herself. "I guess the police will."

"I should call him," Beth mumbled against her pillow. "Christ, I can't believe she's gone."

"Who the fuck would want to kill her?" Sheri said rather loudly. "I mean, some random guy she just met? Why would he kill her?"

"You hear about this happening all the time," Amy said. "She was at the wrong place, wrong time. Crazy fucking people in this world." Her head rolled to the side. "I think I'm going to throw up."

Nina went to her quickly and pulled her to her feet. "Come on. Bathroom."

They didn't make it to the toilet before Amy's multitude of drinks—and dinner—splashed onto the bathroom floor. She turned away from the sight, feeling her own stomach revolt.

"Jesus Christ, Amy!" Sheri nearly yelled. "That's so gross. You clean that shit up."

"Oh, shut up. I feel like—"

More retching sounds followed, and Nina went to the hotel door. "I'll be right back."

No one acknowledged her and she slipped from the room, heading to her own, which was just down the hallway. Once inside, she went into her bathroom. She stared at herself in the mirror. Her eyes weren't ones she recognized. They seemed almost blank. Emotionless. That was funny, wasn't it? Her emotions seemed to be all over the place, and she felt like she had only a tenuous grip on them.

Jones was dead. Murdered. Their annual, happy, carefree weekend was now ruined for all time. Jones was the fun-loving one. Always had been. Sheri was the next most rambunctious of the group. She and Tammy were the more responsible ones. Amy and Beth were somewhere in between.

She splashed her face with water several times, then lathered soap in her hand and scrubbed her cheeks, her forehead, hoping to rub away the last hour. After she washed the soap off, she leaned on the counter, head held low. She saw her tears fall more than she felt them. She was too numb to feel anything.

She turned away from the mirror and stripped off her clothes. She turned the water on in the shower to almost scalding and stepped in.

* * *

Quinn pointed at the monitor. "There. That's her."

Tony Lawrence, the manager, was a scraggly-looking young man. His hair was long and silky, touching his shoulders, and a full beard and mustache covered his face. A shell necklace circled his neck, and both ears were pierced. His head was bobbing to the music that was still playing in the background.

"Yeah, man. He gets around."

"The guy she's dancing with? You know him?"

"Sure. That's Wayne."

"Wayne got a last name?"

Tony shrugged. "Don't know, man. But he's here all the time. Every weekend for sure."

She twirled her index finger in a circle. "Play some more. I want to see her leave."

After two more dances, Sharon Downey and the man named Wayne were holding hands as they went to the entrance and out of the club. She glanced at the timestamp—11:32.

"Any of your employees might know this guy? Know his last name?"

Tony nodded. "Yeah, man. Sully might know. Come on."

Sully was the bartender, a young woman who looked barely old enough to legally serve alcohol. She gave a bright smile when they approached.

"Yeah, Sully. This is Detective…sorry, man, what was your name again?"

Quinn sighed. "Stewart."

"Yeah, Detective Stewart."

"Is this about that poor woman?" the bartender asked.

Quinn nodded. "Did you serve her?"

"Oh, sure. She had at least three 'ritas. Then Wayne bought her a couple of shots."

"It's Wayne she's interested in. You know his last name?" Tony asked her.

"Wayne?" The woman shook her head. "Wayne didn't kill her. Wayne—"

"Just need his last name," Quinn interrupted.

"It's Hoffmann. Wayne Hoffmann. But—"

"Thanks. He's a local, I'm assuming."

"Yes. Well, he actually lives over in Aransas Pass, but he's here on the island all the time."

"You know his routine? What other clubs he might frequent? What kind of car he drives?"

She shook her head. "I don't know what he drives. I hear him talk about the Mustang Club a bit. But if he's chasing women, he either comes here or to The Lagoon."

She raised her eyebrows. "Does he chase women a lot?"

Sully laughed. "Wayne thinks he's god's gift to women, yeah. He's a big flirt. He's also got a body that most women salivate over. He can pretty much pick and choose who he wants." As if realizing how that sounded, her smile disappeared. "But Wayne would never do this. He's harmless."

She gave a fake smile. "Thank you, Sully." She turned to Tony. "Mr. Lawrence, we're going to need a copy of that security video."

"Sure thing, man."

Silva had the crowd pretty much dispersed by the time she went back outside. The ME's van was parked next to the boardwalk and beyond the circle of lights she could make out the gurney as they pushed it along.

"Quinn? You got anything?" Sergeant Fields met her on the street. "Apparently no one saw a goddamn thing out here."

"Got a name, yeah. Wayne Hoffmann. He lives in Aransas Pass. The security cameras show him dancing with Sharon Downey several times. Got a shot of them leaving the club together at 11:32."

"Let's pick his ass up. Alert Aransas Pass PD."

She glanced at her watch. Three minutes until one. "He's probably still on the island."

"You think he whacks this woman and sticks around? Hell, he probably caught the first ferry back across."

"Maybe. I'm going to head over to The Lagoon. He hangs out there too."

"Okay. Take—" He looked around. "Where the hell is Boyd?"

"He escorted the friends of the victim back to the hotel. He was going to wait there until notified otherwise. I'm going to head over there later to interview them."

"Okay. Take Ramos then."

She saw John Ramos coming up behind the gurney. "I'll let you know if we spot this guy, Sarge."

She jogged over to the ME's van and motioned to Ramos. "John, come on. I need you to take me to The Lagoon. My Jeep is parked a few blocks away."

He nodded. "Roger that. Let's go."

She paused, though, nodding at Dr. Cooledge. "You working the late shift, Randy?"

"Hey, Quinn. How's it going?"

"Well, I was kinda hoping I wouldn't have to ever work a homicide again when I transferred over here."

"Yeah, she was hacked up pretty good. Want me to let you know what I find?"

"If you can."

"Sure. Cell number is the same?"

"Yes. Thanks, Randy."

CHAPTER SIX

Quinn wasn't sure which music grated on her nerves more. The loud pulsing disco or this screeching crap that The Lagoon played. Were there no country music bars on the island anymore?

"What does he look like?" Ramos asked.

"He's about six foot one or two, sandy-blond hair." She scanned the crowd. "Wait here. If he's inside, we don't want to spook him."

She shoved her way through the crowd, her eyes scanning the faces on the dance floor. The perimeter of The Lagoon was bright with blue walls and ceilings. Palm trees were painted in a haphazard pattern on the walls, and a beach scene, complete with sand and water, accented the bottom portion. Inviting, yes. It was a shame the music was so god-awful.

Her gaze was drawn to a young woman dancing with a handsome man. Her hips were gyrating seductively at him. He cupped her, pulling her flush against him as he arched into her. The woman laughed and pulled away. Wayne Hoffmann laughed too and pulled her close once again.

She kept her eyes glued to the couple as she blindly walked among the dancers, getting a few choice words shouted her way. She ignored them.

"Wayne Hoffmann?" she said loudly to be heard over the so-called music.

He turned with a smile. "Yeah?" Then he shook his head. "Sorry. You're a little too old for me."

"As if," she muttered under her breath. She held her shield in front of him. "Police. I need a word with you."

He frowned. "What for?"

"You know Sharon Downey?"

He shook his head. "Doesn't ring a bell."

"You left with her at G.T.'s earlier."

Recognition finally lit his face. "Oh yeah. Was that her name? She just said her name was Jones."

Quinn glanced at the woman who was still dancing. "Find another partner."

Wayne held his hands up. "Hey. What's this about?"

"Let's talk outside."

She grabbed his elbow firmly and led him off the dance floor. At the entrance, he stopped when he saw Ramos.

"What the hell is going on?"

"Outside."

John Ramos was on full alert. One hand on his duty weapon, the other held out as if to grab Wayne Hoffmann if he tried to flee. She led him past the doors and off to the side. She shoved him against the wall of the building.

"Now, tell me about Jones."

He shrugged. "What about her?"

"She's dead. Murdered."

His eyes widened. "Dead?" Then he met her gaze, recognition setting in. "Oh, wait. No. No, no, no. If you think I had something to do with it—no fucking way."

"Got you on the security feed walking out with her. Holding hands. That was at 11:32. About fifteen minutes later, she was found dead on the beach."

He shook his head. "No way. Not me. I left."

"You walked out holding hands and then you left?"

"Yeah. I mean, she was all into me and everything. You should have seen us dancing. I mean, she was *into* me, if you know what I mean."

"So, she changed her mind? You got pissed and—"

"No! That's not what happened. We go outside and start kissing, you know. She was going to take me to her hotel room. She said we'd have a good hour before her friends got there."

"So what happened?"

"I don't know. It was like, one minute she's got her tongue in my mouth and the next she told me to get lost."

"Just like that?"

"No. I mean, she saw someone. I could tell. She was looking behind me. She looked scared. Hell, I thought maybe her husband was there or something. So I split."

"You knew she was married?"

"Oh, yeah. Josh, I think she said." He shrugged. "Wasn't any of my business. I was just out for a good time."

"So, you left there and came here?"

"Yeah."

"What time?"

"Oh, hell, I don't know. Right away. She told me to get lost, so I did. Got in my car and came over here."

Quinn had interviewed her share of potential suspects, and she usually knew when they were lying. In this case, she totally believed Wayne Hoffmann. For one thing, a brutal murder like the one Sharon Downey just experienced—there would be blood. Lots of it. She took both of his hands and held them up, inspecting them. They were clean, his nails perfectly manicured. She dropped them.

"I'll need you to come to the station tomorrow." She glanced at her watch. "Today. Give a statement."

"A statement? It's Saturday."

"Yes, it is. And I need a statement. What you just told me. Let's make it official." She paused. "You're sure you didn't see who spooked her?"

He shook his head. "I didn't turn around." He gave a sheepish smile. "I thought, you know, if it's the husband, I didn't want to get punched in the face."

She sighed. "Yeah, maybe you got lucky." She motioned to the entrance. "Go on."

"Thanks." He paused. "I am sorry about the woman. I mean—"

"Yeah. I want you in the station by nine in the morning. If you don't show up, I'll find you and haul your ass in. Because right now, you're our only person of interest."

"Look, I'm telling you the truth."

"Said every suspect ever."

He smiled at that. "Right. But I didn't do it. And I'll be there *before* nine."

He went back inside, and Ramos came up beside her. "You believe him?"

"Yes."

"I don't know, Quinn. He looked kinda shifty."

She clapped his shoulder as they headed back to his patrol car. "I don't think he's our guy."

CHAPTER SEVEN

Nina sipped on her coffee, watching as the others tried to sober up. They were all in her room now. She'd ordered two carafes of coffee. They had all showered and changed. Tammy had taken Beth with her into her room. Everyone had their own room except Beth and Jones. They always liked to share. It gave them time to catch up, they said.

There was little to no conversation. In fact, it was as if they all felt guilty. No one seemed to be able to meet the others' eyes. Well, she, for one, wasn't going to carry that guilt with her. There was no need to. None of them had done anything wrong.

"Do you want to talk before the detective gets here?"

Amy looked up at her. "What's to talk about?"

She put her coffee cup down. "What happened to Jones wasn't anyone's fault. Not ours, anyway. We were all out for a good time, that's all. Just like every year when we get together."

Beth blew out a breath. "I'm surprised this hasn't happened before."

"What do you mean?"

"We always share a room, so I know what goes on. Last year, she left after we all came in. Didn't make it back to the room until about six that morning. Nearly every year she finds someone to hook up with."

"Really? So, it was like a game to her?" Tammy asked.

"Or were she and Josh really having major problems?" Amy asked.

"The only reason they're having major problems is because Jonesy slept around on him. Not just whenever we get together. But, like, a lot, and he found out," Beth said.

"How in the world did she find time? She has two young kids plus a job," Amy said. "Christ, I only have one kid and it's all I can do to find the energy to have sex with Eric."

"She always had a wild streak," Sheri reminded them. "Remember in high school? She was sleeping with four or five different guys that last spring before graduation."

Beth laughed. "It was actually seven." Then her smile faded. "Shit. I can't believe she got herself killed."

"What do you think happened?" Tammy asked quietly. "That guy she was dancing with. He seemed normal. He didn't look like a deranged killer or anything."

"People are freakin' crazy," Amy said. "You never know nowadays."

A quiet tapping on her door, followed by "Police" signaled the detective's arrival. Detective Stewart had called earlier, saying she was on her way over. Nina went to the door and opened it. The detective stood there along with a uniformed officer. She looked tired, and Nina supposed it had been a long night—and morning—for her too. Nina stepped aside, letting them enter.

"I'm Detective Stewart," the woman said to the group. "This is Officer Ramos." The detective looked at her. "We've reviewed the security footage and identified the guy Sharon left with."

"Jones," Beth corrected. "We haven't called her Sharon since grade school."

"So did you catch the bastard?" Sheri asked bluntly.

The detective ignored that question. "I understand you are all friends, and this was a girls' weekend type of thing."

"We get together every summer," Amy supplied. "Childhood friends."

"Sharon—I'm sorry, Jones—lived in Corpus. What about the rest of you?"

Nina stepped forward. "Amy lives in Dallas. Beth and Tammy live in Houston. Sheri is in Scottsdale, Arizona."

The detective arched an eyebrow. "You?"

"Oh. I live in Corpus too."

"Is this where you normally get together?"

"Nina is the one who usually makes all the reservations so that's why it's down here most years. Plus, Jones lived here too now, so it made sense to meet here," Tammy said.

"Did you call her husband?" Beth asked.

"Yes. Sergeant Fields notified him. I believe he is on his way here." She glanced at her watch. "Probably here by now. I assume you all know him. He'll undoubtedly want to see a friendly face or two."

"Actually, I've only met him one time. At their wedding," Sheri said.

Nina nodded. "Me, too."

"I know Josh," Beth said. "Jones and I...well, our families got together three or four times a year."

Detective Stewart moved farther into the room. "Let's do a rundown of the night. Before you went to the club, where were you?"

"We went to dinner," Nina said. "We walked from here over to Pelican's Bar and Grill."

"Did you meet up with anyone? Any altercations or anything? Feel like someone may have been following you?"

"No. Nothing."

"What about before that?"

"We were here at the hotel."

"Doing tequila shots," Sheri said. "Jones loved her tequila."

"Okay. What about the night before? Were you here then or did you all get to the island yesterday?"

"We all got in Thursday afternoon. And that night was the same," Tammy said. "After dinner, we went out to the club. Good Time Disco. We had such fun, we went again last night."

"Did Jones meet anyone Thursday night? Dance with anyone more than a few times?"

"I don't think so," Beth said. "We all walked back together. I shared a room with her."

"This guy from last night...I interviewed him," Detective Stewart said. "He claims that Sharon—Jones—was going to bring him here to the room. Said that they would have an hour or so before you all got here. Was that unusual for her? Or the norm?"

They all looked at Beth. Beth nodded. "More like the norm," she said quietly.

"You interviewed this guy?" Amy asked. "You got him in jail?"

"No. There's no physical evidence linking him to this murder. Based on his account of things and the timestamps on the security feeds at both places, it would be almost impossible for him to have killed her."

"Both places?"

"After he left G.T.'s, he went over to The Lagoon."

"But they walked out together," Beth said. "Why would he leave?"

Nina noticed there was only a slight hesitation before Detective Stewart spoke. "He said she changed her mind."

Beth laughed. "No. Not Jonesy."

"He said she saw someone she recognized. He thought maybe it was her husband, so he left."

"Josh wouldn't have been on the island. He knows this is our weekend," Beth said. "Besides, he had the kids."

"Could someone have followed her from Corpus? Did she receive any threats that any of you know about?"

Again, they all looked at Beth, who shook her head. "Look, I know Jones was a bit, well, on the promiscuous side, but she didn't have any enemies that I know of. She's married, has two kids, and has a normal job. They live in a nice subdivision— Flour Bluff. Normal."

The detective looked at Nina as if for confirmation. She found herself staring into the detective's blue, blue eyes. She finally blinked, breaking the stare, and nodded.

"How long will you be in town?" the detective asked the group.

"We're supposed to leave Sunday morning, but I, for one, plan to see about getting a flight out today," Amy said.

"Me, too," Sheri echoed.

"I'll stay," Beth said. "Like you said, Josh will probably need a friendly face."

"I'm the only one who drove here," Tammy said. "I may very well pack up now and leave."

Nina sighed. Yes. Their long weekend was shrinking fast. Here it was, after four in the morning on Saturday. They should all be sleeping off their booze and dreaming of brunch and a day on the beach. Instead, Jones was dead and everyone else was jumping ship. She wondered if this would forever put a damper on their friendships. Would this be the last time they got together like this?

"If you would all please give Officer Ramos your full names and contact details, then you're free to go." The detective glanced at her. "May I have a word, Ms. Evans?"

Nina nodded, wondering if she was in some sort of trouble. She got even more nervous when the detective went out into the hallway and closed the door on the others. They stood staring at each other. Nina took in the detective's very short hair, the almost brilliant blue eyes, and the tiny scar above her right eyebrow. How did she get it? Did she fall off her bike when she was young? Fall out of a tree? Had someone hit her? The detective cleared her throat and Nina came back to the present.

"You seem to be the spokesperson for the group."

"Do I?"

"Are you not?"

Nina sighed. "I'm…I'm the responsible one. This weekend is always their chance to get away from their husbands and kids and have some adult fun."

"You don't have that same opportunity?"

"I don't have a husband and kids. That's why I'm usually the one to organize the weekend."

"This is an annual thing?"

"Yes. We all grew up together. Went our separate ways after high school, but we've kept in touch. This is the only time we see each other. Well, other than Beth and Jones. Like she said, their families were friends."

"Beth lives where again?"

"Houston."

"And you can't think of any oddity this weekend? Was Jones acting strange? Different?"

Nina was about to say no. Jones was Jones. But she *was* different, wasn't she?

"Jones was always the life of the party. Especially when we were younger. We're over thirty now, so that has tempered a bit. Yet this weekend, she was back to her old self. Drinking way more than she should. She brought a bottle of tequila and insisted on shots before dinner. She had three margaritas with dinner. At the club, she had more."

"Yes. Three, I believe. Then the guy she was dancing with bought her some shots. I'm surprised she was able to walk."

"She's had years of practice." She waved her hand in the air. "But Jones seemed distracted. Like she was overcompensating and didn't want us to know she was distracted."

"Why do you call her Jones?"

"Maiden name. We've called her Jones since we were kids."

"Okay, makes sense. Distracted how?"

"I don't know. Like she was preoccupied with something."

"Did she make a habit of going out with guys when you got together like this? I believe one of your friends said it was the norm."

"Look, I only see her once a year. I don't know—"

"You only see her once a year, yet you both live in Corpus?"

Nina nodded. "They moved here, oh, three or four years ago now, I guess. But no, we don't see each other."

"Why did they move here?"

"Josh's older brother has a law firm. He made Josh a partner. Downey, Hines, and Downey, I think is the name." She held her hand up. "But I really don't know anything about what her habits are. We simply didn't see each other or even talk on the phone."

"What about here, when you and your friends get together? Was it her habit to pick up guys?"

"Perhaps you should be asking Beth these questions. She always shares a room with her."

Detective Stewart smiled. "Is that a yes?"

Nina blew out her breath. "She wasn't shy about picking up guys, no."

"I see. And what about the rest of you? Is that the purpose of this weekend? Everyone gets away from their husbands and—"

"No! And even if they did, what would that have to do with Jones? I mean—"

"You're right. That has no bearing. I'm simply trying to get a feel for the weekend."

"They're not wild and crazy women. They don't pick up men. They are all happily married." She paused. "Well, Beth did say that Jones and Josh were having some problems. What I'm saying is, they are—"

"Happy, married, normal women. Except for Jones."

"Yes."

"Okay. So, if she told the guy she was trying to pick up for the night to get lost, then what do you think happened to her?"

"Random killing? Wrong place, wrong time?"

The detective studied her. "Could be an explanation. Except for the fact that my guy says she saw someone she recognized and got antsy."

"I can't imagine who she would have recognized."

"Maybe someone followed her here," the detective suggested. "Or simply someone she knew from Corpus."

Nina shrugged. "I don't know. Like I said, I only saw Jones once a year."

Detective Stewart scratched the side of her neck absently. "You get together once a year. You're childhood friends. Do any of you talk during the rest of the year? I know about Beth and Jones. What about the rest of you? What about the others with Jones?"

"No. I don't speak to any of them except during the time we're making arrangements for our long weekend." She nervously waved a hand in the air. "It's weird, I know. And if we hadn't been childhood friends, I doubt any of us would be friends now. We're all so different. Well, Beth and Jones were best friends all throughout school, so there's that. But the rest of us? No. I don't believe any of them talk to each other during the year."

"So why still have these reunions?"

"It's become habit, I guess. We drink and reminisce and laugh, and it *is* a good time. For the most part. Like I said, it gives them all a chance to escape their real lives for a few days."

"For the most part?"

Nina crossed her arms defensively. "Why is this relevant?"

"It's not." Detective Stewart motioned to the door. "Give Officer Ramos your contact information please."

Nina paused. "Do you think it was random?"

"No. Unfortunately, G.T.'s security cameras don't cover the street. We've got footage of them going outside, got footage of them in front of the club. There are security cameras in the parking lot, but Jones and this guy didn't go there. They appeared to be heading up the street, presumably to your hotel."

"And you're *sure* this guy didn't do it?"

"Not positive, no. We'll wait for the ME to give his report. See if there was any DNA evidence left on the...the body. We'll go over all the security footage to see if we can spot someone watching Jones. And we'll interview the husband to see if he might know of any threats his wife may have had. I'm sorry, but there's not a lot to go on. Unless some witness comes forward who may have seen something, that's all we got."

Nina nodded. "I understand."

She went back inside, and the others were all quiet, some still sipping their coffee. She went over to Officer Ramos, giving him her home and office address and her phone number. The detective was leaning in the doorway watching them.

Once the police left, she closed the door with a sigh. She glanced at her watch, seeing that it was a quarter to five. She was exhausted.

"So, she was cute," Sheri said in a singsong voice. "I find really short hair on women to be attractive. Not that I would ever dare cut mine like that. But god, she had killer eyes."

Nina had to agree with that statement, but she ignored her and slipped down on the sofa between Amy and Tammy.

"Incredible eyes. Jonesy would say she was just your type," Beth chimed in.

Nina held her hand up. "We've had a very emotional, traumatic event happen to us. Let's don't try to set me up, huh?"

Amy patted her thigh. "I guess I shouldn't tell you that Jones was chatting up that woman at the reception desk, hoping to entice her to have dinner with us."

"Oh my god! The one with the blue hair? She's probably not even twenty-one yet."

Tammy sighed. "We're getting older, aren't we."

"Yes, we are," Amy agreed.

"These weekends just won't be the same without Jones," Sheri said.

"If we ever get together again, I'd rather it not be down here." Tammy looked at her quickly. "No offense, Nina."

"I agree with Sheri," Beth said. "It won't be the same without Jonesy." Beth's voice cracked. "I can't believe she's gone."

Nina's gaze traveled across her childhood friends, feeling certain that she'd never see any of them again. And as she'd told Detective Stewart, they never spoke on the phone. Was this the turning point? Was this going to be the catalyst that broke up their group?

"I think I'm going to pack up and head home," Tammy said. "I think I want to be with my family tonight."

"Me, too," Amy said. "If I can't get a flight to Dallas today, I'll rent a car and drive. I can't stay here." She glanced over at her. "Sorry, Nina."

"I completely understand. I don't really want to hang around either."

"You all go on," Beth said. "I'll wait for Josh."

Everyone seemed to move at once and Nina got up too. There were long, tight hugs between all of them, and she wondered if they were thinking the same as her. That this would be one of the last times they saw each other.

CHAPTER EIGHT

"No," Quinn mumbled as Willie licked her face. "Go back to sleep."

Another lick and Quinn opened her eyes. Bright afternoon sunlight filled the bedroom. With a groan, she rolled over and reached for her phone. It was 4:23, and with a sigh, she sat up. Willie crawled onto her lap and flipped upside down, exposing her belly. Quinn automatically scratched it.

"Spoiled."

She fluffed the pillows and leaned back, her hand still rubbing against Willie's stomach. She was getting too old to pull all-nighters. She yawned and closed her eyes, knowing it wouldn't take much to fall back asleep. But if she did, she wouldn't sleep worth a damn during the night.

"You hungry?"

Willie didn't budge. Quinn smiled at her, then let her thoughts drift back over the previous night. She wasn't sure what to make of Josh Downey. Maybe he was in shock. Maybe he handled grief differently, but he didn't seem as distraught as she would have imagined him to be. Of course, by the time she'd interviewed him, he'd had time to absorb the news. Then again, maybe anger overrode his grief.

They had let him watch the video of his wife dancing with Wayne Hoffmann in the hopes that he might recognize someone in the crowd, the same someone who Sharon had recognized. But as she watched him watch the security feed, his eyes never strayed from his wife. No, he didn't think Sharon had had any threats. No, she didn't have enemies that he knew of. No, she hadn't been acting strange lately. And no, he had no idea who could have killed his wife.

Daylight on the beach had offered no clues. There were far too many footprints to attempt to sort them out. A broad search in all directions did not turn up a murder weapon. It had been low tide when Jones had been killed. The killer could have very well walked to the surf and flung the knife into the Gulf. If so, it was already buried in sand as the tide came back in.

Wayne Hoffmann had shown up at ten minutes to nine, looking fresh and alert. No doubt he had gone home last night and slept like a baby. He'd given his statement and even offered to take a lie detector test if they wanted. She had sent him on his way.

Now, there was nothing to do but wait for the ME's report. While toxicology would take a few weeks, she wasn't really interested in that. By all accounts, Sharon Jones Downey should have been drunk on her ass. Yet on the security feed she appeared to be perfectly sober, no clumsy steps in her gait at all. She'd been stabbed numerous times, including a violent wound to the neck. What she hoped was that the killer had cut himself in the process and his blood would be mixed with hers. Or maybe he had left behind some fibers, some transfer evidence.

Or maybe they would have nothing. Maybe this new murder would join the other one, the one of the businessman who had washed up on shore, half his head blown off. Maybe they would now have two unsolved murders in the tiny town of Port Aransas.

She closed her eyes and sighed. Not so tiny, really. The local population was barely three thousand souls. But beach houses and condos filled the island, most all of them rentals. With the numerous hotels along the beach, the summer and holiday population rose to twenty thousand most summer weekends. Even then, the crowds who came here weren't rowdy. Well, not counting the few weeks of Spring Break, that is. But most of the time, it was just families out for a good time. Most staying for a week of fun, some renting a place for a month or even the whole summer. It was a mostly peaceful, friendly crowd that made her job easy. The Beach Patrol Unit featured her and the three officers she'd handpicked to fill out her team. They patrolled the beaches between Port Aransas to the state park boundary, nearly six miles. For the most part, it was a relaxing job that bordered on boring—checking vehicles for beach parking passes, trying to curb underage drinking, making sure dogs were leashed, and mostly just being a presence out there. The three officers alternated shifts, and each had two days off a week. During the busy Spring Break weeks, she and her team were usually out from dawn to dusk daily. Nighttime patrol was done by the other units. Her team was responsible for daytime hours only. It was a cushy job to be sure, and it certainly beat a murder investigation. But "detective" was the other hat she wore and right now, the murder of Sharon Jones Downey took priority over beach duty.

CHAPTER NINE

Nina leaned back in her chair, staring out her office window to the pair of oak trees at the back near the fence. They were large enough to keep the yard shaded on hot summer days. When she had started her business, she ran it out of her house, but that soon lost its appeal. She felt like she could never escape the job and was on duty all the time. When her business had taken off, she bought this place and transformed it into her headquarters.

Amazing how her little venture turned into a successful business and career for her. She'd started out doing the work herself—cleaning newly built homes and getting them ready for the new owners to move in. She had had exactly one client, and she worked her ass off. She now had four teams with four members on each, and most of the major builders in Corpus were now clients.

This fixer-upper of a house, located in an older neighborhood near Lexington Park, was used mostly to store their inventory. She'd converted two of the bedrooms into offices, one for herself and one for Lisa, her assistant. She had turned the open kitchen area into a lounge. The third bedroom now had multiple shelves lining all four walls and housed the various cleaning supplies they needed.

In the last three years, she even built up enough capital to purchase four new vans, complete with advertising on each side. That had brought in more clients, and she'd branched out into regular housecleaning duties, serving some of the most expensive neighborhoods in Corpus.

She stood up and went to the window, absently noting that the grass needed to be mowed. That was one chore she hadn't outsourced. While she had a yard service at her home, she enjoyed tending to it here. The yard, both in front and in back, was rather small, and it didn't take much effort to mow it. She'd even put in some flowers around the back patio. When the weather was nice, her teams used it to eat breakfast before going out on their assignments.

She supplied a meal each morning, often either she or Lisa—her part-time assistant—picking it up on their way in. Sometimes, but not often, she would cook it here for them. Nothing too fancy. Scrambled eggs and pan sausage. Breakfast tacos. Sometimes fruit and yogurt to go with it. Not this morning, though. No. This Monday morning she was still feeling a little out of it. She'd stopped at Whataburger and picked up assorted breakfast sandwiches and taquitos for the crew. No one seemed to notice that she'd been overly quiet. Lisa had their schedules printed out and placed in their trays by eight-thirty each morning. After breakfast, everyone gathered their supplies and headed out in the vans. She wouldn't see them again until they returned, usually about three o'clock. By then, she would already have their next day's schedules set and she'd take off too, leaving that for Lisa to print out and distribute the next morning. She'd lock up and head to the home she now owned on the north side of Oso Bay, a mere five-minute drive from the office.

She purchased it after she and Allison split. It was a newer home and she'd done nothing more than have the walls painted. The previous owners had apparently been into dark colors, and she'd positively hated the scheme they'd used. It was almost enough to make her not buy it, but she'd fallen in love with the backyard and the view of the bay. She had grand plans for it, but so far all she'd done was have a large deck built onto the existing porch. She wanted an outdoor cooking area, but she'd not gotten around to that project. Maybe during the winter months when she didn't use her deck as much. Yeah. Maybe she'd start it then. For now, she made do with the gas grill.

She turned from the window and went back to her desk. God, what a gloomy Monday it was. She'd been in such a funk, she'd even skipped her morning beach walk—a rarity for her. Beth had called her yesterday. She'd come here to Corpus and stayed with Josh overnight on Saturday. From what Beth had learned from the police, they had absolutely no suspects in Jones's murder. What she'd said about Josh, though, troubled her.

"He alternated between being a total zombie, to crying, to acting like nothing at all had happened. And then when he told me about Jones cheating on him, he got angry and basically just bashed her."

"So maybe their marriage was already falling apart. And now he finds out his wife was taking another man to her hotel room. Can you blame him?"

"Oh, I know. And then he told me that he'd caught her not even a month ago with someone. He said he was planning to file for divorce and for custody of the kids."

"Oh, wow. Well, you knew her better than anyone. Why was she cheating on Josh in the first place?"

"She told me she didn't love him anymore and wasn't happy. Wasn't fulfilled. From what I gathered, she'd had three or four affairs this last year alone. Josh, of course, doesn't know about the others, and I certainly didn't tell him."

Nina shook her head. Jones had everything. A handsome, successful husband. A good job in her own right. Two beautiful kids. And a huge, expensive house with an elaborate swimming pool. She supposed the old saying was true. Money couldn't buy you happiness.

Her office phone rang, chasing away her thoughts of Jones. She reached for it with a sigh, but she heard Lisa pick up from the office across the hall. "Bayside Cleaning. How may I help you?" She sighed again, then moved to her desk, telling herself she needed to snap out of this.

Whatever *this* was.

CHAPTER TEN

Quinn and Willie ran along the beach, heading south, away from her beach house and toward the state park. She still couldn't believe she'd taken up jogging. At first, it was only a walk and a slow one at that. She had never been a runner. After she'd moved here and got Willie, it was only natural that they take daily walks. It didn't take long for the walking to evolve into a leisurely jog. As Willie grew, their pace increased. Still, it wasn't anything to brag about. Three miles on a good day but normally only a mile out and then a mile back.

Dawn was fully upon them, but the sun was still below the horizon. Didn't matter. There were clouds blocking any sunrise views. The beach was still fairly empty except for the constant cries of the gulls and terns as they started their day. She kept an eye on the dunes. Sometimes, if she was lucky, she'd catch a coyote or two making their way to their daytime hiding place. No coyotes this morning, but a very lovely heron stood high on a perch, the breeze rustling its feathers. Far up ahead on the beach she could see someone walking. Whether toward her or away, she couldn't tell from this distance. Other than that, she'd only passed a man and woman out early for shell hunting.

It was three weeks now since the murder of Sharon Jones Downey. The newness of it had worn off around town, but it was still talked about at the station. Jones had been wearing one of those fitness trackers. They had been able to download the information and were able to tell exactly when it stopped registering a pulse. It went dead at 11:46 p.m., exactly fourteen minutes after Sharon Downey and Wayne Hoffmann had left the club together. Luckily for Wayne, the timestamp at The Lagoon showed him entering there at 11:52. The Lagoon was a good fifteen minutes away, so there was no way he could have committed the murder and gotten there in six minutes. Not that she thought he had, even though Sergeant Fields continued to suspect him.

Other than that, they had nothing. No stray fibers, no unusual bruising. No witness had come forward. Toxicology had been interesting. Besides the alcohol, she also had cocaine in her system. Quinn wondered if the others in her group knew that. Or her husband. That, too, was strange. She hadn't heard a word from Josh Downey since he'd given her the feed from his home's security cameras. It was like he'd washed his hands of the whole thing and wasn't concerned if his wife's murderer was brought to justice or not.

And that, of course, led her to suspect that perhaps *he* had been the killer. Of course, the security camera said otherwise. And a quick track of his cell phone showed it at his home address up until the time Sergeant Fields had called him. His statement to her had been that he'd stayed home with their two young children while his wife took off for the weekend. His security camera and phone corroborated that.

Considering that they had no leads—or evidence— whatsoever, there would probably be no conviction in the case. No. Sharon Jones Downey would most likely go down in the Port A police annals as Murder Mystery Number Two, a crime never to be solved.

She was tiring and so was Willie, so she slowed her jog, finally stopping and bending over to catch her breath. They were close enough to the mile-and-a-half mark to claim it, she thought. Willie immediately went into the surf and lay down, letting the waves wash over her long, golden coat. It would be a wet, sandy mess by the time they got back home. Quinn took the water bottle from her waist belt and took a drink. The dog came over then, looking at her expectantly. She cupped her hand and poured some in for her, letting her lap it up.

She glanced up, seeing a woman walking toward them along the surf. She didn't seem to be paying them any attention, but nonetheless, Quinn dutifully clipped the leash on Willie's collar. She was a cop. She should at least obey the leash laws she tried to enforce.

She was about to turn around and head back when the woman stopped walking. Quinn met her gaze, recognition setting in.

"Detective Stewart," the woman greeted.

Quinn nodded. "Good morning, Ms. Evans."

"Nina," she corrected.

Christina "Nina" Evans came toward her, reaching down to touch Willie's head. How could she not? The dog was practically dancing beside her, her tail wagging wildly.

"Willie," Quinn introduced.

"He's beautiful."

"She."

Nina raised her eyebrows. "Why Willie then?"

"Actually, her name is Willow. Somewhere along the way, it became Willie."

Nina smiled at her, then sighed. "I don't suppose there's any news."

"No. Nothing. I'm sorry." She turned and started walking back toward her house.

Nina fell into step beside her. "I've seen you out here before. Well, I mostly recognize Willie."

"Yes." She pointed up ahead. "I have a beach house about halfway between here and the Port A beaches."

"A beach house? Must be nice."

"It's old. One of the original ones." She raised her eyebrows and smiled. "You've seen me and Willie, but I haven't seen you out here before. I'm sure I would have remembered." She smiled broader. "My hobby."

"Your hobby?"

"Watching beautiful women. I'm on Beach Patrol so I see my share."

Nina stared at her. "Are you flirting with me?"

Quinn laughed. "I must be horrible at it if you have to ask."

Nina continued to stare at her. "I guess I haven't been flirted with in a while."

"No?"

"No. And I usually take my walks on Padre Island—the Seashore. I have a yearly pass there. I come here to the state park a couple of times a week, though, just for something different." She hesitated, looking out into the Gulf before speaking. "Have you talked to anyone?"

"You mean your group? No. I interviewed the husband. Beth was there waiting for him, but I didn't speak to her."

"I haven't heard from anyone. Well, Beth called me that Sunday, but nothing since then. I mean, other than the funeral. They were all there, but it was quite subdued, and everyone left right away."

"Beth and Jones were best friends, you said. How was she when she called?"

"Still upset. And questioning Josh's reactions."

Quinn nodded. "Yes. He didn't seem too distraught, if that's a good word to use." She shrugged. "Maybe he was in shock."

"Yes. Probably."

They were quiet as they walked in the wet sand, just out of reach of the racing waves. They were both barefoot and Willie walked between them, her tongue hanging out as she smiled.

"You didn't know him?"

"Josh?" Nina shook her head. "No. I only met him the one time at their wedding."

"And how well did you still know Jones?"

Nina smiled at her. "Is this part of your investigation or a genuine question?"

Quinn smiled too. "Both."

Nina sighed. "Jones had changed a lot. Yet, sometimes, not at all. In high school, she had quite a reputation and not in a good way. She used to say she was sleeping her way through the senior class. I have no idea how she was in college. Probably the same." She bent down to pick up a shell. "Despite her wild side, she was very smart and studious."

"Did you all see each other in college? I mean, like this. Grab a weekend here and there."

"Yes. Not everyone made it the first couple of years, but we got together. After college is when it became a little easier to organize a weekend where we could all make it."

"So, she changed?" Quinn prompted.

"Yes. Her friends in 'real life,'" she said, making quotations in the air, "were very different than us. Not to mention Josh came from a wealthy family. We all grew up in an older, middle-class neighborhood in Sugar Land. That was suddenly beneath her, and she shunned her family. Pretended they didn't exist, I think."

"She became better than the rest of you?"

Nina laughed. "She *thought* she was. I think that's because no one else bragged about their own life as much as Jones did. Sheri owns a very successful real estate company in Scottsdale. So successful, in fact, that she's opening an office in Tucson. Tammy owns three childcare centers in Houston. Amy works in the tech industry and is in a management position. Beth is the only one who doesn't work. Stay-at-home mom with three kids."

Quinn raised an eyebrow. "You failed to list your own accolades."

Nina waved a hand dismissively. "I have a small business in Corpus. But my point was, Jones put herself on this pedestal and none of us ever tried to knock her down."

"Why not?"

Nina again waved her hand in the air. "When we were in middle school, Jonesy's father got sick and could no longer work. Her mother had never had a job—was always a housewife. They were living on his disability and barely making ends meet." She shook her head. "No. They *weren't* making ends meet. They became a charity case for their church and received food stamps. Jones was embarrassed by it and compensated by sleeping with any willing boy in school, of which there were plenty."

"So, you all let her elevate herself above the rest of you now?"

"Something like that, I guess. But the last couple of years, it was like she'd reverted back to that old person she used to be. Not as haughty. She let her hair down." She shrugged. "And apparently she'd been having affairs behind Josh's back."

"Really? I guess he didn't know, huh?"

Nina glanced at her. "Beth told me that Josh had caught her not even a month before she died. Said he was going to file for divorce."

Quinn kept her comment to herself. She'd asked Josh Downey point-blank if his wife had been sleeping with anyone and he'd said not that he was aware of.

"Did she know that? I mean about the divorce?"

"I don't know. Beth didn't say."

She stopped walking, surprised that they'd made it almost to her house. Willie knew where they were and was tugging on the leash. Quinn unsnapped it from the collar.

"I live up there. The blue one." Then she smiled. "The shabby blue one. Not the fancy one two past it."

Nina laughed. "It doesn't look so shabby. And you have decent space between your neighbors. I bought a house on Oso Bay last year where the homes are crammed together like sardines. And I'm not quite sure my view is worth the close neighbors."

Quinn hesitated, her head tilted. "You want to come up for coffee?"

Nina seemed to hesitate too, then she shook her head. "I better get back. But thanks."

"Sure. Well, maybe I'll see you around."

Nina nodded, then turned to go. But she stopped and looked back at her. "Are there...well, any leads? Any investigation?" She held a hand up. "I'm sorry. I guess you can't divulge stuff like that."

No, normally not. But—

"There's not much, to be honest. I went through all of her social media accounts, but it was all pretty tame. Mostly just family and kids' stuff. No red flags. Josh offered me nothing, so I had no idea about her affair or the impending divorce." She shrugged. "No evidence at the scene. That's where we stand."

Nina nodded. "I understand."

"If I broached the subject of the affair with Josh, do you think he'd cooperate? Perhaps give us the name of the guy? Maybe it was a friend of theirs or something."

"Oh, I have no idea."

"Sure. Okay. Well, enjoy your walk."

"Thanks, Detective."

"It's Quinn."

Nina nodded, then rubbed Willie's head a few times before heading back down the beach. Quinn stood there watching her, feeling Willie leaning against her leg. She reached down to ruffle her head much like Nina had just done, then trudged through the sand up to her house. At the bottom of the stairs, she looked back. Nina was bending down, picking up another shell, no doubt. The wind blew her dark hair around her face and Nina tried to tame it before walking on. For some reason, that brought a smile to her face.

"She's cute," she murmured to Willie.

CHAPTER ELEVEN

Nina took her time walking back to her car. It was too pleasant a morning to rush, and it was Lisa's turn to pick up breakfast for the crew. She was in no hurry. She did think it a little odd that she had run into Detective Stewart—Quinn. She had seen the woman and dog running before but had paid them no mind. Now that she'd seen her up close again—and those dazzling blue eyes—she was reminded of how attractive the detective was. The shorts and skimpy tank top only added to the allure.

She normally took the S.P.I.D.—South Padre Island Drive—across the causeway to Padre Island and over to Whitecap Beach or even farther down at Malaquite Beach if she had the time. On other days she would cross Packery Channel to Mustang Island and park by the jetty and walk from there. Today, however, she'd driven farther north on Mustang to Newport Pass and parked on the beach by the wooden posts—bollards—that were used to prevent vehicles from driving on that section of beach. It was a nice, long walk to the state park, and she seldom ventured very far past it. She rarely had the time. Today, though, she'd started out earlier than usual and hadn't been concerned with the clock. Her staff usually got there around eight-thirty and by nine were heading out on their assignments. Lisa could handle things if she was late.

Before she ran into Quinn and Willie, she'd been mindlessly walking, her head still filled with thoughts of Jones and the others. They had hardly talked at all at the funeral. There had been tears and there had been tight hugs, but they hadn't talked. She'd picked up the phone a handful of times to call Beth, but she'd convinced herself that if Beth had something to share, she would have called. And since she hadn't heard anything from the police, she figured she wasn't needed for anything there. Apparently, their investigation had turned up nothing.

She did wonder why Josh hadn't told Detective Stewart about Jones's affair. She also wondered if Josh knew about the three or four others that Beth had mentioned. Beth didn't seem to think so. My god, she still couldn't believe that Jones was dead. Couldn't believe that she'd seen her like that, lying on the beach.

Yes, that was what haunted her the most and what she couldn't seem to get out of her mind—the image of Jones lying up against the dunes, her beautiful blond hair caked with blood and sand, her eyes open and staring up at her in a silent plea for help.

She shook her head as she ran back along the beach, trying to chase Jones from her mind. Her vision was blurred by tears, and she stumbled in the sand. She stopped running, walking instead into the surf. She turned her face toward the Gulf, letting the breeze dry her tears.

She needed to snap out of this. Maybe she would call Beth after all. Maybe Beth was having a hard time too. Of course, Beth had a husband to turn to for comfort. She wrapped her arms around herself and closed her eyes. Was that it? She had no consolation? No support? No one to bare her soul to? Was that why she felt so out of sorts?

She let out a deep breath, then continued toward the small four-wheel-drive SUV that she'd bought specifically for beach driving. She would call Beth this afternoon, she decided. Just to talk. And maybe she'd call the others too and see how they were all getting on.

CHAPTER TWELVE

"What makes you think she was having an affair?"

"Mr. Downey, I mean no disrespect here," Quinn said. "I've spoken to the women your wife was with here in Port Aransas that weekend. All lifelong friends. I believe the consensus was that she'd had an affair and you found out."

"That's what they say?"

"Yes. Now, my question to you is, do you know the man's name? I'd like to interview him."

"Whatever for?"

"We don't think her killing was random. We think she knew her assailant."

"She doesn't have any friends on the island. She wouldn't know anyone there. I told you that already."

Quinn sighed. "I just need his name."

"Fine. It's Patrick Engleton."

Quinn scribbled down the name. "Did you know him?"

"No. She met him at some gym."

"What gym was that?"

"The Island Gym."

She nodded. "That's the one off the S.P.I.D.? The one with the big lighted palm tree?"

"Yes. And she'd been acting very strange for the last several months. More than that—six or eight months. Maybe even longer. So, I got curious."

"You hired a private investigator?"

"I did. A man in my position, I can't afford to let my wife make a mockery of our marriage. I followed her to the gym. Caught them exactly where I was told they'd be."

Quinn tapped her desk with her fingers. "When I asked you, you said you had no knowledge of an affair," she reminded him.

"I was embarrassed, Detective Stewart. Can you blame me? I've given my wife everything. Anything she ever asked for, she got. This is how I get repaid?"

"I'm not judging you or your wife, Mr. Downey. Or your relationship. I'm trying to find her killer. Now, do you know how long this affair was going on?"

"According to him, only a few weeks. She was rather noncommittal. Like she didn't really care that I'd found out."

"A couple of weeks only? And that prompted you to consider divorce?"

There was a long pause before he spoke. "How do you know about that?"

"Like I said, I interviewed her friends."

"Beth, no doubt. She would have been the only one Sharon would have told." She heard him sigh rather loudly. "Yes. As you know, I'm an attorney. I spoke with one of my colleagues to begin divorce proceedings. This affair may have been going on for only a few weeks, but based on her demeanor for, like I said, the last six or eight months, I knew he hadn't been the only one."

"Did you discuss it with her?"

"Divorce? Of course. I caught her having sex with another man," he said loudly. "And yeah, I asked her if there'd been others. She just smiled at me. That was it. That was pretty much our discussion. I moved into one of the spare bedrooms, and we basically didn't talk for the last month. And she didn't seem to care. Even with our children, she had little interaction. It was like she was in her own separate world. One that didn't include me and the kids."

"I'm sorry. I know this is painful for you to talk about. I get it. But I'm trying to cover all the bases."

"I understand. And I'm sorry I wasn't truthful with you. But this guy, Patrick Engleton, he's young. Maybe twenty-one, if that. He almost shit in his pants when I caught them." A humorless laugh followed. "Had he been wearing any, that is. He was just happy to get the hell out of there. I seriously doubt he's your guy."

"Thank you for the information, Mr. Downey. If anything turns up, I'll be sure to let you know."

"Sure. Thanks."

She stared at the phone long after the call ended. Her first assumption appeared to have been correct. Josh Downey didn't seem to care whether they found his wife's killer or not. Apparently, the love in that family had disappeared not only for Sharon Downey, but her husband as well.

CHAPTER THIRTEEN

Nina sat at the bar, still nursing the rum and Coke she'd ordered forty-five minutes ago. The ice had melted, and it was watered down, but she had no interest in another. In fact, she had no interest in even being there.

"You're sure quiet tonight," Jennifer said. "You want to get out of here? We can go to my place and watch a movie or something." Then she grinned and wiggled her eyebrows. "I've got a good bottle of dark rum."

"I'm sorry. I just—" She lifted a hand. "I don't know what's wrong. Long week." That was a lie. She knew exactly what was wrong.

"So? You want to leave?"

Nina reached over and squeezed Jennifer's arm. "I'm not up for it tonight, Jenn. I think I'm going to head home."

The disappointment was evident on Jennifer's face. "I can come with you, keep you company." Then she leaned closer. "Make you breakfast," she said in a near purr.

Casual dating is what she would call what she and Jennifer did and even that was a stretch. They both went out with other women. While she hadn't been interested in sleeping with any of them, she knew that Jennifer did. Jennifer had been up front with her about that. It wasn't an issue and there was no jealousy involved. There was no jealousy because there was no emotional attachment. She never would have thought that she'd end up like this—someone with a fuck buddy.

But after she and Allison had ended things—well over a year now—she'd been in no hurry to jump back into a serious relationship. She'd met Jennifer on the beach one Sunday morning, two weeks before she and Allison officially called it quits. She'd enjoyed Jennifer's company, and she was a distraction from the breakup even though Jennifer hadn't made it a secret she was trying to get her into bed. A month later, she succeeded. Nina had made it clear that she wasn't looking for anything more than that and Jennifer had been agreeable. They'd been seeing each other on and off since then.

It was no longer very enjoyable for her, however, and she'd declined the last few times Jennifer had asked her out. She should have declined this one too. She needed a friend. Someone to talk to. Jennifer wasn't that person. Whenever they got together, it was only for sex. There was little talking between them—before or after bed.

She stood up and pulled some cash from her pocket and placed it on the bar. "There's a cute brunette over there watching you. You should stay."

Jennifer turned to look, then smiled. "Yeah. Maybe I will." She quickly downed the rest of her drink. "See you around, Nina."

"Sure. See you around," she repeated, but Jennifer had already walked away.

She turned and headed to the door. She felt restless, and despite her assertion that she would go home, she really didn't want to. She sat in her car, watching the traffic speed by on the S.P.I.D. She glanced to the north, seeing the lights of the city twinkling over the bay. Instead of turning left and crossing the causeway to head home, she turned right and stayed on Padre Island. A short time later, she turned left to Mustang Island and Port Aransas. She drove past the state park, then took one of the beach access roads to the right. It was fifteen minutes past ten. After what had happened to Jones, she knew she had no business being on the beach alone, not at this hour. But she parked anyway. There was a half-moon, already far in the western sky. Its light reflected off the water and she stared out into the Gulf, listening to the waves as they rippled the moon's glow. The breeze felt nice against her face, and she started walking.

She knew where she was going, she just didn't know why. This section of beach wasn't accessible to vehicles and some of the beach houses that lined the dunes had lights on. Her eyes adjusted to the darkness, and she had no problem seeing. The blue house came into view, but there was no welcoming light on the deck. A Jeep was parked under the stilted beach house, but that didn't necessarily mean Detective Stewart was home. She walked toward the stairs, hearing the soft strumming of a guitar. She stopped and listened. It was quiet and soothing, and she smiled.

Instead of going up the stairs, she sat down on the lower step and leaned against the railing. She closed her eyes, letting the sound of the guitar lull her into a peaceful daze. It was a minute or two before the music stopped, yet she didn't move. She felt too content to move. A voice above startled her, though.

"You gonna come up or stay down there?"

She leaned her head back, seeing Quinn Stewart looking down at her. "How did you know I was here?"

"Security camera. You scared the crap out of me. For a minute there, I thought you were my ex."

Nina stood. "I need to talk. Do you mind?"

"Come on up. Want a drink?"

She was about to decline but nodded. Quinn disappeared then, and she hesitated only a moment before climbing the stairs to the top deck. Despite no porch light, the wall of windows on the deck let out enough light from inside to hide the shadows.

Willie was there to greet her, and she smiled at the exuberant welcome she received.

"Hey, girl," she cooed, rubbing briskly on Willie's head.

"She loves having company."

Nina turned. "She's very sweet."

Quinn was holding two cocktail glasses with a lime wedge on each. She handed one to her before going to sit down. There was no sign of a guitar. Quinn motioned to the other chair. It was only then that she realized they were both old-fashioned rocking chairs.

"I haven't been in a rocker since I last visited my grandmother."

"Yeah, they're nice. Cedar. Handmade." Quinn motioned to the chair again. "Have a seat."

Nina sat down then and leaned back, trying to relax. She took a sip of the drink. Rum. The lime made it unexpectedly crisp and refreshing.

"Nice."

Quinn smiled. "I guessed rum for you." She held her own glass. "I prefer bourbon. Not that I drink much anymore."

Nina nodded. "I hope I'm not intruding."

"Not at all. I was just—" She shrugged. "Relaxing."

"Have you played the guitar long?"

"No. About two years. I'm pretty raw. In fact, I think you're probably the first person who has heard me play."

"It was…soothing. Peaceful," she said, thinking back to how she felt earlier.

Willie was lying next to her chair, her tail wagging against the deck boards. Nina automatically reached down to touch her.

"Is everything okay?"

Nina looked over at Quinn and sighed. "No. I'm having a really hard time with Jones's death. For one thing, I can't get the image of her out of my mind."

"That's right. I forgot you saw her out on the beach."

"Yeah. And it's something that I can't unsee, you know." She sighed. "I don't have anyone to talk to about it."

"Family?"

She shook her head, thinking of the brief conversation with her mother. "I don't have a close relationship with my parents, especially at the moment. And they weren't friends with Jones's parents, so…" She turned to her. "I hope you don't mind that I barged in on you."

"Not at all."

Nina sighed. "I feel like I've lost a part of me…a part of my life." She put the rocker in motion. "I told you that we didn't see each other or talk during the year, but at least I knew they were there. I've known these women my whole life. I don't remember a time when we weren't all friends."

"Who were you closest to?"

"Right now, not anyone more than the others." Nina took another sip of the drink. "Our relationships shifted over the years. When we were kids, Amy and I were close. The older we got, the more we veered apart. Senior year of high school, I was best friends with Tammy. We were both a little more reserved than the others. Tammy had very strict parents and she didn't dare do anything wrong. And I was hiding, trying not to bring attention to myself."

"Because?"

"Because I was gay and was terrified to tell any of them. But the six of us were always together in some form or fashion. Our houses were all within two blocks of each other. Anyway, I feel kinda disoriented now. I don't know why, exactly. I feel like I've probably lost lifelong friends. Forever." She wiped at a tear that leaked out of the corner of her eye. "I needed someone to talk to and, well, there's not anybody."

"Okay," Quinn said easily. "I'll be that person."

"Besides, you've met all these women. You know about—"

"Sure. You don't have to explain."

"Thank you."

Quinn nodded. "Do you really think that's what's going to happen? That you won't see them anymore."

"Yes. And truthfully, when I was around them, I felt like we'd changed so much, all we had left were our childhood memories. Those memories still bound us. But now? I feel a responsibility to keep us together and I don't think I can anymore."

"Why you? Why not the others?"

"Because they all have lives, and I don't." She laughed quietly. "I didn't mean to insinuate that because I don't have a husband and kids I don't have a life. Other than Beth, they all juggle a career, a husband, and kids. I always felt like, if I didn't organize these weekends, who would?"

"When next year comes around, organize another one, see who shows up."

Nina shook her head. "I don't think so." She pushed the chair into a slow rock again. "I spoke with Amy this week. And Beth too. Just to see how they were getting on. Amy is totally over it and basically blames Jones for what happened. And Beth is still grieving, and now she seems to be going through some kind of an identity crisis."

"How so?"

"She said she feels old and frumpy, and she thinks life is passing her by. She doesn't have a job, she's a mother to three kids—the oldest one is eight—and her husband got promoted to regional sales manager at the beginning of the year. Since then, he travels during the week." She glanced over at Quinn. "She said he's been different since his promotion. She only sees him on the weekends, and he's like a stranger to her. To top that off, he hasn't been interested in sex."

"Ah."

"Yeah. So, she's convinced he's got a woman on the side and it's because she's now old and frumpy."

"You're all what? Thirty-two? I certainly wouldn't call that old. But yeah, she did look a little...well, I don't even know if I would say frumpy really. She just looked...kinda normal. Nothing splashy."

"Beth and Jones were the complete opposite, yet the best of friends. Jones was always up on the latest fashion. Always chic. Making up for the hand-me-downs she wore as a kid, I think. And Beth? No." She shook her head and smiled, remembering Beth's drab style. "Beth couldn't care less about what was in style. She's still that way." She pointed at herself—baggy shorts and a simple blouse. "I'm much the same. I dress for comfort, not fashion."

Quinn laughed lightly. "Are you saying you think you're frumpy too? Because I beg to differ."

Nina matched her smile. "No." Then her smile disappeared. "Beth is troubled now, and even though we've always gotten along, I'm not a good sounding board for her. Jones was her person. I can't relate to what she's going through. Apparently, her husband has been home more since the thing with Jones, but she said he's still acting very weird. And she's terrified that he's having an affair and is going to leave her. The opposite of Jones, to hear Beth tell it. When Josh said he was going to file for divorce, it hardly fazed Jones, like she just didn't care one way or the other."

"Right. That's what he told me."

Nina glanced quickly at her. "You called him?"

"Yes. Told him I knew that his wife was having an affair. He finally came clean with me. Gave me the guy's name."

"Oh, wow. He knew who it was?"

"No, he didn't know the guy." Quinn stood up and went to the deck railing. "I shouldn't really be discussing the case with you, you know."

"I'm sorry. Of course."

Quinn remained at the railing, where a beam of moonlight seemed to illuminate her face. She had a rugged attractiveness to her. More handsome than pretty. Her dark hair was cut nearly brutally short. So short that the wind from the Gulf didn't even move it. The style looked sensational on her and even in the darkness, she could imagine her brilliant blue eyes. When they'd met the other day on the beach, she'd tried so hard not to stare at them. Not sky blue, no. More of a crystal blue. When Quinn turned toward her, she found herself looking into those eyes, hoping to catch a glimpse of the color.

"I guess it doesn't matter. It's not like we have a suspect or anything. The guy she was having an affair with—Patrick Engleton—is twenty-two years old. I ran him through the system. He's never had so much as a speeding ticket. Did a little background check on him. Normal guy, works two jobs. Pretty much lives at the gym when he's not at work. That's where they met."

Nina nodded. "Yes. Jones used to say the only reason she went to the gym every day was to stare at the young men and their buff bodies. It doesn't surprise me that she was sleeping with one of them."

"Yes. And affair is too strong a word, I think. According to Patrick, it was more of a fling that was only two weeks old. Which leads me to believe that there were others before that. According to Josh, Jones had been acting strange—his word—for the last six to eight months."

"Does it matter who she was sleeping with?" Then her eyes widened. "Or do you think one of them is the killer?"

Quinn came back and sat down again. "I believe she knew her killer, yes. That's based on what Wayne Hoffmann said."

"Who's Wayne Hoffmann?"

"He's the guy she was dancing with. The one she was going to take to the hotel with her. He said one minute they were kissing and the next she told him to beat it. He said she was looking at someone behind them, someone she recognized. Someone she was afraid of."

"Afraid of?"

"He said she had a scared look on her face. He thought maybe her husband was there and had caught them. So he left."

"If she was afraid, then why didn't she go back inside the club? Come find us?"

Quinn shrugged. "We'll never know."

"How do you find out who all she was having an affair with?"

"I guess I'm going to have to dig deeper into her past. Our department here isn't large, and we don't have the resources that others have, like CCPD, for instance. I'll probably have to hire out for that."

"Hire out?"

"Private investigator. Using one is not uncommon for a department our size." Quinn arched an eyebrow. "Do you happen to know the names of any of her current friends?"

Nina shook her head. "No. Beth might."

"I don't think that I want to get Beth involved."

"What about her coworkers?"

"Yeah, I've spoken to them. Jones kept her personal life private. In fact, I couldn't even find anyone she went to lunch with." Quinn leaned back and seemed to relax. "I love sitting out here at night. You can't see the Gulf, but you can hear the waves, the surf, feel the breeze, smell the salty air. It's so quiet. I can close my eyes and picture it all as if I'm standing right there."

Nina turned to look at her. "How old are you?" she asked quietly.

Quinn turned too and their eyes met in the shadows. "Thirty-eight last month. I'm still getting used to it. It's damn close to forty."

Nina smiled, then leaned back and closed her eyes, doing as Quinn had suggested. She listened to the waves, picturing them as they crashed onto the beach. Judging by the sound, it was high tide or thereabouts. She could hear Quinn rocking slowly beside her and she, too, put her chair in motion. She had heard of occasions like this. A companionable silence. Heard of them but never experienced one. She stayed quiet, wanting to bask in the moment for a little longer. But she should probably head back to her car and leave Quinn in peace. She had barged in on her uninvited after all. With a quiet sigh, she opened her eyes.

"Thank you for the drink and the talk, but I guess I should go," she finally said. "I didn't mean to intrude on you like this."

"No intrusion. I enjoyed the company." Quinn stood. "I'll walk you back."

"Oh, you don't have to. I can manage."

"It's late. I'd feel better knowing that you made it back safely. Besides, Willie will enjoy getting in a late-night walk."

"Okay then. Thank you."

"My pleasure."

CHAPTER FOURTEEN

Quinn knew she was in over her head when she could find nothing more on Sharon Jones Downey than what she'd already uncovered. As she'd told Nina, larger departments had more resources than they did. On impulse, she picked up her cell phone and scrolled through her contacts, coming to Dee Woodard, a detective at CCPD. Dee was at least fifteen years older than she was—maybe more—but they'd been friendly enough with each other to go out for drinks occasionally, even if they seldom worked cases together. From what she recalled, Dee was friends with a private investigator in Corpus.

She paused before punching the number. Maybe she should clear it with Sergeant Fields first. With a sigh, she pocketed her phone and went to his office.

"What's up, Quinn? You've been in the office a lot lately. Tired of Beach Patrol?"

"Not at all. The guys have it under control."

"Then what? Got something new on the beach killing finally?"

"Not really. Dead end still. I've done as much as I can with what we've got. I'd like to hire a private investigator. With your permission, of course."

He frowned sharply. "A private investigator? You sure?"

She went fully into his office and sat down. "A detective friend of mine at CCPD—she's friends with a PI there, a former detective herself. Finley Knight. I'd like to delve into Sharon Downey's past. According to her husband, he suspects she's been having an affair—or affairs—for the last six to eight months. I can't find anything on her socials, but maybe she's got a fake account or something."

"I know you talked to one of the guys she'd been with."

"Right. But he's not the killer. I checked him out thoroughly. Sound alibi. But my thought is that maybe one of these other guys didn't like her calling it off. Or like the fact that she was seeing someone else. So maybe he followed her over here. Maybe he'd been threatening her."

"And you want this PI to try to find some names?"

"Yes. Or at least maybe point me in the right direction. I have exhausted all the resources I know of. Private investigators are pros at this."

He rubbed the stubble on his face, nodding. "Okay. Go ahead. Don't break the bank with our budget, though. I know how much they charge an hour." He pointed his finger at her. "And by the book, Quinn."

"Of course. Thanks."

If she'd known he would have been so agreeable, she would have mentioned the PI a couple of weeks ago. She pulled up Dee Woodard again, this time tapping her number. She answered after the third ring.

"Detective Woodard."

"Hi, Dee. It's Quinn Stewart, Port A Police Department. I don't know if you remember me from—"

"Quinn, sure. How the hell are you?"

"Doing good, thanks. Listen, I'm needing to hire a PI for this case I have. I know you're friends with one. Finley Knight I believe you said her name was."

"Yes, Finn and I are friends. Are you calling to see if she's legit?"

"I'm hoping since she was a detective, she'd be safe to use for an investigation."

Dee laughed. "Yes. Make it clear to her upfront. I've known her to use some unconventional methods sometimes. But yes, she's very good. I use her myself from time to time. Do you want her number? I mean her cell, not the office number."

"If you don't think she'd mind."

"No. Just tell her you talked to me."

"Okay. Thanks a lot, Dee."

"No problem. And we need to get together for a drink sometime, catch up. It's like you left Corpus and disappeared on us."

Quinn nodded. "Sure, let's do it. It's been a while. Thanks, Dee." She ended the call without further niceties. A few seconds later, a text came from Dee with Finley Knight's contact information.

Before she could call her, though, another call came in. This one from her brother. She smiled before answering.

"Mike, what's up?"

"Hey, Quinn. Haven't talked in a while and I wanted to remind you about Bree's birthday party on Saturday."

"Damn. I'm glad you did. I'd completely forgotten."

"Figured you had. You know she'd be so disappointed if you didn't come."

"I wouldn't miss it. What can I bring?"

"Sara said an appetizer. Chips and a dip or something. Don't go to any trouble."

Quinn nodded. "Okay. I'll be there."

"Two o'clock. Don't be late."

"See you then."

She sighed. That meant she needed a birthday present. Now that the kids were older, she'd turned into the worst gift-giver. When they were young, she just got them the latest and greatest toy and they loved it. But Bree was fifteen.

Yeah, she was the worst gift-giver. So, she'd give her money, same as last year.

CHAPTER FIFTEEN

"I'm Detective Stewart," she said as she shook hands firmly with Finley Knight. "Thank you for seeing me on such short notice, Ms. Knight."

"Please call me Finn. And it's no problem. I do some work for Dee occasionally too." Finn pointed to a chair. "Have a seat, Detective. We'll go over it."

"It's Quinn. Quinn Stewart."

A sharply raised eyebrow, then a smile. "Quinn and Finn. That's gotta be a first."

"Yeah." Quinn pulled the folded paper from her pocket and handed it to her. "I wrote down all the particulars. And some of the info that I was able to dig up. I didn't want you searching for stuff that we already knew about."

Finn glanced over it, reading silently. "How far back do you need to go?"

"At least a year. Right now, without any evidence or a motive, her death appears to be random. That's how the paper reported it. Based on what I've found out so far, she'd been having multiple affairs for at least the last six to eight months. I want to know who with and all the information you can get on each."

"You've already been through her social media accounts?"

"Yes. There was nothing there. I was hoping you could find something."

Finn nodded. "She probably has other accounts under different names. May even have a dating profile under a bogus name. If she's having multiple affairs, she has to meet these guys somewhere."

"You can find that out?" she asked hopefully.

"I should be able to, yes. It's going to take some time. Give me a few days to get started. Three or four. I've got a couple of cases I'll be closing in the next two days. Then I can devote my full attention to this."

"That's great. Thanks. I was expecting a week or more."

"And it may take that long, depending on how fast we find her other accounts—if they exist—and how many guys we're running background checks on."

"I understand. It's been over a month since the murder. I'm kinda going at my own pace. The husband is not hounding us in the least. In fact, the opposite."

Finn arched an eyebrow questioningly.

"He was going to file for divorce," she explained. "Her death didn't exactly break his heart."

"I see. And is he a suspect?"

"Not any longer. He was home with their two young kids at the time of the killing."

"Okay. I'll get started on this as soon as I can."

Quinn stood and again offered her hand. "I appreciate it. My cell number is on there," she said, indicating the paper she'd given her. "If you have any questions or anything, give me a call."

"I'll be in touch."

Back outside, she stood by her Jeep for a moment, indecisive. She looked down the dead-end street of Moonlight Avenue, then up into the cloudless sky. It was a gorgeous day, and she should head to the island and get back to her real job—Beach

Patrol. Instead, she searched through her contacts, finding the info she'd put in for Nina Evans. She'd done a little snooping around on the pretense that it pertained to the case. It didn't. She'd simply been curious about the woman.

She found out she owned a cleaning service—Bayside Cleaning—and was fairly successful. She headed there now, hoping to catch Nina. And once more, she'd use the pretense of the case as her excuse for stopping by. When she walked Nina back to her car the other night, Nina had apologized again for popping over unannounced. She'd said she had needed to talk and there was no one in her life to fill that role. That alone made Quinn curious about her, taking that to mean that she was not only single but that there was no good friend to lean on. Or maybe it just meant that there were none who could relate in this instance.

She followed her phone's directions and easily found the address. It was in an older neighborhood with some lots boasting large coastal oaks and others sporting palm trees. There was no sign to indicate that this was Bayside Cleaning and she wondered if she'd gotten the address wrong. She parked in the driveway and got out, looking around before going to the front door. She tilted her head, wondering if she should knock or ring the doorbell. She opted for the bell, pushing it once before stepping back. It was loud and shrill, and it only took a handful of seconds before it was opened. Nina's face registered surprise, then broke out into a smile.

"Oh my god, what are you doing here?" Then the smile faded. "Or do you have news?"

"No, no. I was in the neighborhood." Nina looked skeptical and Quinn smiled. "Really. Kinda."

Nina stepped back. "Come in, please."

"Thanks."

She went inside and Nina closed the door behind her. The inside was open and roomy with not two, but three sofas in the space.

"So you were in the neighborhood?"

Quinn nodded. "I was on my way back to Port A. Close enough. I thought I'd see how you were."

Nina didn't answer. Instead, she waved a hand at the large room. "This is our lounge. I have twenty employees and it gets crowded when everyone is here at once."

She walked through the room and Quinn followed, going down a hallway toward the back. One of the bedrooms had been converted into office. Besides the desk, there was a large table that held a printer and a small copy machine. On a wall hung three rows of trays, all with names on them. Nina went over to the trays and smiled.

"I still do it the old-fashioned way—with paper. If I were a really big company, I would have an app built for me where I could post their daily assignments." Another smile. "But I'm not. Besides, they have to come here anyway for supplies and to pick up the vans."

Instead of sitting, though, Nina motioned her out. "This is my assistant's office. She only works in the mornings. College student," she explained.

Farther down the hallway was another room, a smaller bedroom. This, too, was made into a small office.

She motioned to one of the chairs, then sat behind her desk. "Did you really come by to check on me?"

Quinn sat down too. "I did. Do you mind?"

"Of course not. That was sweet of you."

Quinn met her gaze and smiled. "So? How are you?"

Nina sighed. "I guess okay. Beth called me again. She needs someone to talk to and it appears she's chosen me."

"And you? Have you chosen *her*?"

Nina shook her head. "No. Beth and I were never close enough to have those heart-to-heart talks. All of this has made me realize how superficial our friendships had gotten over the years. When you're kids, you tell your friends everything—your secrets. As you get older, you become more guarded."

"How is Beth handling things?"

"She seems to have recovered somewhat from Jones's death. She mostly wants to talk about her husband and her fears." Nina shook her head. "I'm not the right one to talk to. Like I told you, I can't really relate to all that she's going through. I've hinted that perhaps she should call Tammy or Amy to talk it out with."

"Maybe she's chosen you because you're removed from her life. You're not someone she's going to have to face."

"Yes, that's occurred to me too. I'm more of a sounding board, really. I don't have any advice to give her."

"What about you? When you came over the other night, you said you needed to talk. Do you not have a sounding board?"

Nina looked fully at her, holding her gaze for a long moment. "Not really, no. Allison—my ex—was always the one I could talk to."

"Bad breakup?"

"No, not at all. It was amicable. I initiated it, thinking that she would be horribly upset. Turns out, she'd been feeling the same. It was one of those situations where you make better friends than partners. It was almost too easy to break up."

"She's not around anymore?"

"No. She's seeing someone from San Antonio and moved there right after Christmas. I haven't talked to her in a while. After we broke up, we kinda drifted." Nina raised her eyebrows. "What about you?"

"Me?" She shook her head. "No."

A quick smile. "You said the other night that there was an ex."

"Well, yeah. I mean, everyone has an ex, right?"

"Not something you like to talk about?"

Quinn hesitated for a moment, then shook her head dismissively. "Nothing like that. It was a short-lived thing that never should have happened in the first place. I..." She paused. "Story for another time."

"Okay. And no current girlfriend?"

"Nope. I'm pretty much on my own. Well, other than family. My parents have a summer home in Wyoming and are only here during the winter. But I've got two older brothers and two younger sisters. They all live here in Corpus, and we get together pretty often."

"Nieces and nephews?"

Quinn smiled. "Oh, yeah. I love them. In fact, Bree has a birthday on Saturday. She'll be fifteen. That's my brother Mike's daughter. You have family? You said you weren't close to your parents but—"

"My parents are still in Sugar Land. I have two older brothers but neither lives close. One is in Kansas City and the other in the Atlanta area. I don't get to see them much. Both are married but neither has kids or wants them, as far as I know."

"Well, if you want to be around kids, you should come to the birthday party with me on Saturday. There are ten just in our family alone, not to mention Bree's friends who will be there."

Nina laughed. "Is that supposed to tempt me? Teenagers?"

"Yeah, it took me a while to get used to them. Bree is the oldest and Jeremy is the youngest at five. And lots of others in between."

"So, there are five of you plus your parents, and then ten kids. Wow. That must be quite a houseful at Christmas."

"Boisterous, yes. Saturday will be a backyard grill fest. You should join me."

Nina tilted her head. "Are you asking me out?"

Quinn stared at her. Was she? No. Since Christie, she hadn't asked anyone out. But she smiled. "If I was, would you accept?"

Nina smiled too. "To a teenager's birthday party? That would be a hard sell."

Quinn leaned closer to her desk. "What about dinner then?"

Nina again tilted her head. "So you *are* asking me out?"

"Hypothetically, if I was…would you say yes?"

Nina leaned on her desk and rested her chin in her palm. "Hypothetically?" A quick smile. "Maybe."

Quinn smiled too. "Well, probably wouldn't be proper, seeing as how we met at a crime scene." She stood up quickly, thinking she was getting in over her head. "I should go. I really just came by to check on you." She tapped Nina's desk with her knuckles. "I'll see you around."

Nina held her gaze for a moment, then nodded. "Sure. Thanks for stopping by, Quinn."

CHAPTER SIXTEEN

Nina lay on the chaise lounge on her deck, soaking in the sun. Her sunglasses shielded her eyes as they were fixed on the bay. On this beautiful Saturday afternoon, boats were scattered about as fishermen tried their luck. She loved her view; she just didn't love her neighbors. The ones on her left had three young kids who had a penchant for screaming. The privacy fence between them did nothing to muffle the sound. And the neighbors on her right assumed that everyone in the neighborhood wanted to hear their loud music whenever they were outside. Today, however, it was blissfully quiet, and she was taking advantage of it. If her luck held, she would be able to grill the kabobs she had marinating in peace as well. But she supposed she was asking too much, considering she lived on a street with wall-to-wall houses along the bay, not to mention the fact she was only a few blocks from the S.P.I.D. It was normally far from peaceful. Not like Quinn's beach house. There it had been quiet and serene, the only sounds those of the surf, the breeze, and the gulls. No traffic noise. No city noise.

She smiled thinking of the other woman. Was she at her backyard birthday party right about now? Was she being mugged by teenagers? If Quinn had been serious—if she had been really asking her out—would she have gone? Maybe. Probably.

She didn't have a lot of friends and she wasn't sure what had happened to them. She glanced at the sky, allowing herself a slight eye roll. Yeah, most of her friends were also Allison's friends and they'd all been shocked at their breakup. Afterward, she'd avoided them—and their inquisitions—and had started hanging out with Jennifer. She allowed a quick smile. Hanging out? Was that what they'd been doing? No. They'd been having sex.

Now, after more than a year, most of her old friends had moved on, Allison had moved on, and she'd immersed herself in her business and when there was time—and she was in the mood—she'd hang out with Jennifer. And once a year, like clockwork, she'd get together with her five oldest friends and reminisce about the good old days. The good old days that were now long gone.

Maybe that's what had her feeling so disjointed, so blue today. She'd alluded to it when talking with Quinn—and she'd certainly thought it—but now that Jones was gone, she feared those old friendships were gone too. She could sense that. Could hear it in Beth's voice, in Amy's. She hadn't talked to Sheri or Tammy, but by their silence, they knew it too. The tight hugs at the funeral as they said goodbye to each other. The lingering glances as they all went their separate ways. Had they been like her, trying to memorize faces and smiles, knowing they most likely would never meet up again?

God, how depressing her life had suddenly become. So depressing that she wished Quinn—a virtual stranger—had indeed invited her to a teenager's birthday party. She shook her head. No. Calling Quinn a stranger didn't seem right. They'd talked too much for that to be the case. But no. *She'd* talked. Quinn had shared very little.

She pictured Quinn's crystal-blue eyes. Yes, she was attractive, but it wasn't solely because of the eyes. A woman like that shouldn't be single. That then made her wonder what kind of baggage she carried. There had to be something, surely. She let out a nearly wistful sigh. If Quinn asked her out, then yes, she would go. For one thing, she hadn't been on a real date since Allison. And two, she liked her. Quinn was easy to talk to, had a pleasant personality and she could quite possibly drown in those blue eyes of hers.

The ringing of her phone chased thoughts of Quinn away and she reluctantly let them go. She sighed rather heavily. Jennifer. It was Saturday. Was she wanting to get together tonight? She took a deep breath before answering, hoping she sounded appropriately cheerful.

"Hi, Jenn."

"Hey, Nina. What are you doing?"

Nina locked her gaze on a fishing boat bobbing in the bay. "I'm out on my deck, enjoying the sunshine."

"Oh, okay. Good." A pause. "Listen, I wanted to talk if you've got a second."

Nina frowned. Jennifer sounded nervous, which was so unlike her. "Sure. What's up?"

"Well, remember the last time we went out…at the bar?"

"I do."

"And remember you left early?"

"Right."

"Well, that woman there, the one I went to talk to…well, we kinda hit it off."

Nina leaned her head back and stared into the sky, wondering how she felt. "That's great, Jenn."

"Yeah. And so…" A long pause.

Nina laughed. "Are you breaking up with me?"

Jennifer laughed too. "It's been a while for us, you know."

"You're right. It has. I haven't been—"

"Interested," Jennifer finished for her.

"To be honest, Jenn, our arrangement just wasn't fulfilling anymore." *Had it ever been?* "And I guess I'm not cut out for a sex buddy." She again allowed herself another quick eye roll. Lord, but she was sounding older by the minute.

"So, you're okay if I don't call you anymore?"

Nina was surprised by the relief she felt. "I'm okay, Jenn. What's her name?"

"Marsha. We've been…well, together almost every night and I really, really like her."

"Good. I think that's wonderful. Glad you found someone."

"Thanks, Nina. Maybe we'll run into each other out at the bar or something."

She nodded, knowing they probably wouldn't. She only ever went to the bar to meet Jennifer. "Sure. Take care, Jenn. I hope things work out for you."

This time as she stared at the bay, she saw nothing. She was trying to assess how she was feeling. A bit empty, she supposed. Jennifer had been the only intimacy in her life in the last year. And even though she admittedly had tired of their arrangement, at least Jenn was still there. Oh, why hadn't she nurtured any friendships? Why had she let the old ones slip away with Allison?

"I was busy with my business," she murmured quietly. That was true, of course. And the women who worked for her, she would call some of them friends. Certainly not close friends but she sat in on the morning gossip sessions before everyone headed out to work. She knew about their lives, their husbands, and kids. They, however, knew little about her or her life. None knew about Jones's death, for instance. So no, she supposed they weren't really friends, were they? She was the boss, that was all.

She blew out her breath and closed her eyes, the long, lonely weekend suddenly looming like a heavy dark cloud on this bright sunny day. Maybe that's why the thought of being at a teenager's birthday party was sounding like fun right about now.

She allowed a smile to form. Not so much the birthday party. Maybe it was just the prospect of being in Quinn's company.

CHAPTER SEVENTEEN

Quinn had just pressed the last of the ground beef into another patty when her security camera beeped at her. She tapped the alert on her phone, smiling as she saw Nina Evans standing at the bottom of her steps, looking up. She washed her hands quickly, then went to the sliding door. Willie beat her out and met Nina halfway up the stairs.

"Hey, girl," she heard Nina coo to the dog.

She leaned against the railing, watching them. "You out for a walk?"

Nina looked up then and met her gaze. "Sort of."

"Well, come on up."

"Are you busy? I mean, do you have company? Am I intruding?"

Quinn gave her a quick smile. "Not at all."

"I don't have your cell number and I—"

"It's okay. Come on up." She started walking away, then turned back toward her. "Want a drink?"

"Yes, please."

She left the sliding door open as she went back into the kitchen, wondering what Nina was doing there. Not that she minded—it was a pleasant surprise. She opened the upper cabinet and took out the rum and bourbon. She didn't normally drink anything on Sundays, and she eyed the glass of tea she'd been sipping on. With a shrug, she took out two glasses for their drinks, hearing Nina and Willie come inside. She glanced over at them.

"Feel free to look around."

Nina's gaze went to the platter of burger patties instead. "I'm sorry. I guess I'm interrupting dinner."

"No, not really. I grill patties every Sunday. Have them for lunch during the week."

Nina nodded, then, instead of checking out the house, she turned back to the windows. "Your view is fantastic. I bet it's awesome to watch storms come in."

"You said you had a house on the bay? I guess you get a few storms too." She grabbed the platter of burger patties and quickly shoved it into her fridge.

Nina joined her in the kitchen. "Storms from the Gulf lose their punch by the time they cross the island and hit Oso Bay." She smiled quickly. "Not that I would mind that during a hurricane."

She handed Nina her drink. "Surprisingly, when Harvey hit, they only had some minor roof damage here. Some of the newer houses down the way got hammered pretty good I'm told. The guy who did the inspection when I bought it said this old house was rock solid." She picked up her own drink and headed back out to the deck. "Not that I'd want to go through a storm like that."

"Were you living on the island then?"

"No, thankfully. I was still in Corpus."

"Oh? You used to live in Corpus?"

"Yeah. I worked for CCPD."

Nina sat down next to her in the same rocker she'd used the last time. "Really? Were you a detective there also?"

"Eventually, yeah. But it lost its luster."

"How so?"

Quinn took a sip of her drink, then held it up. "This. I was drinking way too much and staying at the bar way too late. I basically hated my life."

"Was this before the ex or after?"

Quinn laughed. "Christie. Before and during." The smile left her face as she remembered that time in her life. It seemed like so long ago. It was also something she'd not talked about to anyone, and she didn't think now was a good time to go there. "So, what's going on? I know you didn't come over to talk about my ex."

Nina stared at her for a long moment. "You don't like to share much, do you?"

Quinn shrugged. "Not a whole lot to share."

Nina continued to stare at her, but she didn't push. Instead, she put her rocker in motion. "How was the birthday party?"

Quinn laughed lightly. "You would have hated it. In fact, it was too much for me and I cut out early." She reached over and touched Nina's arm, tapping it lightly. "And I know you didn't come over to talk birthday parties."

Nina let out her breath. "I had an awful weekend."

"Oh yeah. Wished you'd gone to the party with me after all?" she teased.

Nina turned to look at her. "Yes, actually."

"Tell me why you had an awful weekend. What happened?"

Nina shrugged. "Nothing, really. Jennifer has a new girlfriend and I realized that I don't have any friends. And, well, Tammy called and that was..." She paused. "Depressing."

Tammy was from their group, and she almost asked about the call, wondering if there was some news about Jones. But instead, her curiosity took over. "Jennifer?" she asked as nonchalantly as possible.

Nina leaned her head back. "I'm embarrassed to say."

Quinn started rocking too. "Someone you dated?"

"Dated? No, that would be stretching it." She blew out her breath. "I met her out on the beach one morning on one of my walks. About two weeks before Allison and I broke up." Another deep breath. "And a few weeks after that, I slept with her." Nina turned her head to look at her. "Jennifer and I didn't really date. We just—"

"Had sex?"

"Yes."

"Nothing wrong with that. Or did you fall in love, and she didn't?"

Nina laughed. "No, no. Jennifer was perfectly happy with our relationship. I wasn't. In fact, it's been several months since… well, since we'd slept together. It wasn't fun for me anymore." She waved her hand in the air. "Jennifer and I weren't friends. That's what I've come to realize. We never talked about anything meaningful. In fact, we rarely talked at all." Nina turned toward her. "I need a friend."

She nodded. "Okay." Then she smiled. "Are you picking me?"

Nina smiled too. "I am. Do you mind?"

"Not at all. I'm flattered. I haven't made many friends lately. None, actually."

"Why is that? I find you easy to talk to. Don't others?"

"Maybe I haven't been receptive," she admitted, knowing that was the truth.

"Why not?"

Quinn knew the reason for that too, but did she really want to get into her past with Nina? Did she want to bring up her old habits? No. "Had other things going on," she said evasively. "Moved from CCPD to over here. I lost touch with people." There. That was as good an excuse as any, she supposed.

"How long have you been a cop?"

"Right after college. I'd always wanted to be one." She smiled. "I watched too many TV shows, I guess." She took a swallow of her drink. "I was a little on the wild side. Rebellious middle child, my mom likes to say—wild as the devil."

"Really? I don't see it. Tell me."

"About my wild side?"

"Yes. It occurred to me that you know a lot about me, and you've shared next to nothing about yourself."

She took another sip of her drink, thinking back to her teenage years. Yeah, she'd had a wild side. "I had a fake ID and was cruising the bars when I was sixteen."

"No curfew?"

"I worked at a restaurant busing tables. I always volunteered for the late shift on Friday and Saturday nights. As soon as I got off work, I'd hit the bars for an hour or so, then go home."

"Alone at the bars at sixteen?"

"Sometimes. But there were three or four of us, usually. All underage. All drinking." She shook her head. "One of my older brothers—Mike—caught me out one night. I was seventeen, he was nineteen."

"Told your parents?"

"Nope. He threatened to." She laughed. "I remember what a smart-ass I was that night. I asked him how he was going to explain to them what *he* was doing at the bar. Because like me, he had a fake ID and was drinking too."

"Ah. You teamed up?"

"We did."

"And you never got busted?"

She smiled quickly. "No. But my partying carried over into adulthood." She held her hand up. "Old history. I partied way too much when I was younger." She shook the ice in her glass. "I allow myself one, sometimes two of these. That's it. Now, what about Tammy?"

Nina rocked beside her silently for a moment. "She called this morning. Beth—thankfully—has turned to her now instead of me for her marital advice. She told Tammy that she'd spoken to me so that's why Tammy called. She's really worried about Beth. Between Jones's death and her marriage, Tammy says Beth is spiraling into a deep depression. Tammy urged her to see a therapist, but Beth won't hear of it. She's afraid they will want to medicate her."

Before she could reply, her cell rang. "Excuse me," she said before going inside to retrieve it. "Yeah, this is Quinn."

"Yes, this is Finley Knight. Sorry to call outside of business hours, but I'm about finished with my report, and I found some discrepancies in what you told me. I'll email the final report to you either tomorrow or Tuesday, but I thought I'd give you a heads-up."

Quinn looked out to the deck, watching as Nina petted Willie's head. "No problem, Finn. Sure. What did you find?"

"Well, first off, I was able to find her alternate social media accounts—Facebook and Instagram. I also found her on two different dating sites—Casual Dating for Adults and Match. The name she used was Ingrid Cloudcroft."

She frowned. "Casual Dating for Adults? God, I'm out of touch. I've never heard of that one."

"Yeah. It's a totally sex-focused dating site. Caters to swingers and those interested in casual sex hookups."

"Great," she murmured.

"The main issue I have is with Patrick Engleton. According to what I found, they first met online—through Match—about a month before she started showing up at his gym. The first confirmed meeting was at a restaurant—Big Moe's. Then I've got them at a motel two nights later. That was all twenty-six days before she first went to his gym. I also found four other guys that she met with."

"So, Patrick lied to me. He didn't meet her at his gym, and he hadn't known her only two weeks."

"Right. About six weeks."

"Guess I need to pay him a visit in the morning."

"I'll send the detailed file on all the others, like I said, tomorrow or Tuesday. I've got when and where they met up, plus backgrounds on them all. Interesting stuff."

"Great. I appreciate it, Finn. Appreciate the call too."

"No problem. Let me know if there's something else I can do for you."

"Thanks."

Yeah, Patrick Engleton had lied to her, but her gut told her that Patrick didn't kill Sharon Jones Downey. She set her phone down on the counter, then went back outside. Nina looked at her with raised eyebrows.

"Sorry. That was the private investigator I hired."

"Oh? For Jones?"

She hesitated. Should she be discussing this with Nina? Probably not.

"You ever heard of Ingrid Cloudcroft?"

CHAPTER EIGHTEEN

"You ever heard of Ingrid Cloudcroft?"

Nina's eyebrows rose. "Actually, yes. Well, I mean, I don't know her, but I've heard of her."

Quinn sat back down beside her. "Who is she?"

"She's a friend of Jones's, I guess. She was talking about her that weekend when we were together. Apparently, she's a *naughty* friend."

"Naughty?"

"That was what Jones called her."

"What do you take that to mean?"

She stared out into the Gulf, trying to recall what Jones had said about her. "She said she did things that even Jones herself wouldn't do. That could mean anything, but I assumed she had been talking about sex."

Quinn stood up then and went to the railing of the deck. She looked out at the water, then turned around to face her again.

"I'd like to discuss this with you, Nina, but I need your assurance that you won't share anything with the others."

Quinn seemed so serious, and she simply nodded. "Of course."

"Ingrid Cloudcroft was apparently Jones's alter ego."

"What? No. She said she was a friend of hers."

"She had Instagram and Facebook accounts under that name. She also used it on a couple of dating sites."

"But how do you know it was Jones?"

"The private investigator found it. I'm sure through IP addresses and whatnot. I would imagine the profile pictures were of her." Quinn moved back to her chair. "When I interviewed Patrick Engleton, he said he and Jones had only been seeing each other for two weeks. But the evidence says that they'd been meeting up for the last six weeks prior to her death. He was twenty-two. Jones was thirty-two. I don't know the ages of the other guys that the PI found yet. There were four others. But Wayne Hoffmann was also in his early twenties. Was that her pattern? Younger men?"

Nina shrugged. "I…I don't know. I do know that Josh turned forty this year, but still, he's an attractive man. But yeah, maybe she was trying to hang onto her youth." She leaned back and put her hands on her head. "I just can't believe all of this. It's like she was living two lives."

"Yes."

Nina turned to her. "But why?" She held her hand up. "I know you can't possibly know the answer to that."

"Maybe she was really unhappy with her life and, like you said, wanted to go back to when she was younger. From what you've told me, I'm assuming she was, well, promiscuous."

"That would be putting it mildly," Nina said with a laugh. "The belief among the rest of us was that she wasn't simply sleeping her way through the senior class in high school."

"What do you mean?"

"She was doing it for money. I told you her family had little."

"You think she was prostituting herself for money to help her family?"

"No. Jones wasn't that noble. She kept the money for herself. Her family had none yet Jones was suddenly wearing new clothes and was always in the latest fashions. I'm convinced that's how she put herself through college too."

"Do you think her husband knew anything about her past?"

"Highly doubtful. I don't know Josh other than what I learned from Jones over the years, but he seems very conservative, very proud of his upbringing, his family name. I'm certain he has no clue how she was in high school or college. I doubt he knows much about her family. They weren't at the wedding and as far as I know, Jones never brought him to meet them."

"Strange, isn't it?"

Nina shrugged. "Is it? Jones was embarrassed by her family. After she left home for college, she rarely went back. All these years that we've been getting together, she never mentioned her family. It wouldn't surprise me if she didn't even speak to them anymore."

"What about the funeral? Were they there?"

"Her mother and one of her sisters. That was all that I saw."

"Are you close with any of the families?"

Nina shook her head. "For as close as the six of us were, our families never were. They all knew each other, of course. We lived in the same neighborhood, had sleepovers. But our parents never socialized. Now that I think about it, that is a little strange, I guess. I mean, they were friendly with each other, but it wasn't like there were dinners or parties or anything like that where they mingled." Nina looked at her. "Does that have a bearing?"

"No, not at all. My questions are driven more by curiosity is all. I'll talk to Patrick Engleton tomorrow. And I should get the report from the PI in a couple of days. That'll tell me more, of course."

"Is that something you'll have to share with Josh?"

"Only if I have questions for him. Or he asks. Judging by his silence this last month, I doubt that will be the case." Quinn stood up then. "Let's freshen our drinks then we'll go around to the front deck and catch the sunset."

"I was thinking earlier how you must have a beautiful sunrise here over the Gulf. My view is to the north, but certain times of the year, I get a full sunrise too." She waved toward the water. "You have nothing here to obstruct your view though."

"Not of the sunrise, no. That won't be the case in the front, but I've got a sliver of a view between some of the houses." She motioned with her head. "Come on." Then Quinn paused. "Or do you need to get back?"

Nina hesitated too. Was she intruding? She'd popped over unannounced after all. "No. But you were in the middle of grilling burgers and—"

"I only do that because I have nothing else to do on Sunday evenings. I can grill them just as easily tomorrow."

She stared into those blue, blue eyes, wondering if Quinn was being truthful. Again, it struck her that a woman this attractive should not be single. That thought was spoken out loud before she could stop it.

"Why are you single?"

Quinn laughed. "Why are *you* single?"

Nina smiled too. "You first."

She followed Quinn inside and leaned against the counter and watched as she added first ice, then a bit more liquor to each glass before topping them off with Coke. The statement Quinn made wasn't something she was expecting.

"I wasn't a very nice person in my younger days. I used people."

Nina's eyebrows shot up questioningly.

"Women," Quinn clarified. "I partied and I had a lot of one-night stands, and I didn't much care about anything else, including my job."

Quinn handed her the drink, and she again followed her, this time going around the wraparound deck to the front. Two chairs, separated by a small table, faced west—and some of the neighboring houses. She waited for Quinn to sit, then took the other.

"I was thirty-four, I think, when I met Christie. The whole situation was totally unfair to her. My sisters were reminding me that I was getting older and needed to settle down. I was telling myself I was getting too damn old for the bars and random sex." Quinn sighed. "So I asked Christie to move in with me."

"Here?"

"No. I was still in Corpus then. Had a little house near the campus. Anyway, I stopped going to the bars, stopped drinking every damn night, stopped acting like I was still twenty-one. Of course, the thing with Christie didn't last because I wasn't remotely in love with her." Quinn glanced at her. "I asked her to leave. We were having dinner one night and I told her I didn't love her, and I wanted her to leave."

"She was upset?"

"Yes. And I'm not sure why. She couldn't possibly have been happy. I was miserable and brought no joy to the relationship and most likely made her miserable too."

"Okay. Then what?"

"I thought that would be a great time to change my life. I quit the force there and joined the Port A Police Department. I started going to the gym, sold that house and bought this place, got Willie."

"And no one since?"

"No." Quinn smiled. "I'm embarrassed to say this, but I've not been out on a date or slept with anyone since then. Penance for my earlier years, maybe."

Nina laughed. "Self-imposed penance or your reputation is such that no one will go out with you?"

"Self-imposed. I didn't like myself very much and I was trying to figure out who I really was."

She asked the obvious question. "And have you?"

"I think so. I've realized that I'm a lot more introverted than I thought. I'd been drinking and partying since I was sixteen. Booze made me more outgoing than I truly am. Booze made me the life of the party."

"And with your looks you could have any woman you wanted?"

Quinn seemed genuinely embarrassed by the question. "With my looks?"

"Don't pretend that you don't know how attractive you are. My god, your eyes alone must have had the girls swooning over you."

Quinn smiled sweetly. "Swooning?" Then she arched an eyebrow. "Are *you* swooning, Nina?"

Now it was her turn to be embarrassed, but she didn't shy away from the answer. "I find you attractive, yes. And I'm sure you've heard this your whole life—your eyes are the most brilliant blue I've ever seen."

Those eyes were holding hers, then Quinn looked away, her gaze now on the sunset they had scarcely regarded.

"Yes, my whole life," she said quietly. "When I was young—a child—strangers would stop and comment on them. It was unwanted attention, and I was mostly embarrassed." Then she smiled. "As I got older, I quickly learned to use them to my advantage."

Nina smiled too. "With the ladies?"

Quinn nodded. "Like I said, I wasn't a very nice person."

"That's your version of using people? Seduce them with your looks, your eyes, then forget about them."

"Exactly. And despite that fact, some came back for more."

Nina laughed. "That good in bed, huh?"

Quinn's face turned crimson, and she held up her hand. "Okay. That's enough on that subject."

Nina was still smiling as she leaned back, following Quinn's gaze to the fading sunset.

CHAPTER NINETEEN

Quinn had looked through her notes first thing that morning. Patrick Engleton hit the gym each day at six thirty a.m. and again at four thirty p.m. He held two jobs—mornings he did janitorial work at the university and then at one o'clock he logged in for four hours at a barbeque place on the S.P.I.D. only a few blocks from his gym. And he had dreams of being a personal trainer, he'd said. She was on her way there now, hoping to catch him before he left for work.

It was nearly seven and traffic was already getting thick. As she stopped at the traffic light on the S.P.I.D.—known this far south as Park Road 22—she glanced to her left, wondering if Nina was out taking a beach walk this morning. She tapped her fingers on the steering wheel, smiling as she thought of the other woman. Nina needed a friend and had picked her. She wondered when the last time that had happened was. The older she got, the less interest she had in meeting new people. She didn't mind her own company—and Willie's, of course—but if she craved conversation, all she had to do was call up one of her siblings or pop over to their house. Or she could start going to the gym again and reacquaint herself with those she'd met there. She glanced up, meeting her eyes in the rearview mirror, and smiled. For some reason, she'd lost her motivation for the gym.

The light turned and she drove on, her mind still on Nina. She liked her. And she had enjoyed the impromptu visit yesterday. Nina had stayed to watch the sunset, and she and Willie had walked her back to her car again. She'd also given Nina the gate code for her neighborhood so that—if she wanted to visit again—she wouldn't have to park way up the beach and walk down. She could pull right into Quinn's driveway. In fact, she thought she might invite her over for steaks sometime soon. And yes, it would be a date. It had been a long time, sure, but this was also something completely different. She'd never once been on a date with someone who she hadn't met at a bar. In fact, every date she'd ever been on had ended at a bar too.

She saw the sign for Island Gym, the giant palm tree flashing with colored lights, and she moved into the lefthand lane, waiting for a break in traffic to turn into their parking lot. Apparently, people were much more dedicated to their exercise routine than she was—the lot was nearly full. As she went up to the entrance she thought that, yeah, she needed to get back into the swing again.

At the front counter, a pretty young blond woman smiled brilliantly at her.

"Welcome to Island Gym. Are you interested in a membership?"

Quinn assumed her attire and lack of a gym bag clued the girl that she wasn't a regular there. Instead of answering, she pulled her shield out of her pocket and showed it to her.

"I'm Detective Stewart. I'm looking for one of your members. Patrick Engleton."

The girl's smile disappeared. "Oh. Is something wrong?"

"Just need to speak to him. Have you seen him this morning?"

"Well, actually, no. I mean, he's usually here every morning, but I haven't seen him yet."

Quinn glanced through the glass walls, hearing the clanking of weights being slammed around. "Any of his friends here?"

"Maybe...maybe you should speak to my manager," the girl said in a nervous voice.

She hopped off the stool she was sitting on and quickly disappeared into an office. Before long, a man came out. He obviously used his own gym. He had a barrel of a chest and his biceps bulged under his Island Gym T-shirt.

"I'm Billy Olson. How can I help you?"

"Yes, I'm Detective Stewart. I'm looking for Patrick Engleton. The last time I spoke with him, he said he came here every morning and again at four-thirty in the afternoon. I understand he hasn't checked in yet."

"Yeah. Really odd. Pat has been coming here for about three years now. Rarely misses a day."

"Does he have any buddies here that might know where he is?"

"Sandy, pull up the roster. See if Frankie checked in." He turned back to her. "Pat and Frankie lift together most often."

The girl was already shaking her head, but she did as he asked. "I haven't seen him this morning." She shook her head harder as she pointed at the screen. "No. Frankie's not here."

Mr. Olson shrugged. "Pat and Frankie hang out. Other than that, everyone else here is just gym bros. I don't think he's outside friends with anyone else."

She pointed to the monitor. "Can you tell me if he was here yesterday?"

"I saw him yesterday morning," the girl offered. She then made a few clicks and shook her head. "But he didn't check in yesterday afternoon."

"And that's unusual?"

Mr. Olson nodded. "Like I said, Pat rarely misses. Even on Sundays he comes by."

She pulled out one of her cards and handed it to him. "Thanks. If you happen to see him would you tell him that I need to speak with him again?" She smiled. "He's not in any trouble. I just have some more questions for him."

He looked at her card. "Oh. You're with Port Aransas Police Department. Not Corpus."

"Yes. I'm just needing some information from him." She smiled again. "Thanks."

"Okay, sure. Well, if I see him, I'll pass this on."

She already had her phone out before she stepped outside into the sunshine. Her call went unanswered, however. Well, she'd buzz by his apartment on the off chance he was there. If he wasn't, then perhaps she'd put in a call to Dee Woodard and have her assist in finding Patrick Engleton.

CHAPTER TWENTY

Quinn double-checked the apartment number, then found the building with FOUR posted near the stairs. She looked to the top and paused just a second before nearly jogging up the steps. It was an open-air stairway and walkway between apartment units on the second floor. A breeze blew up from below and she glanced at the first door she saw—210. She moved down, looking for 216.

The door was closed, but before she could knock, she saw a smear of what appeared to be dried blood on the walkway. She stepped around it to the side of the door, one hand automatically resting on the butt of her weapon as she knocked three times. She paused only a few seconds, then knocked again.

She should really call CCPD, she knew, but instead, she pulled her T-shirt—the navy-blue Port A police-issued one that she normally wore while on beach patrol—out of her jeans and used it to turn the knob. She wasn't really surprised to find it unlocked.

She pulled her weapon from her holster and slowly pushed the door open. "Patrick? You there?" she called. "Police."

There was no sound from inside, and she pushed the door fully open. It only took a second for her mind to register the scene—tall floor lamp toppled, small sofa upended, a kitchen chair flung into the tiny entryway. Her heart pounded wildly as she moved into the apartment, her gun held at the ready. She saw the body sprawled on the kitchen floor. There was blood pooled around his head and torso, and a rope was still cinched tight around his neck.

She went to him and squatted down, lightly touching his cold flesh. Lifeless eyes stared back at her, and she slowly shook her head. Just a kid, really. Twenty-two years old with his whole life ahead of him. Yet he gets mixed up with Jones—Ingrid Cloudcroft—and this happens.

A noise outside the door made her jerk her head around and she stood upright. She turned and faced the door just as someone came inside.

"Police! Drop your gun!"

She froze in place. *Oh, fuck.* "Whoa now. Calm down," she said in a voice that was anything *but* calm. "I'm a cop! I'm—"

"Drop your gun!" he yelled again.

"I'm a goddamn cop!" She stared at him. "Okay, I'm holstering my weapon," she said slowly. She slipped it into the holster at her waist. "Now I'm going to reach for my badge."

They stared at each other, and recognition seemed to set in for both of them, although his name wouldn't come to her.

"I'm Detective Stewart. Port A PD." She finally saw him relax.

He nodded. "Quinn."

She let out a relieved breath when he lowered his weapon. "Yeah."

"Hell, sorry. I didn't recognize you with your short hair."

She ran a hand over it now, his name finally coming to her. "Harmon. How the hell are you?"

He grinned. "Better than you. You looked like you were about to shit your pants."

"No kidding. I was afraid you were going to shoot me." She stepped back. "Got a body. Patrick Engleton."

He came into the kitchen and nodded. "We got a call to do a welfare check. Didn't show up for work. Didn't answer his phone." He looked at her. "What are you doing here anyway?"

She sighed. "He was a possible suspect in a homicide."

"Okay. I got to call it in. You touch anything?"

"No. And I didn't check the rest of the rooms. I just got here." She motioned to the door. "I'll wait outside."

She went back down the stairs, pausing to glance into the sky, seeing white, puffy clouds streaming across. Well, obviously Patrick Engleton hadn't killed Jones. Of course, she never really thought he had, based on her interview with him. There was the matter of him lying to her, however.

She leaned against her Jeep, arms crossed as thoughts raced through her mind. Who the hell killed Jones? And had they now also killed Patrick Engleton? Logically, she needed to consider the husband, but she'd gone over that several times already. He had been at home with his two kids. His security camera proved it. His car pulled into his garage at 5:43 p.m. The nanny left about six. His car didn't leave again until after midnight when Sergeant Fields called him. So, it wasn't the husband.

She took out her phone, calling Finley Knight. She answered on the third ring.

"This is Finn."

"Yeah, it's Quinn." Then she smiled. "Maybe I should call you Finley."

"Maybe I'll call you Quinley."

They both laughed, then she sobered. "I hate to be a bother, but have you by chance finished? I need another suspect. Patrick Engleton was murdered in his apartment. Gonna have to strike him off my list."

"Wow. Who caught the case?"

"Don't know yet," she said as two more police units pulled into the lot. "Just found him."

She heard tapping on a keyboard. "Give me about an hour. I'll email it to you."

"Great. Thanks."

She paced impatiently in the parking lot as a flurry of police came and went, but there was no sign of a detective. Finally, some fifteen minutes later, an unmarked car pulled up. It was with relief that she saw Dee Woodard step out of the car. Dee's hair was showing signs of gray, and she was wearing glasses, but still, she was familiar. She immediately walked over to her.

"Hey, Dee."

The woman turned, a frown on her face. Then she smiled. "Quinn! I hardly recognized you."

"Yeah, I cut my hair off when I moved to the island." She pointed to the stairs. "You mind if I go in with you?"

Dee frowned again. "What's going on?"

"Patrick Engleton. Age twenty-two. I found him."

Dee simply arched an eyebrow questioningly.

"He was a…well, a person of interest in my case."

Dee nodded. "Okay, sure. Come on up then. Tell me what happened."

"Not much to tell. I went to his gym this morning. He's an every morning and every afternoon gym rat. He wasn't there yesterday and didn't show up this morning. Didn't answer his phone so I came over." At the top of the stairs, Quinn pointed down the walkway. "Found some blood smear close to the door. I'm assuming it's transfer from the killer."

Dee nodded when she saw it. "Door locked?"

"No. And no sign of forced entry."

She followed Dee inside where three officers were standing. One of them pointed toward the small kitchen. Quinn hung back, as Dee bent over the body.

"Doesn't look like a bullet wound."

"No," Quinn agreed. "And judging by the blood pool, I'd say cause of death was strangulation. Could have whacked him on the head to stun him, then strangled him."

Dee looked around the kitchen. "Whacked him with what?"

"ME just pulled up," one of the officers said.

"Okay, well, let's get out of his way." Dee motioned to her. "Quinn, you got personal information on this guy you can share?"

"Sure."

CHAPTER TWENTY-ONE

Nina wasn't a news junkie and normally turned the TV off when her crews left each morning at nine. She tolerated the Corpus Christi Morning Show only because the others enjoyed it. Today, however, she was elbow deep in suds when everyone left. She was only halfway listening to the TV as she finished washing the breakfast dishes. While she didn't mind cooking a big breakfast for the ladies occasionally, the cleanup was enough of a reminder as to why she bought it and brought it in more often than cooking.

"Patrick Engleton, age twenty-two, was found dead in his apartment this morning. Corpus Christi Police Department officials declined to give specifics, but they are treating it as a homicide. We spoke with some residents of Manor West Apartments, who were visibly shaken by the incident. We'll have more on this developing story on our noon broadcast."

Nina stared at the TV, her hands dripping water and soap onto the kitchen floor. She moved to turn it off, not interested in the day's weather forecast. She dried her hands on her shirt absently as she went into her office. Her cell was on her desk, and she picked it up, noting that her hands were shaking. Quinn answered almost immediately.

"Hey, Nina."

"Quinn. I just heard something on the news. I didn't know if you—"

"Patrick Engleton?"

She let out a breath. "So, you do know."

"Yeah. I was trying to find him this morning. Went to his gym, then to his apartment."

"You were the one who found him?"

"Yes. The detective who caught the case is someone I used to work with so hopefully I can get with her later today. I'm waiting on the private investigator's report."

"Whoever killed Jones also killed this guy? Is that what you're thinking?"

"Yeah."

Nina gripped the phone tighter. "God, you don't think it's Josh, do you?"

"You always suspect the husband, yes. But he gave us all of his security camera feeds. He never left the house. I also checked his phone. So, it's not him."

She let out her breath. "Okay. Good." Then she paused. "Have you let him know?"

"About Patrick? No. Not until I can tie him to Jones's murder. It could be a coincidence. Unlikely, but I don't want to assume it's connected."

"Okay. Well, I'm sorry I bothered you. I didn't know if you'd heard or not."

"It's certainly no bother, Nina." She paused. "I enjoyed our visit last night."

She found herself smiling. "Me too."

"Do you like steaks?"

She moved to the window and looked out into the backyard, still smiling. "I do. I'm particularly fond of ribeyes."

"What a coincidence. So am I." Another slight pause. "If I offered to grill steaks out on the deck, say, Friday night, would you be interested in joining me?"

Nina laughed quietly. "Are you asking me out?"

"I am."

She could hear the smile in Quinn's voice and could picture her blue eyes. She nodded. "Okay. I accept."

"Great! I'll talk to you later then."

She went to her desk and sat down. Just like that, she had a date with Quinn Stewart. Then she frowned. What did that mean? She hadn't been on a date in years, not since she met Allison. Would there be kissing? Would Quinn expect her to stay the night?

"Good lord, we hardly know each other," she murmured out loud.

Yet she probably knew Quinn better than she had Jennifer when she'd fallen into bed with her. The difference, of course, was that she and Jennifer had not dated. There were no get-to-know-you dinners or long talks watching a sunset. She had known from the beginning that she and Jennifer were not compatible in that regard. She shook her head now. Why on earth had she thought she needed someone to have sex with?

Well, she knew why. After Allison, she didn't want the stress of meeting someone new and dating. Jennifer had offered her companionship and a bed partner without the drama of a relationship. The reality was, however, that there was little companionship and, as the months wore on, little sex either. Despite her bout of loneliness over the weekend—which is what drove her to Quinn in the first place—she was thankful that Jennifer had met someone.

A knock on her opened door brought her around and she found her assistant standing there. "Hi, Lisa. What's up?"

"I have an exam tomorrow afternoon."

The stricken look on her face made Nina laugh. "Wish you had skipped summer school?"

"I know. It's like we have an exam every week. Anyway, I've got a study group in the morning. Would you mind if I missed work?"

"Of course not. I'll either go very early or skip my walk entirely and be here by eight-thirty with breakfast. Don't worry about it. Your classes come first."

"Thanks, Nina."

This was the third year that Lisa had been working for her. She only had two more semesters before she graduated. Then she would have to keep her fingers crossed that the next one she hired would be as dependable as Lisa had been.

CHAPTER TWENTY-TWO

Quinn sat at her small home desk, eagerly opening the email that Finley Knight had sent. She scanned through it briefly, then opened the attachments. The first file was a list of names and a thorough background on each. Five men. Her assumption that Jones was into younger men did not hold true as only two of the five were younger than thirty. One, of course—Patrick Engleton—was now dead. Two were over forty, and another—Brad Turner—was thirty-six.

"Turner?"

She pulled up the file on Jones, going back over her notes. Wasn't one of the women a Turner? She scrolled to where she'd put their contact info, finding Beth Turner.

"Oh, shit." She then went back to Finn's spreadsheet, looking at his address. Houston. She glanced back at her notes, seeing the exact same address for Beth. "Well, I'll be damned." Apparently Beth's fears had been right. Her husband *was* having an affair with someone. That someone was her best friend.

The two younger men, Patrick and Scotty Fritz—age twenty—both met Jones on the Match dating site. The two men in their forties, William McDonald from San Antonio and Nathan Poole from Corpus, met her on the adult dating site. That led her to believe that Patrick and Scotty Fritz were actually looking to meet someone for a potential long-term relationship, whereas the other two were only looking for a hookup for sex. And Brad Turner? Yeah, he already knew Jones. No need to meet on a dating site.

She read his section more thoroughly. It seemed they met often but not strictly here in Corpus. Finn showed they'd met for an afternoon tryst in Victoria, which would have been a near midpoint for them both. Met there three times, in fact. Other than that, Brad came to Corpus, and they hooked up at a Best Western six times and at a Hyatt five times. This was all within the last six months—fourteen times, the most recent being the Tuesday before the fateful weekend. Far more often than she met the other guys. Had Jones been in love with Beth's husband? Was that why it appeared to be more than an affair? Christ, what did she know about it? Maybe hooking up twice a month *was* an affair.

Nathan Poole had met with Jones three times. The last one being two weeks before she was killed. William McDonald, the guy from San Antonio, had been to Corpus twice to meet with Jones. The last encounter was more than a month before her death.

She leaned back in her chair, arms folded behind her head. Her gaze was on the surf, but she wasn't really seeing it. Where should she start? She needed to interview these guys, sure, but she thought maybe she would get with Dee Woodard first.

She sat forward again, taking her mouse and clicking through the commands to print out Finn's report. Then she picked up her phone to call Dee.

CHAPTER TWENTY-THREE

Quinn felt a little uncomfortable sitting in a bar at four in the afternoon, even though it was one she'd been to a hundred times before, it seemed. Dee had ordered a scotch, and she remembered a time when she would have done the same. Today, though, she ordered a beer. A light beer at that.

"It seems like when you left CCPD, you dropped off the face of the Earth, Quinn. I don't think anyone has seen you in a couple of years. Or did you find new hangouts over on the island?"

Quinn took a sip of her beer. "Not really. I got old and slowed down."

Dee laughed. "I know the feeling. Is it true you're on some Beach Patrol assignment?"

She laughed. "Yeah. I get to wear shorts and hang out on the beach all day driving a souped-up off-road vehicle."

"Yet you retained your title?"

"Detective? Yeah. I moonlight as a detective. Other than a burglary now and then, I don't really wear that hat much."

"And then a murder happens on your beach…"

"Yeah. Kinda ruined things."

Dee took a swallow of her drink. "Why was he your number one suspect?" she asked of Patrick Engleton.

Quinn pushed the beer to the side. "When I interviewed him, he said that he and Jones—that's my victim—had met at his gym two weeks prior and it was a short-lived affair. Finn found out that they'd been seeing each other for six weeks and that they'd met through a dating app. Lying to me doesn't make him guilty, but it did make me curious as to why he would lie."

"And you think his death is related to your victim?"

"I do. I'll give you the short of it. Sharon Jones Downey was on the island for a girls' weekend with some childhood friends. It's a yearly thing they do. They are all about the same age—early thirties—married with kids, professional jobs. Probably all upper-middle class. Except my victim had a secret life. She went by Ingrid Cloudcroft on dating sites. Finn found five men that she'd been seeing recently. Two men are in their forties, and they met on an adult sex site. Two were in their early twenties and she met them on Match. One of them is now dead."

"And the fifth?"

"Yeah. The fifth one is her best friend's husband."

Dee grimaced. "Does the friend know?"

"I'm assuming not. The friend is one of these women who was here for the weekend."

Dee took a sip of her scotch. "The victim's husband? Surely you started there."

"He was at their home with the kids at the time of the murder. Verified by security cameras and phone records. But yes, he was the obvious suspect. He caught her at the gym with Patrick Engleton. He was going to file for divorce. And there wasn't a whole lot of grief over the killing." She reached for her beer. "But I think one of the guys on my list is the killer."

"Gonna share your list with me?"

"Of course. The two that live here in Corpus will be easy to interview. There's one in San Antonio and the best friend's husband is in Houston. The guy from San Antonio I would put at the bottom of the list. He only had two hookups with her, and the last one was more than a month before she was killed."

"Maybe he wanted more, and she wouldn't meet him. Pissed him off."

Quinn nodded. "True. I didn't think of that. But this site—it's called Casual Dating for Adults—is for sex, not relationships. The people on the site don't pretend otherwise. If she turned him down, he could easily find someone else."

Dee frowned. "Casual Dating for Adults? I've never heard of that."

"Me either, but it's very real," she said with a smile. "Finn sent me the profiles of both of those guys as well as Ingrid Cloudcroft." She shook her head. "And it made me blush."

"Why Ingrid Cloudcroft?"

Quinn shrugged. "I guess she thought it would be safer than using her real name."

"Okay. What about the best friend's husband? Maybe he fell in love with her, then found out she was sleeping with these other guys."

"And in a jealous rage, he kills her? I guess we could speculate that about all of these guys. But would any of them kill her and then go after all of her other lovers? For that matter, how would they know who these other guys are?"

Dee smiled. "Same way you did. Hire a private investigator."

She nodded. "I've got four guys left now that Patrick is dead. Two in Corpus and I'm going to interview them tomorrow in person. Or at least I hope to. The other two I'll do a phone interview and try to feel them out."

"Are you checking their phone records?"

"They're not suspects yet. I doubt I could get a warrant."

Dee smiled as she knocked back the rest of her scotch. "Finn wouldn't have that restraint." She quickly held her hand up. "Not that I'm condoning it, but I have had her do that for me before."

"Get evidence first, then worry about a warrant later?"

"Yes. It hasn't come back to bite me in the ass yet."

"I doubt my sergeant would go for that. I'm surprised he so readily agreed to use a PI in the first place."

Dee leaned closer. "Let me have the list. I'll get Finn to pull phone records on the four of them. Might get lucky and one of them was at Patrick Engleton's apartment. Or in your case, out on the island when your victim was killed." At her hesitation, Dee continued, "If we find someone, then we'll know on who to concentrate our efforts. We can pull footage from traffic cams and see if we can spot him that way."

Sergeant Fields would have her ass, but she nodded. "Okay. But I still want to interview them the old-fashioned way."

"Of course. But as far as my case goes, I have no reason to even know of these guys. I'll see what Finn can find, then go from there."

CHAPTER TWENTY-FOUR

Quinn stood by patiently as Scotty Fritz painstakingly washed his hands at the filthy sink. The rag he used to dry them looked equally dirty. As if reading her mind, he held it up.

"Stained. It's been washed." Then he grinned. "Or so they say."

Scotty Fritz looked anything *but* a killer. And after learning all she did about Jones, she couldn't see her with this young man. He had a handsome face and reddish-blond hair that hung across his eyes. But his jeans and shirt were smeared with grease and his hands looked to be permanently stained as well. No, a car mechanic did not seem like Jones's type. But maybe Ingrid Cloudcroft liked him.

"I just have a few questions, if we could go someplace private," she said.

"You're with Port A police, you said?"

"Yes."

He rubbed what appeared to be peach fuzz on his young face. "I haven't been there in a while," he offered. "You catch somebody speeding in a truck like mine or something?"

She offered a quick smile. "Nothing like that." She looked around. "Is there an office where we can talk?"

"Yeah, but David is probably in there." He jerked his thumb out past one of the bays. "Step outside?"

"That's fine."

The morning sun was already heating up but like most days along the coast, there was a breeze blowing from the Gulf. She turned to him, deciding to get right to the point.

"You know Ingrid Cloudcroft?"

He frowned as if thinking, then a big smile lit his face. "Oh, yeah. Ingrid. She was hot. She was fun." He held his hand up. "I mean, yeah, we met up a couple of times. She's a little older than what I'm looking for but hey, she offered and I'm not stupid," he said with a laugh. Then his smile faded. "Wait a minute. She didn't say that I, like, assaulted her or something, did she? She was the one who wanted to do kinky stuff, not me."

"When was the last time the two of you got together?"

"Oh, yeah, it's been a while. I don't remember the date." He shrugged. "Well over a month, I'd guess. I haven't heard from her."

She knew from Finn's notes that it had been ten days before Jones was killed. "You met online?"

He grinned. "Yeah. Because women like that don't normally come on to me. She's a little above my pay grade if you know what I mean."

"Right. She's also dead."

His eyes widened. "Oh, man. *No.* What happened?"

"She was murdered. About six weeks ago."

He actually looked crestfallen, then his gaze met hers. "No," he said with a quick shake of his head. "You're not thinking that *I* had something to do with it, are you?"

"Where were you on Friday night, May twenty-fourth?"

"I don't remember. That was a long time ago. Friday night? I was probably out at one of the bars. Me and my buddies hang out at a couple of them."

"I tell you what, if you'll give me permission to check your phone records for that night, then that'll clear you." She smiled quickly. "Providing it doesn't show you on the beach, that is."

"Yeah, yeah. Sure," he said quickly. "You look at my phone. If we go to bars, we stay here in Corpus. If we go to the beach, we normally go to Padre, not Mustang. I haven't been to Port A recently."

She pulled out a piece of paper she'd printed out earlier—a consent form to search his phone records. He readily signed it.

"I got nothing to hide, officer."

"Detective," she corrected. She folded the paper again and shoved it in her back pocket. "Thanks for your cooperation, Scotty. If this checks out, I don't suppose you'll hear from me again."

"Okay, sure."

She turned to leave, then stopped. "One more thing. Another guy that Ingrid hooked up with was murdered in his apartment a couple of days ago."

"Whoa."

"Yeah. Might want to watch your back."

CHAPTER TWENTY-FIVE

Nina smiled as she glanced at her phone, seeing Quinn's name. "Hi," she answered.

"Hey. Am I interrupting?"

"No, no," she said as she leaned back in her chair. "Just making out schedules for tomorrow."

"Good. Feel like lunch?"

"Sure. I guess that means you're in Corpus."

"Yeah. I'm in the mood for fried shrimp. You know a place?"

She stood and grabbed her keys from the corner of the desk. "As a matter of fact, there's a great place not too far from my office. Right off the S.P.I.D., south of Oso Bay." The doorbell rang just as she went into the kitchen. "Hang on a second."

She opened the door hurriedly, only absently wondering who it could be. She laughed as Quinn stood there smiling at her.

"Hi."

"Hi yourself." Then she saw the large, white bag Quinn was holding.

"So? Lunch?" Quinn prompted.

Nina smiled at her. "I see you found Paula's Seafood. How did you know it was my favorite?"

"Is it your favorite? Good."

Nina stepped back, letting Quinn inside. "It's close to both here and my home. I go there far too often."

"That's right. You said you live on Oso Bay. Nice."

"It's convenient. And I have a great view." She led Quinn into the kitchen. "Well, not as great as yours. Besides, I hate my neighbors."

"Oh, yeah? I've got great neighbors. On one side, it's a retired couple who only spend winters there. On the other, it's a weekend place for a couple who live in San Antonio."

She laughed. "No wonder you say you have great neighbors. They're never there."

"Yeah. That's a plus," Quinn said with a smile. "Bobby and Theresa are the ones who live in San Antonio. I think it's five or six more years, then they retire and move here." She shrugged. "But I get along with them, so it's no big deal."

Nina grabbed two paper plates from her stash under the bar. "There are some water bottles in the fridge."

She took the plates and their food to the small breakfast table while Quinn got two waters for them. There were two large containers, and she opened them both, revealing a mass of fried fish and shrimp, along with fries and hushpuppies that were buried beneath the seafood.

"I didn't know if you had a preference for fish or shrimp, so I got the mixed platter."

"I like them both. In fact, this is normally what I get too."

She smiled as Quinn stole a hushpuppy from the pile and popped it into her mouth before sitting down. There was no awkwardness between them for it being the first time they'd shared a meal. She relaxed as she shoved two fries into her mouth before scooping out a portion of the fish and shrimp onto her plate.

"I used to eat at Paula's when I lived in Corpus. It reminds me of this little dive of a place on the island—Buster's. Local hangout and it looks like a biker bar from the outside. I don't think tourists dare go there," Quinn said before dunking a shrimp into the small tub of tartar sauce.

"Is that your favorite place to go to?"

Quinn bit the shrimp in half. "Hard to screw up fried shrimp, but yeah, I go there a lot. Enough that they know me by name."

"You said the other day that you worked Beach Patrol."

"I do."

"Yet you're a detective?"

"I was a detective at CCPD. Had my fill. It wasn't something I wanted to do anymore."

"I'm assuming doing beach patrolling was a demotion?"

Quinn smiled. "I guess it depends on how you look at it. It's very tame, for the most part. But Port A needed a detective, so we compromised. I still got the Beach Patrol gig, but I play a detective when warranted."

"Which is not often?"

"No."

"No crime?"

Quinn dipped a fry into the ketchup. "Not a lot of crime, no. Certainly not murder. The weeks around Spring Break get kinda crazy, though." Quinn smiled at her. "Are you questioning whether I know what I'm doing?"

"Not at all."

"There are standard procedures to follow, steps to go through. And ideally, you'd like there to be some physical evidence on the body or some DNA left by the killer."

"And there's none in this case?"

"No." Quinn paused, her gaze thoughtful. "Any of your group do drugs?"

"Drugs? No, I wouldn't think so." She smiled. "Well, I mean, pot, sure. College, you know."

"Cocaine?"

"Oh, no. Never. Why?"

Quinn glanced over at her, then picked up a piece of fish with her fingers. "Tox report showed Jones had cocaine in her system."

Nina's eyes widened. "Jonesy? Cocaine?"

"You didn't know?"

She shook her head. "I had no idea. She loved her tequila. That was her drink of choice. Always. Other than beer and cheap wine when we were in high school, that is."

"What about the others?"

"Cocaine? I wouldn't think so. I mean, these are all happily married, *normal* women with kids. All of them are very upper-middle class. Sure, if I had to pick one out of the group to do drugs, Jones would be it. The others? No way," she said with a shake of her head.

Quinn bit into the fish, then put it down. "I don't guess it matters much anyway. The fact that she had cocaine in her system has little bearing."

Nina frowned as she too took a piece of fish, but her mind was on Jones. For as much alcohol as she'd had that night, she should have been falling down drunk, yet she wasn't. Was it because of the cocaine?

"Are you shocked?"

Nina looked up. "Yes. I think I am. I guess I'm realizing that I didn't really know her at all."

"The whole Ingrid Cloudcroft thing is pretty wild."

Nina leaned closer. "Gonna share what you learned?"

Quinn smiled. "You mean like gossip? Tell all her dirty secrets?"

Nina sighed. "I keep forgetting your job, I guess, and think of you as a friend. So yes, gossip."

Quinn bit into another shrimp. "I guess me telling you about her won't compromise the case. If we think the same person who killed Jones also killed Patrick Engleton, I suppose CCPD will crack the case before me."

"Are you discounting your skills?"

Quinn laughed. "Skills? No, they just have a bunch more resources than we do. The info that I had to go to a PI for, they have people in-house that can do most of that."

"Okay. So, what did you dig up on Jones?"

Quinn wiped her mouth with a napkin, then wiped her fingers. "Well, Ingrid Cloudcroft was on a couple of dating sites. One, Match, is very common and pretty normal, I guess. The other—Casual Dating for Adults—is quite the opposite."

"I've never heard of that one."

"Right. Me either. It's basically a sex site. The casual dating part is really casual sex. And judging by what I've read about it, more into your kinky kind of sex—bondage and spankings and stuff."

Nina was sure she had a glassy look on her face. "*Jones?*"

"Yeah. So, I have the names of five guys she's been out with more than once. Two are from this sex site. I've not yet interviewed those guys. Two others she met on Match. Both of them are young, early twenties. Patrick, but of course he's dead. The other, Scotty, mentioned that Jones—or Ingrid—was into kinky sex."

"Just wow."

"These two from this other site, one lives here in Corpus. The other in San Antonio. I think she only hooked up with him twice and the last was about a month before she was killed."

"You said five. Who's the other?"

Quinn met her gaze and Nina locked on those blue eyes. Then Quinn arched one eyebrow. Nina frowned slightly, then her eyes widened.

"Oh my god," she whispered. "Beth's *husband*?" she guessed in a near whisper.

Quinn nodded. "Yeah."

She leaned her head back and closed her eyes. "Oh my god," she murmured again. "You have *got* to be kidding."

"No. And it's something I probably shouldn't have shared with you, and it goes without saying that you can't—"

Nina held her hand up. "I wouldn't mention that to anyone, least of all Beth." She buried her face in her hands. "I can't believe it! What the *hell* was Jones thinking? That was her best friend! I mean, like forever." She stared at Quinn. "Or did Brad initiate it?" Then she shook her head. "No. From how Beth describes him, he doesn't seem the type."

"I've not interviewed him either. I was going to call him after lunch." Quinn reached for a shrimp. "What's he like?"

Nina shrugged. "I don't know him. I first met him at their wedding. He was at Jones's funeral, but I didn't speak to him. He's nothing flashy. Just a normal guy. Jones was more into looks." She waved a hand at her. "You've seen Josh. Handsome. Articulate."

"Yet the four of them were friends?"

"I couldn't say how close Brad and Josh really are. It could just be a default relationship because of Beth and Jones. But their kids are close in ages, and I've learned from Beth that they play well together." Nina leaned away from the table, her head nearly spinning. "Oh my god, you don't think *Brad* killed her, do you?"

"You know what, at this point, I'm not sure what the hell to think. I assumed one of these guys got jealous and killed her. But now that Patrick is dead, is that guy going after the others too?"

"How would he know about the others?"

"Through a PI like I did or maybe Jones told him, which is doubtful. Hell, I don't know. This is a crazy case."

Quinn's phone rang and she offered a quick "Excuse me" before answering. Nina was too shook up to listen, her mind on Jones…and Beth. Good lord, but if Beth found out, it would send her over the edge, she was sure. Quinn laughed and she glanced over at her, seeing the corners of her eyes crinkling as she smiled. Obviously not a call related to the case. When Quinn looked at her, her eyes still smiling, Nina felt an unexpected flutter in her stomach.

"Can I bring a date?"

Nina's eyes were still held by Quinn, and she simply couldn't look away.

"Okay, I'll let you know."

Nina waited, watching as Quinn picked up her water bottle.

"Do you have plans for the Fourth?"

"The Fourth of July?"

"Yeah. It's coming up, you know."

"I haven't even thought about it, no."

"That was one of my sisters, Maggie. She always organizes a family outing at the beach. She and my oldest brother have small campers, so they pull them out there and stay overnight. The kids have tents."

"On Mustang Island near you?"

"No. Padre. We go to the National Seashore. She reserves a couple of camping spots. We'll set up a volleyball net and horseshoes. Some will fish. Just a good time getting together, drink a few beers." Quinn arched an eyebrow. "You want to go with me?"

Did she? "Yes," she said without much contemplation.

"Great. It'll be an all-day thing," she warned.

"Okay. I'm game." She took the last shrimp on her plate. "Who are your siblings?"

"Names? My oldest brother is James. We call him Jim. He's forty-two. Then Mike—Michael. He's forty. My sisters are Susie and Maggie—Susan and Margaret. Ages thirty-six and thirty-four. Susie is the youngest."

"And you're thirty-eight, you said? All two years apart. Planned that way or just luck?"

Quinn laughed. "Planned. If you ever meet my mom, you'll understand. She's extremely organized."

"They all have nicknames. Why don't you?"

"Quinn is actually my middle name."

"Really? Then what's your first name?"

Quinn made a face. "It's Rachel," she said dryly.

Nina couldn't help but laugh. "No. Rachel so does not fit you."

"My mother started out calling me that. I'm two years older than Maggie and the first girl. So, she was determined to make me a little ballerina. I, on the other hand, only wanted to tag along with my big brothers. When Maggie was old enough and showed an interest in dance, my mother finally gave up on me. By then, my brothers were calling me Quinn and it just stuck. I haven't been called Rachel since I was, oh I don't know, nine or ten." Quinn picked up her last piece of fish. "I'm stuffed, but I can't let this go to waste."

"I know. Lunch was very good."

"Yeah, thanks for letting me pop over, but I really should get back to work."

Quinn got up to clear the table, but Nina stopped her. "I can get that. And there's some fish left in mine. Do you want to take it?"

"No, you keep it." Quinn went into the kitchen to wash her hands. "Are we still on for Friday?"

Nina smiled at her. "Steaks I think you promised me."

"Yeah. Come over about six?"

"I'll be there."

She went with Quinn to the door, then leaned against the jamb as she watched her drive away. She liked her. She liked her a lot. Then she let out a deep breath and went back inside. Her upcoming date with Quinn—and the invitation to spend the Fourth with her and her family—took a back seat to the news she'd learned about Jones.

"Ingrid Cloudcroft. Good lord," she murmured.

She almost wished Quinn hadn't told her, because she didn't quite know how to process the information. Yes, Jones was living two separate lives, apparently. And for god's sake, she'd been having an affair with Beth's husband. What the hell had she been thinking? What the hell had Brad been thinking?

And poor Beth. She was already feeling insecure and anxious about her marriage. If she found out about this, it would kill her.

CHAPTER TWENTY-SIX

Quinn tapped her fingers impatiently on her leg as the phone rang. Finally, it was answered in a hurried voice.

"Hello."

"Yes, hello, is this Brad Turner?" she asked.

"It is. Who's calling?"

"I'm Detective Stewart with the Port Aransas Police Department. I have a few questions. Is this a good time?" There was a long pause, and Quinn pulled the phone from her ear, wondering if they'd been disconnected. "Mr. Turner?"

"Yes. Sorry. I suppose this is about Jones?"

"It is." She heard a rather loud sigh, and she wasn't sure if she should try to be tactful about the whole thing or just come right out with it. "How long had you been having an affair with her?"

Again, there was a lengthy silence. "An...an affair? What makes you think—"

"Come on, Mr. Turner, let's don't play games. Let me ask the most obvious question. Where were you on the night of May twenty-fourth?"

He gasped. "Surely to god you don't think I killed her?"

"Did you?"

"Of course not! I…I loved her. Why in the world would I kill her?"

"I take it your wife doesn't know."

"About the affair?"

"That. And that you loved her."

"No. But I don't think my marriage is any of your concern," he said a bit testily.

"Okay. Again. Where were you on May twenty-fourth?"

"I was here. We have three children. Beth was away with her friends for the weekend. I had the kids."

"Can anyone verify this?"

"Friday night, we went out for burgers. Then we went to my mother's house, and we watched a movie. It was late when we got home. Beth called me with the news sometime after midnight."

She nodded. "And your mother will vouch for this?"

"Of course. It's the truth."

"I'll need her number."

"Am I a suspect?"

"I'm just trying to eliminate suspects at this point. I understand the sensitivity of this, Mr. Turner. I'm not looking to cause you any grief with your wife. As you said, your marriage is none of my business."

"I understand. And I hate to even think this, but are you sure Josh didn't kill her?"

"Did Josh know of your affair?"

"No, of course not. I mean, Jones wouldn't have told him, no."

"You called her Jones?"

"My wife and her…well they were friends. I always knew her as Jones."

"Did she ever want you to call her by another name?"

"Another name? Why? Or do you mean Sharon? I just always knew her as Jones so that's what I called her."

"How invested were you?"

"What do you mean?"

"I mean, were you planning to divorce your wife?"

"I was totally in love with Jones. But she was married too. I never considered divorcing Beth."

She shook her head, wondering how relevant these questions were, or if it was any of her business. She went a different route. "Do you have any reason to think that Jones was having an affair with anyone else?"

There was a long silence before he answered. "When she and I first started out...well, our affair, yes, she was seeing someone else. She told me that. But after we got together, she said she had ended it. And the guy was pretty upset by it."

"Did she tell you a name?" she asked hopefully.

"No. And I didn't ask. I didn't want to know."

"Okay. Did you know Patrick Engleton?"

"No, that name is not familiar. Why? Do you think she was seeing him?"

She ignored his question. "Did you know that Josh was planning to divorce Jones?"

"No. Not until Beth mentioned it recently. Jones never said a word to me about it."

"Okay. Well, thank you for your time, Mr. Turner."

"Wait. My wife...there's no reason for her to find out, right? I mean—"

"I have no interest in your marriage. If I have more questions, I'll be in touch. Thanks."

She disconnected, then set her phone on her desk as she quickly pulled up the notes from Finley Knight. Were any of these men the one Jones had been seeing before she hooked up with Brad Turner? The timelines didn't seem to match. She and Brad had been seeing each other for more than six months. These other guys were more recent. Regardless, just as she knew in her gut that Patrick Engleton wasn't the killer, she knew Brad Turner wasn't either. And young Scotty Fritz wasn't the killer. That left the two men Jones had met on the adult dating site—William McDonald of San Antonio and Nathan Poole of Corpus.

She picked up her phone, putting a call in to William McDonald.

CHAPTER TWENTY-SEVEN

Nina waited while the security gate opened, then drove into Quinn's neighborhood, which looked completely different from this side of things. Nearly every house had at least two palm trees planted in their neat, but small lawns. As she wound to the right, she could see glimpses of the Gulf water between the houses. She followed Quinn's directions, going to the last street, aptly named Gulf Side. She spotted the now familiar blue beach house with the Jeep parked under it. Next to the Jeep was a utility vehicle of some sort. As she got closer, she recognized the Port Aransas Police Department logo on the side. Was this what Quinn used while doing her beach patrolling?

She parked behind the Jeep and got out, pausing to look around. It was an odd mix of houses. Some older, some newer. Most were modeled after traditional beach houses, but others had adobe siding with more neutral colors. Their spacing was staggered, giving those behind the beachfront houses a better view of the Gulf.

She turned to look at the Gulf now. It had been a hot, sunny day but here at the water's edge, the breeze was refreshing, and she lifted her face into it. She brushed the hair from her eyes before going around to the passenger's door. She had thought about bringing a bottle of wine, but she got the impression that Quinn wasn't a wine drinker. Instead, she brought dessert—a decadent chocolate cream cheese pie with whipped cream on top.

She paused at the bottom of the front steps, wondering if she should go around to the back as usual. But then Willie was there at the top, smiling at her, and she smiled back at the dog, who was wagging her tail so exuberantly her whole backside was wiggling.

"Hi, girl," she cooed when she got to the top, taking the time to rub the dog's head before going to the door. Quinn opened it before she could knock.

"Hey. Whatcha got there?"

She smiled at Quinn, noting again how brilliant her blue eyes were as the sun hit them. "Hi. Dessert. Very fattening."

Quinn lifted the lid to peek inside. "I vote we skip the steaks and go right to this."

"No way. I've been thinking of that steak all day."

She followed her and Willie inside, getting her first look at this part of her house. Here there weren't wall-to-wall windows like the back that faced the Gulf. Instead, two large windows on either side of the door were it. A big flat-screen TV hung on a side wall and a sofa and recliner faced it. The other side wall contained a large bookshelf that held nary a book. Assorted collectables sat about in it instead. She went over to it, glancing at several unique seashells and other items from the sea.

"This here is an old Japanese fishing float," Quinn said, picking up a round glass ball about the size of a softball.

"What are they used for?"

"They used to tie them to fishing nets to keep them afloat. They would wash ashore on the West Coast. Not sure how far south they'd go, but this one was found on the Oregon coast."

"By you?"

"No. Someone gave it to my dad years ago. I was always fascinated by it, so he gave it to me when they sold the house."

"That's right. You said they only live here during the winter months."

"Yeah. They usually come in November so we can have a big family Thanksgiving gathering." She carefully placed the glass float back on the shelf, then motioned down a hallway. "The spare bedroom and bath are back there. My bedroom is on the opposite side." She started walking and Nina followed. "Half-bath here," she said, pointing to a closed door.

They were then in the kitchen and small sitting room, and she put the pie on the counter. "You spend most of your time in here?" She motioned to a desk that was tucked into one of the corners.

"My tiny office. And I don't watch TV much unless it's football season. I mostly hang out on the deck."

"And watch the waves?"

Quinn smiled. "I've killed many an hour doing that." She went into the kitchen and opened one of the cabinets. "Want a drink?"

"Yes. Thanks." She glanced down at Willie who was sprawled out on the cool tile floor. "She was on the deck when I drove up. Do you worry about her running off?"

"Not anymore. When she was a puppy, I had the area under the house fenced off and I kept her there when I was gone."

"The area where you park?"

"Yes. The fence extended out into the lawn there and she was fine with it. But now that she's older, she just stays inside when I'm gone. If I let her out when I'm here, she's good at staying on the deck. She's learned that if she gets off the deck without me, she gets put back in the house."

She took the drink Quinn handed her. "Thanks."

"You want to stay inside or go out?"

"No, let's go out. I don't want to miss a second of this view."

They settled in the rocking chairs, which were well out of the sun this late in the day. To her surprise, Willie lay down beside her chair, not Quinn's. She dropped her hand down to pet her.

"What's your view like on Oso Bay?"

"The view itself is nice although nothing like this, of course. I can see the university in the distance, and I can see beyond Ocean Drive to Corpus Christi Bay. I like to sit on my deck and watch the sailboats."

"You say all of that as if you don't really like it there."

Nina nodded. "As I told you, I have the worst neighbors. And I can hear traffic noise from the S.P.I.D. And the naval station is close enough to buzz the bay with their jets."

"Ah. So not quiet and peaceful then."

"On rare occasions only. I was enamored with the view, though. In hindsight, I should have looked around more before I bought it."

"Well, I lucked out with this place. I told the realtor what I wanted and what I could afford. This place had come on the market like two days before. It was a little more than I wanted to spend, but after looking at some of the prices on others around here, I snatched it up."

"The inside looks nice. Did you do anything to it?"

"Not a lot. I redid the bathrooms—new fixtures, new flooring. The kitchen had recently been remodeled so I didn't make any changes." She sighed. "And I need to have the outside painted. I'll probably do that in late summer."

Quinn raised her eyebrows at Nina. "Tell me about your family."

"My family?"

"I know you have two brothers. What else?"

Nina took a deep breath. "You mean my parents?"

"Yeah. You said you weren't really close with them. Tell me."

She leaned her head back and stared overhead, then turned, and gave her an apologetic smile. "I don't see them or call them nearly enough, I know. The drive back to Sugar Land isn't even that long. Three hours and some change." She sighed. "My mother is still in denial. About me being gay," she explained. "She's very active in her church and is determined to set me straight. She always has some nice man she wants me to meet. The last time I went for a visit, she had invited another couple and their son to dinner."

"Trying to set you up?"

"Yes." She laughed at the memory now, but at the time, it wasn't funny in the least. "I was trying to be polite to him, but his overtures were too much. Completely over the top, as if my mother had coached him on what to say and do. I told him and his parents, right there at the table, that apparently my mother had failed to mention that I was gay and asked him to please stop hitting on me. He was completely shocked. His parents were speechless, and my mother was stricken with embarrassment. These were people from her church. My dad got up and went into the kitchen and came back with a bottle of wine, acting as if nothing out of the ordinary had happened. 'Who wants more wine?'" She laughed. "God, you could have heard a pin drop, as they say. So, I held my glass up and said, 'Fill me up' and he did."

Quinn laughed too. "I take it your mother was pissed at you?"

"To say the least. However, I was equally as pissed, and I didn't give a damn if she was mad or not."

"You cleared the air?"

"No. We don't ever clear the air. It gets swept under the rug with all the other things and eventually we'll pretend that it never happened. That was only like six or seven months ago and our relationship is still a little frosty."

"That's too bad."

"I suppose you were one of the lucky ones whose parents and family were accepting right from the start?"

"Yeah. Our family has always been close, and we've always talked about everything. That was no different."

Nina was caught up in her eyes again and she couldn't pull away. "I'm sorry I keep saying this, but your eyes are almost too beautiful."

"Thank you." Then Quinn fluttered her lashes teasingly, causing her to laugh.

"How many women have you picked up with only a look into your eyes?"

"Countless."

"I imagine so."

"Makes me seem very shallow. And I suppose in my younger days I was."

"But you are practicing abstinence now," she reminded her.

Quinn laughed. "Is that what I'm doing?"

"Isn't it?"

"I think I was just taking a break from it all."

"Were you faithful?"

Quinn arched an eyebrow. "Faithful? With Christie?"

"Yes. Or did you cheat on her?"

Quinn shook her head. "No, I didn't cheat on her. I told you, I quit going to the bar, quit hanging out with my usual drinking buddies. It was hard, I won't lie. I was used to..." She waved a hand in the air. "Well..."

"Used to having anyone you wanted?"

Quinn groaned. "God, that makes me seem so conceited."

"Why conceited if it's the truth? You're attractive. You can't help that."

"My personality is completely different when I'm drinking."

Nina motioned to the drink she held. "How so? I haven't noticed you change."

"No. I only have a drink or two now. I'm talking about being at the bar and drinking for hours."

"Do you start dancing on the tables?"

Quinn laughed. "Actually, yeah, I was known to get pretty wild. And because of that, I tended to attract women who liked that sort of behavior." Her smile disappeared. "I didn't like that person. I didn't even *know* that person." Quinn turned to look at her. "After Christie, I knew I couldn't go back to that. I didn't want to go back." She shrugged. "It's been refreshing really. The best thing I did was to get out of Corpus. Things are slower here on the island. I'm at peace with my life now."

"I can't picture you as that person dancing on tables. You seem so grounded."

"Grounded? Is that another word for boring? Or mature?"

Nina laughed. "Not at all. It was a compliment. But I guess you felt like you were living two different lives. Maybe that was how Jones felt."

"I don't know. Jones seemed to morph into Ingrid Cloudcroft willingly and intentionally. My two lives were based on whether I was sober or not. That always determined who I was."

Nina didn't want to pry but… "Were you an alcoholic?"

Quinn leaned back, obviously considering the question. "It wasn't like I woke up in the morning and needed a shot of whiskey to function. It wasn't like that." Quinn glanced at her quickly, then away. "I don't know if I had a party problem or a drinking problem. One caused the other. Which came first?"

"Yet you still drink."

"Compared to what I used to do, these few cocktails I have on the weekends makes me nearly a teetotaler."

"Do you think Jones needed her tequila before becoming Ingrid? Or even cocaine?"

"You would know that better than me."

Nina stared out into the Gulf, noting the sky showing signs of evening. She thought back to their last couple of days together. She could see Jones clearly, the tequila bottle held tightly in her hand. "Yes. I think she did." She turned to Quinn. "Speaking of Jones, did you find out anything more?" Then she held her hand up. "I'm sorry. I shouldn't expect you to tell me how the case is going."

"Well, we've already broken that rule, haven't we? Several times, I believe." Quinn stood up. "Let me start the grill."

Nina watched her go. "Does that mean there's nothing new?"

Quinn paused at the door. "I spoke with Brad Turner."

"Oh, wow."

"I'll tell you about it. You want me to refreshen your drink?"

She held the glass out toward Quinn. "I think so, yes."

* * *

Quinn had offered to move around to the front to catch the sunset, but she had rather stay in the back and watch the Gulf. So, Quinn had motioned her down the steps toward the beach. From a closet under the stairs, she took out two folded canvas chairs, handing one to her.

"We can sit out until dark."

"What about the grill?"

"Yeah, it'll be nice and hot for the steaks."

She followed Quinn and Willie to a spot she assumed they used often because Willie stopped and lay down before Quinn even had her chair set up. She put her chair next to Quinn's and sat down too. They were both looking out into the Gulf, the waves bringing in the reflection of the sun's last colors of the day.

"You do this often?" she asked quietly.

"Not nearly enough." Quinn turned to her. "I'm glad you enjoy this."

"And I'm glad you do."

"Yeah. I get pretty wild on Friday nights. If you weren't here I'd be drinking herbal tea. Decaf at that."

Nina brought her gaze from the water back to Quinn. "Are you apologizing? Or do you really think you're boring?"

Quinn smiled at her. "I guess I don't know how to be on a date. It seems boring, yes."

Nina reached over and touched her arm, letting her hand rest there. "I would much rather be here with you, sharing this quiet time, sharing steaks later, than to be out at a restaurant or worse, at a noisy bar." She smiled at her. "This is heaven to me."

Quinn stared at her as if trying to see if it was the truth. Her eyes weren't quite as brilliant in the approaching darkness, but nevertheless, she found herself caught in them. Then Quinn relaxed again, the corners of her eyes crinkling as she smiled.

"Brad Turner said that he was totally in love with Jones."

"Oh, good lord. Really? Beth would just die if she knew that." She grasped Quinn's arm tightly. "You're not going to tell her, are you?"

"No. That's between them. But there were five guys. One is dead. I've interviewed two others. I don't think either of them are the killer. So that leaves two more. The one guy who lives in San Antonio and the other one here in Corpus. And perhaps someone we don't know yet. Brad mentioned that Jones had been seeing someone before she and him got together. Said she ended it once they started their affair."

"This all just blows my mind. But I'm certainly glad you don't think Brad could be involved. I mean, I don't know him, but it would totally devastate Beth."

"I haven't been able to contact those other two, though. I've left a couple of messages. If I don't hear from them this weekend, I'll probably get Dee to help me locate Nathan Poole. He's the one who lives locally."

"Dee?"

"Detective Woodard with CCPD. She's the one I know from when I worked there."

"And are the two of you...friendly?"

Quinn laughed. "Is that a subtle way to ask if we've slept together?"

"Okay, yes it is."

Quinn shook her head. "No. Dee is married to the job as far as I can tell. She's probably early fifties and I don't recall her ever dating anyone." She stood. "Come on. Let's get those steaks on."

CHAPTER TWENTY-EIGHT

Quinn paused at the door, watching as Nina leaned on the deck railing, her gaze out over the now dark Gulf. The usual breeze blew around them and Nina absently brushed the hair out of her eyes. As if sensing her watching, Nina turned, a smile on her face.

"I guess you can tell that I love it here."

Quinn smiled too. "I wish I drank wine."

"Why?"

Quinn moved up beside her. "It seems like the romantic thing to do. Out here with the sound of the surf, the moon, the stars. Seems like we should be holding a wineglass or something."

"And decaf tea just wouldn't cut it?" Nina teased.

"No. Maybe brandy." She turned to face the Gulf. "Thanks for coming over. It was nice to share dinner with someone. And that dessert was awesome."

"You're welcome. The steak was excellent, as I've already told you." Nina turned to face the water too. "I like to cook outside. When I bought my house, I had visions of an elaborate outdoor kitchen and having every meal out there."

"But?"

"But I have noisy neighbors and it's rarely peaceful. Therefore, I've not done a single thing with enhancing the deck."

"No space at all between houses?"

"Very little. Which would be fine for those who enjoy the view of the bay from *inside* their home. And there are quite a few like that. They have enormous windows facing the water, as do I. But I much prefer to be outside." Nina turned and smiled at her. "Which is why I love your place. Quiet. Peaceful. No screaming kids next door."

"Yeah, I'm lucky in that regard. This little neighborhood here is pretty much all retired folks or weekend or seasonal only. And because I'm a cop and they feel safe with me living here, they bring me cookies and stuff like that."

Nina laughed. "Perks of the job?"

"The biggest perk is getting to wear shorts as I buzz around the beach. Well, that and spying pretty girls in bikinis."

"So, what does your job really entail?"

"I am technically the Beach Patrol Commander. I have three officers who work for me."

"So not a demotion then?"

"Not really, no. It was a new position that was created, and I applied for it."

"And the detective part?"

"Part-time job," she said with a quick smile. "Our little police force here rarely needs detective work. Certainly not for a murder." She heard Nina sigh beside her.

"It still feels a little surreal, you know, that Jones got herself killed. I can't decide if it would be easier to accept if it had been a random killing. To think that her actions with these guys may have caused it...well, it's...like I said, surreal."

"I imagine it is. And to be honest, when it first happened, I had little hope of finding the killer. There simply was no evidence to go on."

"But now?"

Quinn nodded. "I feel confident we'll find him, because I'm certain whoever killed Jones also killed Patrick Engleton. If one of these five guys is the killer, is his plan to eliminate the others? I hesitate to call it revenge. Jealousy? Maybe." She turned to face her. "I had assumed one of these five guys was the killer. But one is now dead. Scotty Fritz is barely twenty years old. He didn't do it. I don't think Brad Turner did it. So that leaves two possibilities. It's just that on paper, neither of them makes sense."

"How so?"

"For instance, William McDonald. In my mind, he doesn't really fit. Jones was with him only twice and the last time was well before she was killed. I don't see what motive he would have. I don't see the jealousy part."

"Maybe she turned him down."

"Maybe. Or maybe there's another player that we don't know about yet. The one before Brad."

Nina leaned closer. "And you're *sure* it's not Josh?"

"Everything that's happening fits the husband perfectly. But he didn't kill Jones. As far as checking his whereabouts when Patrick Engleton was killed—that's on Dee. I'm not working that case."

She turned to face the Gulf again, letting the quiet sink in. For it being late June, the temperature was pleasant. Of course, being here on the water with the constant breeze, it was never unbearably hot, especially in the evenings. She chanced a glance at Nina, who was also staring out into the darkness. Whether Nina would admit it or not, surely this had to have been a terribly boring first date.

Should they have gone inside and watched a movie? Maybe sat together on the sofa and held hands? Should she offer a nightcap? Should she—

"I should get going," Nina said, breaking her train of thought. "We don't normally work on Saturday, but I've got a crew going out in the morning."

"Okay, sure." Quinn turned. "I'll walk you down."

She was surprised, though, when Nina put a hand on her arm and moved closer. She was even more surprised when Nina's lips brushed her cheek, ending at the corner of her mouth.

"I enjoyed tonight," Nina said quietly. "Thank you."

Quinn stared at her for a long moment, conscious of her pulse beating triple time. "I'm...I'm sorry."

"Whatever for?"

"For not knowing all the proper protocols for a first date."

Nina gave her a rather sweet smile. "Are you afraid to kiss me?"

"I didn't know if it was allowed."

Nina laughed quietly. "You are too cute." Then the smile faded. "But yes, it's allowed, Quinn."

Quinn's gaze dropped to her lips, then back to her eyes. God, when was the last time she'd kissed someone?

"Are you afraid?"

Quinn swallowed. "I'm...out of practice." She took a step back. "With all of this."

Nina tilted her head, studying her. "You usually seem so sure of yourself. Is that an act?"

Quinn bit her lower lip, embarrassed. "I'm not used to doing this sober."

Nina's expression softened. "Then we should take baby steps." She smiled then and linked their arms. "And I'll let you walk me down."

Quinn felt herself relax, wondering why she was feeling so insecure. Yes, she was normally very sure of herself. Especially these last few years. But dating? Being with women? There was always booze involved. Maybe that's why things with Christie didn't work. When they'd met, she'd still been partying, drinking. She'd only stopped all that when Christie moved in with her. Because she wanted to change, she wanted to settle down. Christie was perfect for her while she was drinking. But sober? No. Christie wasn't who she wanted to be with. She found that out right away, but by that time, she was stuck. Stuck for months, that is, until she'd found the courage to end things.

Now, as she walked Nina down the stairs, she felt some of her confidence return. She didn't know how to date women like Christie sober, no. But Nina? Yes. Nina didn't know her any other way. And apparently Nina liked her for who she was now. She certainly liked herself better.

When they got to Nina's vehicle, they paused, hearing Willie whimpering at the top of the steps.

"Come on down." Quinn beckoned the dog.

Nina ruffled Willie's head when she joined them. "I never had a dog. Never even had a pet, actually."

"No? We had two dogs and a cat in the house when I was a kid. But Willie is the first for me as an adult. I wasn't home enough before to consider having a pet." She smiled. "Or mature enough."

Nina paused before opening her door. "Thank you again."

Quinn met her gaze and held it. It was dark and quiet, the sound of the surf muted somewhat on this side of the house. She leaned closer and placed a light kiss on Nina's lips. She was shocked by the fluttering of her stomach. "I enjoyed the evening too," she murmured quietly.

Instead of opening the door, Nina moved closer to her. Their bodies were as close as they could get without touching.

"Can we try that again?" Nina whispered.

For being a grown-ass woman, the feelings she was getting reminded her of the teenage crush she'd had on Monica Reddson when they'd shared a kiss at sixteen. Now, like then, she felt her body trembling head to toe, felt her breath being sucked out of her as Nina moved closer. When their lips met this time, there was a little more urgency, a little more fire. Their thighs were touching, their stomachs, their breasts. Yet neither reached a hand out to touch the other. When a tiny moan escaped Nina's mouth, Quinn felt a tightening between her thighs, and she took a shaky step away.

Nina, too, seemed disoriented as she put a steadying hand on her car. "So that was nice."

Quinn smiled. "Yes. Very."

Nina's hand found hers then, and she squeezed it. "When will I see you again?"

"Well, the Fourth is Thursday. You still want to go to the beach with me?"

"Absolutely."

"Good. It's an all-day thing, like I said. I'll pick you up about nine. That should get us there in time for brunch. Then it's a playday on the beach until the grill comes out and we'll do burgers and hot dogs."

"What can I bring?"

"Oh, nothing. I'll bring everything for us." She paused. "You drink beer?"

Nina hesitated. "Do you?"

Quinn smiled. "I'll have a couple."

"Okay. Then I'll have a couple too."

Quinn opened the door for her, allowing Nina to get inside. "Goodnight, Nina. Drive carefully."

Nina nodded. "See you Thursday."

Quinn stood there, watching her drive away. Willie leaned against her leg, and she absently reached down to pet her.

"I think I like her." She looked at the dog. "Do you?"

Willie's tail wagged, causing Quinn to laugh. "Come on. Let's go up."

She paused on the stairs, though, turning to catch Nina's taillights. Yes, she liked her. And yes, she was a grown-ass woman with butterflies in her stomach. What in the world was wrong with her?

CHAPTER TWENTY-NINE

"You seeing anyone, Quinn?"

Quinn looked over at Dee who was driving them to Nathan Poole's house. It was a sunny and warm Monday morning, and she was surprised by the question. Dee seemed to notice her hesitation.

"I mean, when you were on the force here, you had quite the reputation." Dee laughed. "I used to be jealous, but at my age, there was no way I could have kept up with you."

The embarrassment that she normally felt when anyone brought up her past didn't surface this time for some reason. Instead, she gave a playful laugh.

"Yeah, I used to get around."

"So is that a yes?"

Quinn shrugged. "Maybe. It's kinda new." She glanced at Dee and smiled. "I actually met her through this case, but I don't know if I would call it dating." Was it? She'd run into Nina on the beach one morning, then Nina had been to her house three times now. And she'd been to her office a couple of times, once for lunch. And they had plans for the Fourth. Was that dating? Did the kisses they'd shared constitute dating? She smiled at the memory. Yeah, maybe.

"Is she a part of your investigation?"

"No. She was friends with my victim, that's all."

"One of the ones who was with her for that fateful weekend?"

"Yeah. Only she's not married with kids like the others."

Dee turned into a residential neighborhood with most of the houses starting to show signs of age.

"Are you seeing anyone?"

Dee shook her head. "No. I mostly hang out with Finn and her partner, Rylee. And I forgot to tell you, Finn pulled phone records on all the guys on your list. None of them registered anywhere near Port A on the night of your murder. And none with Patrick Engleton either. Of course, as Finn said, if you're going out to kill someone premeditated, wouldn't you leave your phone at home?"

"True. That's providing the killer was taking forensics into consideration."

Dee slowed, then pulled to the curb. "Here."

"Car in the driveway," Quinn murmured. She pulled up her notes on her phone. "Plates match Nathan Poole's vehicle."

"Okay. Let's go see why he's not answering his phone."

Quinn paused at the car before following Dee along the front sidewalk. The car was locked, and nothing looked out of place. Dee was waiting for her, then rang the doorbell. After ten seconds, she rang it again. Quinn moved off the small front porch and stepped into the shrubs, moving her face against the window. The drapes were pulled closed, so she went to the edge, hoping to peek inside.

"Anything?" Dee asked.

"Not from here, no. Let's go around back."

A privacy fence blocked their way, however, and the gate was locked. Dee eyed the fence, then her. "You're younger than me. Want to climb over?"

"Locked gate. Locked house. Don't you think we need a warrant or something?"

Dee smiled. "Yeah, but I've been hanging out with Finn too long. She taught me to break the rules."

"Okay. Your call. I'm just along for the ride."

"Great." She motioned to the fence. "Hop over."

"Been a while since I've done this," she said as she tested the sturdiness of the fence.

She stepped back several feet, then took a running start. Her foot landed about halfway up, and she grabbed the top with her hands, using her feet to propel her over. She landed with a thud and only barely managed to keep her footing.

"Can you open the gate?" Dee asked.

"Yeah. It's just latched. Hang on."

She pulled the pin out, then flipped the latch up. Dee opened the gate and smiled.

"Thanks. Because there was no way I could have hopped over the fence like you did."

They went around to the patio, and she noted that the stainless-steel gas grill was opened, revealing a well-used grate. She moved past it, holding her hand out, but it was cold. The back of the house had a sliding glass door, and Dee paused at it, knocking several times on the glass. Quinn moved closer, again holding her face against the glare to peer inside. It only took a second to register the body on the floor.

"Got a body!"

Dee tried the door, but it was locked. "Shit." She, too, peered through the glass. "Is it him?"

"It's too dark inside to tell."

"I'll call it in."

Quinn nodded, but she was already looking around. Did people still leave keys hidden outside? While Dee stepped off the patio, phone held to her ear, she lifted the mat. No key. She glanced around, spotting a long-dead potted plant in a reddish terra pot. She lifted the pot, seeing the dull shine of a house key. "Bingo." She snatched it up, then showed it to Dee. "Should we wait on backup?"

Dee shook her head. "No. See if it works."

The key slipped into the lock easily, and she nodded when she heard the muted click. They both unholstered their weapons, then Dee motioned for her to open the door. It slid quietly along the tracks, and Dee stepped inside first.

Quinn glanced at the body on the floor beside the table. It was a woman dressed in pajamas and a robe. There were blood stains on her torso. Dee went farther into the house and Quinn bent down, touching the woman's neck. Dee looked at her questioningly, and Quinn shook her head.

"Police," Dee called loudly. "Anyone home?"

The house was eerily quiet, and she could hear each breath she took. She followed Dee into the living room, listening for sound. There was nothing. Dee pointed down a hallway where she assumed the bedrooms were. The first one was neat and tidy and appeared to be unlived in. The second one was obviously a boy's room. The bed was unmade, and clothes were scattered on the floor. There were posters on the walls of sports figures, but she only recognized one—LeBron James. A bookshelf displayed numerous trophies; all appeared to be for basketball.

Dee went toward the closet. "Check under the bed," she instructed quietly.

Quinn did, finding nothing but a baseball bat and glove that had been shoved near the wall.

They went back into the hallway and down to the last door. Master bedroom, she assumed. Dee pushed the door open, and they both stood there, staring at the bloody mess. A naked man—Nathan Poole, she assumed—was tied to the bed. The once white sheets were covered in long-dried blood. A knife was still sticking out of his chest.

"Jesus Christ. His penis was cut off," Dee murmured.

Quinn stared at the mangled mess, then tore her eyes away. "Wonder why Patrick Engleton was spared that fate?"

"Cause of death is obviously not the same." Dee looked at her. "Are we sure it's the same killer?"

"It has to be. And don't forget, my victim was also stabbed."

Dee pointed to the body. "He left the knife. You think he brought it with him or took it from their kitchen?"

"I don't think you come with the intention to kill and don't bring a weapon." She studied the knife. "But would he use the same weapon that he used on Jones and then leave it?"

"Well, if it's the same killer and this is now his third victim, he's got to be more than slightly deranged, don't you think? Maybe he no longer cares if the killings are linked."

Quinn didn't think that was the case. He was being too careful. He was in and out of Patrick Engleton's apartment without anyone seeing him. And judging by the state of these bodies, they were killed over the weekend. Again, he came and left without the neighbors getting suspicious.

"Wonder where the kid is?"

Dee shook her head. "Well, I hope to hell he hasn't been kidnapped."

"Or worse."

They heard the squealing of tires outside on the street. "I think my guys are here. I'll let them in the front door."

Quinn nodded, but she was still staring at what remained of Nathan Poole.

CHAPTER THIRTY

The street was lined with police units, the ME's van, and the forensic team's van. Feeling like she was in the way, Quinn went out into the backyard, her mind still whirling. Dee had spoken to a woman who lived next door. According to her, the Pooles' son had been picked up by the grandparents on Saturday morning. The Pooles had still been alive Saturday afternoon because she remembered speaking with them in the front yard. That was the last the neighbor had seen of them.

Quinn scrolled through her notes, finding the phone number for Scotty Fritz. It rang five times before it went to voicemail. She felt her apprehension grow as she went back to her notes, finding the name of the auto shop where he worked. She called that number.

"Gillespie Auto, this is David."

"Yeah, I'm looking for Scotty Fritz," she said quickly.

"No. Scotty just left. Had something come up. Can I help you?"

"No. I'm Detective Stewart, Port Aransas Police. I really need to speak to him. Do you know if he went home?"

"Couldn't say. He got a call. Seemed real shook up and said he had to go. Is he in some kind of trouble? I mean, he's a good kid. He—"

"How long ago did he leave?" she asked as she headed back to the house.

"Oh, I don't know. Thirty minutes. Forty-five."

"Okay, thanks."

The house was a flurry of activity, and she spotted Dee talking to the medical examiner. She hurried over to her.

"Well, hey, Quinn. Didn't expect to see you at a crime scene here in Corpus."

"Randy," she greeted Dr. Coolidge. "You remember my victim out on the beach?"

"Sure do."

"We think this is related."

"I see. I'll compare wounds, strike patterns, sure."

She nodded, then took Dee's arm. "You got a minute?"

"Not really, no. What's up?"

"Scotty Fritz. He's not answering his cell. I called the auto shop where he works. They said he got a call and took off. I'm going over to his house."

Dee shook her head. "I don't mean to be a hard ass, Quinn, but you don't work for CCPD any longer."

"I know that. But let's say he's a suspect in my murder investigation. I can—"

"You already told me you interviewed him, and he didn't do it. He gave consent for phone records. Remember?"

"Right. I'm still going."

Dee stared at her. "Oh yeah? How are you going to get there? You rode over here with me."

"Shit."

"Forgot that, huh? Okay. I'll send a unit. You ride along." Dee pointed her finger at her. "And you let them go in first. I don't need my ass chewed by the captain."

"Fine. Thanks. Let's go," she said impatiently.

Dee went over to an officer, speaking quietly to him. Quinn tapped her fingers on her leg, silently urging them to hurry. Dee finally motioned her over.

"Hernandez will drive you, Quinn."

"Thanks." She looked at him. "Ready."

"Yes, ma'am."

Quinn glanced at Dee and rolled her eyes. "What is he? Twenty?" she asked in a whisper.

Dee smiled. "Yeah, the older we get, the younger everybody looks. And don't do anything stupid, Quinn."

"Yeah, yeah," she said as she followed after Officer Hernandez.

* * *

"How big of a hurry are we in?"

"Silent run. Code 2," she said, indicating he should use his lights but no siren.

"Then hang on."

He took off with a squeal of his tires and she was flung back against the seat. Thankfully, he wasn't a chatterbox and he drove swiftly and confidently through traffic. She stared straight ahead, not really seeing anything. She was picturing the names of the five guys in her mind. Yes, the list was getting shorter. Patrick Engleton and Nathan Poole were now dead. Young Scotty Fritz was not answering his phone. Brad Turner lived in Houston, and she imagined he was safe. The other, William McDonald, was in San Antonio. Was he in danger? Hell, for all she knew, he could be the killer. But like Nathan Poole, she'd been unable to contact him. If he wasn't the killer, was he already dead? Had he spent the weekend the way Nathan Poole had?

Hernandez slowed as he turned onto Rivercrest. "Here's the street."

"It's a duplex."

"They're mostly all duplexes."

"Yeah, it's 1308-B," she said. Then she pointed. "There."

He pulled along the curb and they both got out. There were numerous cars parked along the street. A dog was barking a couple of yards over and she jumped when a car's engine backfired.

Hernandez laughed. "Yep. Gets me every time too." He led the way up the driveway, walking around the truck that was parked there. "Detective Woodard said for me to go first."

"Right." She held her phone up. "I'm going to call him again."

Hernandez nodded, then pounded on the door. "Police! Scotty Fritz? You there?"

The phone again went to voicemail, and she pocketed it. "Knock again."

He did. "Police! Open up!"

She jerked her head around when she heard glass breaking—a window?—from around back. She ran in that direction. There was a chain-link fence on the side, and using her hands, she scaled it in one leap.

"Goddamn it! Let *me* go first," she heard Hernandez yell behind her. She ignored him.

A man ran ahead of her, jumping the fence into the neighbor's yard much as she had. He cut up, ducking under a tree branch, then jumped the fence again. "He went back to the front," she said loudly. "Go back around!"

She jumped the fence as he had, still giving chase. But ferocious barking from the back of the neighbor's house sounded, and she turned to see a huge black dog, teeth bared, running toward her.

"Oh, fuck!"

She had a split second to determine she could not outrun the dog. She turned, racing back to the fence. She clumsily jumped it, her foot catching the top, and she tumbled to the ground in Scotty Fritz's backyard mere seconds before the dog slammed against the chain links. She rolled to her back, scooting away from the fence as fast as she could. The dog's big paws were hanging over the top as he growled viciously at her. She got to her feet and held a hand up, backing away slowly, never once taking her eyes off the dog.

"Good doggie," she said amid the slobbering growls directed her way.

She turned then and hurried back over the fence on the other side, going back into the front yard. Hernandez was there, looking around.

"Where is he?" she asked tensely.

"Hell if I know. I saw a dark-colored car round the corner. Could have been him."

She scanned the street, but there was no movement whatsoever. Even the dog had stopped barking. "Fuck!" she yelled.

"So that was him? The guy who lives here. The guy you were looking for."

"No. That wasn't him." She slowly turned back to the duplex. "Come on. Let's look inside."

The front door was locked, so they went around to the back again, using the same broken window that the guy had jumped out of. The dog came up to the fence, barking loudly at them. She ignored it, more afraid now of what they would find inside than she was of the dog. An image of Scotty's handsome young face flashed in front of her.

"Signs of a struggle," Hernandez murmured quietly, motioning to the tipped-over chair.

She nodded. She had her weapon out as did he. When they came to a hallway, she stepped around him.

"Check in there," she said, pointing to a doorway. She went to the next room where the door was ajar.

"Clear in here," he said.

She stuck her head inside, her breath catching as she saw him. She hurried over to him. There was blood on his torso. She felt at his neck, shocked to find a weak pulse. "Alive. Call it in."

"Copy that," he said as he fumbled with his radio. "Dispatch. Need a 10-52 at my location."

Quinn gently lifted his T-shirt, seeing the wound in his chest. "Stabbed. Not shot." She went to the drawers there and pulled one open. She grabbed a white T-shirt and held it to his wound, trying to stop the bleeding.

"Look for a knife. The guy wasn't running with one. Maybe he tossed it."

Hernandez nodded, bending down to look under the bed, then he went out into the hallway. Quinn looked around too. There were ropes lying on the bed. Apparently they had interrupted the killing. No doubt young Scotty had been about to meet the same fate as Nathan Poole.

With a sigh, she sat down beside him. The white shirt she'd grabbed was now soaked with red. She lifted it up, seeing blood still seeping from his chest. *Goddamn.* She pressed down harder, trying to get it to stop.

"Hang in there, Scotty. Help is on the way."

She closed her eyes to the scene in front of her, silently praying that he'd make it through this.

CHAPTER THIRTY-ONE

Quinn looked on helplessly as the paramedics lifted Scotty Fritz's body onto the gurney and covered him. *Goddamn.*

"Did you know him?"

Quinn turned to the man who had introduced himself as Detective Wegman. "Met him once, but not really. And where's Dee?"

"She's still at the other scene. Captain assigned me this case."

Quinn shook her head. "It's the same killer. Dee needs to be here."

He smiled—a smile that seemed a bit condescending to her. "I know you used to work for CCPD. I was still on patrol then."

"Ah. So, you're a new detective." *Great.*

"Right. And even though you think they may be related, we'll wait for the forensic team and medical examiner's report. I won't jump to conclusions just because *you* say they're related."

She stared at him for a long second. "I don't mean to be disrespectful, but...you're an idiot." She pointed at the bed. "Same ropes on the bed as Nathan Poole. Scotty Fritz is on the same list. It's—"

"What list?"

She ran a hand through her hair. "That's why Dee needs to be here! She already knows all this," she said loudly.

"Well, she's not here," he said equally as loudly. "I'm in charge. And I need some information from you. Hernandez said that you chased some guy over the fence, but then he disappeared. Did you get a good look at him?"

Quinn thought about simply walking out on him, but that would solve nothing. She glanced at the blood on the floor, the blood on her hands, the bloody T-shirt the paramedics had tossed aside. Scotty had never stood a chance.

"Detective Stewart?"

She sighed. "White guy, light brown hair. He was wearing slacks, not jeans. Like khakis or something."

"Age?"

"Hard to tell since I didn't see his face." She walked out into the hallway, looking for the bathroom so that she could wash up. "Did Hernandez find a knife?"

"No. No weapon was found."

"The guy wasn't running with one. Maybe it was something small then. Like a switchblade. Something he could hide in his pocket." She pushed open the bathroom door. "It'll be tough to find security cameras in a neighborhood like this, but I'd go door-to-door, checking for them. Might get lucky."

"I've got two teams already checking."

Quinn scrubbed the blood on her hands, watching as the porcelain sink turned red. She looked in the mirror, seeing Wegman behind her. "How does he control them?"

Wegman raised his eyebrows. "What do you mean?"

She grabbed a towel that had been tossed haphazardly on the countertop. "I mean, you've got a guy threatening you with a knife, why not run. Why let him tie you up?"

Wegman shrugged. "What are your thoughts?"

Quinn sighed. "My thoughts are that I need to be discussing this with Dee." She pushed past him, wanting to get out of there. Of course, she had no vehicle.

"Like I said, Dee doesn't have this case. I do."

"Fine. Hernandez was here the whole time. Any info you need, ask him. He works for you." She met his gaze. "I don't."

She pulled her phone out of her pocket as she walked outside into the sunshine, ignoring him as he called after her. The day had become blistering hot, it seemed. She now remembered why she'd left CCPD in the first place. Well, one of the reasons. She hated working homicides. She held her hand out and saw that it was trembling. She closed her eyes, trying to push away that old familiar feeling. More than two years since she'd felt it, and it came back in a flash.

Instead of going back to that place and time, she thought about her current life. She opened her eyes, looking into the blue sky again. Yes, she had a job she loved now—Beach Patrol. Shorts. The breeze. The surf. And pretty girls in bikinis. She took a deep breath, trying to stay in that safe place and not picture herself in a dark bar with half a dozen shots of whiskey already in her. She turned her attention to her phone, calling Nina. Yes. Because Nina was also in that safe place.

CHAPTER THIRTY-TWO

Nina smiled when she saw Quinn's name pop up on her phone. "Hey," she answered pleasantly. "What a nice surprise."

"Hi. Listen, are you busy?"

She glanced at the two monitors and the spreadsheets up on both. "Nothing I can't stop. What's up?"

"It's been a hell of a day and I kinda need a ride."

She frowned. "What's wrong?"

"My Jeep is at police headquarters. I rode with Dee. Detective Woodard," she explained. "We got separated and I need to get out of here. Can you come get me?"

She noticed that Quinn's voice lacked her normal pleasantness. She sounded, well, like she was about to cry. "Of course I'll come. Where are you?"

"I'll text you the address. Thanks, Nina. I...I need to see you. To talk. I'm sorry."

"Don't be sorry. I'll be right there."

She saved the work she'd been doing, then locked her computer. A quick glance at the clock showed it was nearly noon. Lisa would be leaving soon. She grabbed her keys, then stopped off at Lisa's office.

"Hey, I need to run out. Do you mind locking up when you leave?"

"Oh, sure, Nina. No problem."

"Thanks. I'll see you tomorrow."

She hurried out, wondering if she should be concerned about Quinn. She had been around her enough to know that Quinn wasn't herself. And she needed to talk? Wonder what that was about?

Well, it didn't matter. Quinn had reached out, and she would go to her. With that, she opened the text. She tapped the address, waiting for the map app to load. It wasn't a street name she was familiar with, so she blindly followed the directions, her mind still on Quinn as she sped away.

Twenty minutes later she pulled into a rather shabby neighborhood mixed with older homes and duplexes. Judging by the conditions of the yards, these were all rentals. She saw Quinn leaning against a police car and pulled up to her. Their eyes met through the windshield, and Quinn's normally brilliant blue eyes were clouded.

She unlocked the door, letting Quinn get inside.

"Thanks for coming," Quinn said as she fumbled with the seatbelt.

Nina stared at the blood on her shirt. "Quinn? Are you hurt?"

Quinn leaned her head back and sighed. "No. I want a drink. I want to go to a bar. A dark bar where nobody knows me. And I want to drink. A lot." Quinn rolled her head slowly toward her. "That's why I called you. Because I *don't* want to do that."

She let out a relieved breath. "So, you want to go talk somewhere?"

Quinn met her gaze. "Can we go to your place?"

Nina stared into her eyes, wondering what it was Quinn was asking. It didn't matter. Quinn had reached out to her. She obviously needed her. It didn't matter what she wanted. Did it?

She nodded. "Yes."

She pulled away, aware that Quinn had again leaned her head back and closed her eyes. Instead of asking the hundreds of questions running through her mind, she kept quiet. She drove a little faster than the posted speed limit, now in a hurry to get home.

CHAPTER THIRTY-THREE

The street they turned on—Ennis Joslin—was familiar to Quinn. This was the street she used to take to the house she owned by the campus. Nina turned well before her old neighborhood, though, taking a left on Sandpiper, then a right as the street wound between houses crammed together so close she could barely see Oso Bay beyond them. The houses were newer and well-maintained. Four or five houses down, Nina turned into a driveway. With the push of a button on her rearview mirror, the garage door opened, and she pulled inside.

They sat quietly in the car, neither making a move to get out. Quinn finally turned her head.

"You weren't kidding. The houses *are* close together."

Nina smiled at her. "Sardines, remember."

Nina opened her door, and she followed suit. She wasn't sure why she expected Nina to console her. For that matter, she didn't even know why she needed consoling in the first place. It wasn't the first homicide she'd worked. Maybe it was the damn list. Maybe she should have been trying to protect these guys instead of thinking of them as possible suspects. And Scotty Fritz? Damn, but for some reason seeing him like that, feeling his life slipping away from her as she tried to stop his bleeding—well, that was like a kick in the gut.

"Quinn?"

She looked up, realizing that she was still standing by the car, unmoving. "Yeah. Sorry."

She moved then, noting how neat the garage was. Not cluttered as some people kept them. She followed Nina through the door that opened into a large utility room. Beyond that was the kitchen. Like the garage, the kitchen was neat and tidy, nothing seemed out of place.

"Do you want some lunch?"

Quinn shook her head. "I don't think I could eat anything."

Nina came closer, stopping just in front of her. "You have blood on you," she stated quietly.

Quinn nodded, then swallowed before speaking. "It...it's from Scotty Fritz. The young guy on the list." She met Nina's eyes. "He was just twenty years old. Still a goddamn kid," she said, her voice cracking.

Nina didn't say anything. She just took a step toward her and gathered her in her arms tightly. Quinn was shocked by the tears that burst from her, tears that shook her, drawing out sobs as she clung to Nina. Nina still said nothing. She just held her close, rubbing one hand lightly against her back.

Embarrassed, Quinn pulled away, going to stand by the sink. She looked through the window at Oso Bay. "I'm sorry. God, I'm sorry. I don't know what's wrong with me." She cleared her throat and wiped a hand under her nose. "Shit."

She felt Nina move closer, but she didn't touch her. "Do you want to take a shower, Quinn? Get out of that bloody shirt? I'll find you something else to wear."

Quinn turned to her. "Will a shower make everything go away?"

Nina tilted her head thoughtfully. "Will a drink?"

Quinn smiled then. "Not just one, no. Why do you think I wanted to go to a bar?"

Nina smiled too. "I'm glad you didn't."

Quinn sighed. "Yeah." She met her gaze then, seeing concern there. "Maybe I will take you up on that shower."

"Of course. Come on."

It wasn't the spare bath that Nina led her to. Instead, she took her into her bedroom and pointed toward the large master bath. The shower was a huge walk-in box with glass walls. There were not one or even two, but three shower heads and an overhead one as well.

"Wow," she murmured.

Nina laughed quietly behind her. "I know. Definitely like bathing in the rain." She opened a cabinet and took out a thick towel. "I'll leave a clean T-shirt on the bed for you. We can talk when you get out."

It wasn't a "we can talk if you want" tone, it was a "we *will* talk" tone. She nodded. "Yes. Thank you."

Nina touched her arm and squeezed it gently before leaving and closing the door behind her. Quinn turned and looked at herself in the mirror. Blood on her shirt, yes. Lots of it. But it was the look in her eyes she didn't recognize. No. That wasn't really true. She *did* recognize it.

She turned away from that look and stripped off the bloody shirt.

CHAPTER THIRTY-FOUR

Nina was trying not to worry about Quinn, but she couldn't help it. The blood on her shirt and Quinn's words could only mean one thing. Scotty Fritz was dead. Did she find him? Was he the second of Jones's lovers to be killed?

She opened the fridge, glancing around inside. Quinn had said she wasn't hungry, and she wasn't sure she was either. Besides, her mind was too jumbled to try to fix something. She opened the freezer, eyeing the frozen pizza she'd picked up on a whim weeks ago. She took it out and quickly read the instructions before turning the oven on.

She then filled two glasses with ice and added water to each. Nothing exciting, certainly, but it would have to do. She pulled out the pizza stone she rarely used and put it in the oven to heat, then quickly took down plates and set the table for their lunch.

She had just put the pizza in the oven when Quinn came in. She looked more like herself now. Her eyes were brighter, not quite as troubled as before.

"Feel better?"

"Much." Quinn arched an eyebrow. "Decided we needed to eat something?"

Nina shrugged. "Something to keep me busy." She motioned to the table. "Let's talk."

Quinn nodded. "I was reminded today of why I left CCPD. I always wanted to be a cop. Always. I told you that before." She pulled out a chair and sat down. "I don't have the right makeup, though, to handle…murder and all that goes with it. I knew it back then. Corpus is not a huge city, but it's still a city with city problems. Three or four homicides every month. Then there's assault, rape." She sighed. "It wears on you. Takes a certain kind of person to work that."

Nina sat down too. "Is that why you started drinking?"

"No. The drinking came first, I think. The job just escalated it. More and more. It's how I coped. How a lot of cops cope. You know the saying, one drink is too much but a thousand is never enough."

"Did you quit your job because of the drinking then?"

"I quit because I was killing the part of me that was *me*. I wanted to be a cop to help people. To be one of the good guys. That's not how it was for me, though. There were too many tears, too much sadness, not enough joy, not enough thanks given for the job we do. I lost my love for it, really. And yes, I was drinking a lot. I didn't like who I was becoming." She shook her head. "No. Who I *had* become. I didn't like that person because that person wasn't *me* anymore. I was totally prepared to walk away. It just so happened that Port A had an opening." Quinn smiled. "Beach Patrol. Now what horrors could ever happen on beach patrol?"

Nina matched her smile, then it faded. "But then Jones came to town."

"You know, when it happened, I thought, well, I'll get to work a homicide again. Refresh my skills. Only it turned complicated very quickly." Quinn sighed heavily. "Dee and I went out to Nathan Poole's residence this morning. I had been trying to contact him and the other guy in San Antonio all weekend."

"Two of the guys on your list?"

"Yes. They were both from the adult dating site." Quinn took a sip of her water. "Anyway, we got to Nathan's house, found him and his wife dead. He had been tied to his bed and basically tortured. Thankfully their kid was with the grandparents. Now we've got Patrick Engleton *and* Nathan Poole dead." Quinn tapped the table nervously. "So I tried to call Scotty Fritz. Was going to warn him or something. Hell, tell him to get his ass out of town."

"Scotty was the one who met Jones on the Match site?"

"Yeah, him and Patrick. He was only twenty. Cute kid. I had already met with him, got his statement. Cleared him by his phone records." Quinn leaned her elbows on the table. "Dee was tied up at the scene with Nathan, so when I couldn't reach Scotty, she sent a patrol unit out to his house. I rode along."

Nina watched as Quinn folded her hands, her thumbs tapping together quickly.

"We knock on the door. Nothing. It's locked. The bastard was still in the house. He crashed out of a window in the back and took off running. I gave chase, but he got away." Quinn looked at her. "Neighbor's dog about had my ass."

She was quiet for a long moment. So long that Nina reached across the table to still her hands. "And Scotty?" she asked gently.

"Stabbed. He was on the floor of his bedroom. He was bleeding out. I couldn't stop it. And I watched him die and I couldn't do a goddamn thing about it." Quinn met her gaze and there were tears there again. "He was just a fucking kid who hooked up with the wrong person."

"Jones."

"Ingrid," Quinn countered. "Not Jones. Brad was the only one sleeping with Jones. The rest were with Ingrid." She rubbed her eyes with her fingers, trying to dry them. "I feel helpless. These guys on my list are getting killed one by one. Three down. Two to go."

"You no longer think one of them may be the killer?"

"The only one I haven't talked to is Willian McDonald. Yeah. He could be the killer. Or he could be already dead."

The timer on the oven sounded and Nina got up and peeked inside to see if the pizza was ready. She pulled it out and put it on top of the stove to cool.

"I'm sorry, Nina."

She turned around. "Sorry for what?"

"For dumping on you like this."

"I wouldn't exactly call it that, but isn't that what friends are for? To be there when they're needed?"

Quinn met her gaze. "We're new friends."

Nina smiled at her. "Yes we are. We're also more than friends. Or have you forgotten the kiss?"

"I most definitely have *not* forgotten the kiss."

"Good."

Quinn got up then and peered around her shoulder. "That does look pretty good. I guess I can force down a piece or two."

Quinn was close and all Nina had to do was turn. She did. Their eyes held for a long moment, then she moved closer. Quinn's arms went around her, and they stood that way, holding each other, saying nothing. It felt nice. It was an intimate hug, not a hug between friends, and neither of them pretended it was. Because of that, she let her mouth find Quinn's. She was shocked by the instant arousal she felt as Quinn kissed her. She forgot all about the pizza as she deepened the kiss, opening her mouth to Quinn, letting her tongue lightly brush with Quinn's.

They moaned simultaneously, and this, too, fed the fire she was feeling. Her body moved closer, her hips pressing tightly against Quinn as they kissed harder. Quinn's hands cupped her from behind, arching against her. She pulled Quinn even closer, her body rocking wildly as Quinn's thigh slipped between her legs. Yes, she forgot the pizza completely and was about to suggest they go into her bedroom when Quinn's phone rang. *Oh god no.*

They both groaned loudly as they pulled apart. They stood there staring at each other, both still gasping for breath. She wondered if her eyes were as feral as Quinn's. Then Quinn looked away from her, fumbling in her pocket for her phone.

"Yeah, Stewart," she answered.

Nina smiled at the huskiness of her voice, at the pulse that she could see beating rapidly in her throat. She turned away and stared out the kitchen window, taking a few deep breaths to try to settle her arousal. *Oh, good lord.* When was the last time she'd had a make-out session in her kitchen? If she had, she didn't recall it. Certainly not one that had her on the verge of an orgasm.

"Okay. I'll meet them out front."

Quinn cleared her throat and Nina turned back around. "You have to go?"

"Yes. I'm sorry."

"No. *I'm* sorry," she said with a smile. "At least they called now and not, say, fifteen minutes later."

Quinn held her gaze. "Is that where this was going?"

"Wasn't it? My god, I was...well." She stopped, too embarrassed to tell Quinn that only a few more seconds of that would have had her screaming her name as she climaxed.

Quinn tilted her head, a slow smile forming on her face. "Yes," was all she said.

She then took a step away from her as if afraid she might continue what they'd started. "Dee is sending a unit over to get me. I need to give a statement. And..." She took a deep breath. "And see where we are with all this. I'm sort of in the way, you know."

"What do you mean?"

"I don't work for CCPD, as I was told twice today. Not my jurisdiction and these are not my cases. I would imagine after three killings, Dee's captain will have a mini-taskforce or something."

"And you won't be involved?"

"I can't really offer them much. They already have the list of names. That's all I was going on."

"So, what do you do next?"

"I think I'm going to pay Josh Downey a visit. Let him know everything that has happened, see his reaction."

"But you cleared him."

"I did. But hell, he's got money. Maybe he hired a hitman or something."

"When will I see you again?"

Quinn smiled. "Well, are we still on for Thursday?"

"Yes." Then she smiled too. "That long, huh?"

"I'll see how the next couple of days go." She pointed at the pizza. "I'll take a couple of pieces with me, if that's okay." Then she plucked at the T-shirt. "And I'll return this. I threw mine in the trash."

CHAPTER THIRTY-FIVE

"I know I can't offer anything that you can't get yourself, but what's the real reason your captain doesn't want me involved?"

Dee took a swallow of the scotch she'd ordered. They were at the bar they'd met at before. And like before, Quinn had ordered a beer. Even so, she had yet to touch it.

"He wants Wegman and me to team up. Doesn't see a benefit to having you involved," Dee said bluntly.

"He knows about the list?"

"Yes. He knows about your case too. I believe his words were that you should concentrate on that and let us handle things here."

"Damn. Did I cross paths with him before and I don't remember?"

"Pointer. He was promoted to captain last January. He's very regimented. I used to think Mabanks was a stickler, but this guy…" Dee said with a shake of her head. "And it didn't help any that you pissed Wegman off." Dee laughed. "Called him an idiot, I hear."

Quinn sighed. "I was frustrated."

"No doubt. Anyway, I'll keep you in the loop, Quinn." Dee swallowed the last of her scotch. "Now, tell me your thoughts on Scotty Fritz."

"My thoughts?"

"Wegman mentioned you were questioning how our killer is able to subdue these guys enough to tie them up. What are your thoughts?"

"The only thing that will make you not run from a guy with a knife is a guy with a gun."

"So, he kills with the knife but holds them with the gun. Okay. How does he get inside their house?"

"Scotty got a phone call while at work. The guy I spoke with said he seemed shook up and said he had to go. I'm assuming the killer called him. But what did he say to him? What did he say that would make Scotty go home? Did he know the guy would be there waiting for him?"

"We're running his phone records, so if anyone called him this morning, we'll find it and go interview them." Dee raised her hand, signaling she wanted another drink. "We've got three dead guys from your list. Nathan Poole was bound by ropes to his bed, then tortured and killed. Judging by the ropes left at Scotty Fritz's house, he had the same in store for him, only you got there first. But Patrick Engleton? No. Completely different." Dee nodded as the bartender brought over another glass. She picked it up, then paused. "Maybe we have two killers."

"Patrick was stabbed too," she reminded Dee.

"And strangled and bashed in the head with something."

"See if the rope used for strangulation matches these."

Dee nodded. "Yes, they'll check for that. But if it's the same killer, why change?"

"Maybe because he's getting better at it. Gaining confidence. He killed Jones with five stab wounds to the neck and torso. She was a slight, petite woman who probably offered little resistance. Especially if she knew him. Patrick Engleton was next. He would have put up a fight. He was a bodybuilder. He was strong."

"Hit him in the head first to disable him. Then kill him."

Quinn shrugged. "It's a theory, I guess."

"Okay, then let's go back to your list. Two guys remain. Brad Turner of Houston and William McDonald of San Antonio."

"McDonald seems to be in the wind. I've been calling him since Friday."

"You think he could be our killer?"

"Or he's already dead."

Dee nodded. "I'll check into him more. Work. Family."

"Finn supplied his work info. I called there on Friday too. They said he was traveling for a conference in Austin."

"Then if he's traveling, I'll solicit Finn's help with locating him. I don't know how she does it, but she can find anybody." Dee killed the rest of her drink. "And I don't mean to question your instincts or anything, but are you *sure* Brad Turner checks out?"

"His alibi is his mother and his three young kids."

"And that was good enough for you?"

"So you *are* questioning my instincts then?" Quinn gave her a brief smile. "No, I don't believe that Brad Turner is the killer. Not of my victim and not of these guys. He's a regional sales manager for his company. He travels, which I thought would have been an opportunity for him to be here without it causing suspicion. Since the murder of Jones, he's been sending his assistant out and he's been working from home."

Dee nodded. "Okay. Good enough."

CHAPTER THIRTY-SIX

Quinn leaned against the railing of the deck, looking out into the nighttime. Willie was pressed against her leg, also looking into the darkness. The decaf tea she'd started with had been set aside. Instead, her hands were clasped together, her thoughts drifting in and out of the different scenes she'd had that day—the bloody mess of Nathan Poole's bed, Scotty Fritz's young face as the life drained from him, the backyard chase, the damn dog, and the dark bar where she and Dee had talked.

The scene that came to her most often was in Nina's kitchen, however. She closed her eyes now, reliving the heated kisses once again. Of course, what they'd been doing was far more than kissing, wasn't it? Had it only been an escape—a diversion—on her part? Something to chase the awful image of Scotty Fritz from her mind?

No. Because Nina had started it, not her. She smiled a little. It had felt so good, she hadn't wanted to stop. It also reminded her of how long it had been since she'd had someone in her life. More than two years since Christie. That's a long time without companionship, intimacy. She hadn't known she'd missed it.

And now she was, well, a little embarrassed. Maybe embarrassed wasn't exactly right. She tilted her head a bit, listening to the surf. No, maybe it was. She felt like she'd come across as needy. Desperate. And good lord, she'd sobbed like a baby. Yeah, that was embarrassing.

So, she hadn't called Nina. Hell, what would she say? Best to let that little episode in the kitchen get stale in her mind—not fresh like it was now. Maybe tomorrow she'd call Nina. Or maybe she'd wait until she saw her on Thursday for their planned beach day for the Fourth.

She sighed. Yeah. That might be best. Because who knew what tomorrow would bring? Her plan right now was to call Finley Knight and get her to go back over Jones's phone records prior to the affair with Brad Turner. Maybe she could find the guy Jones had been seeing before Brad. Then she was going to pay Josh Downey a visit at his office. A surprise visit. She'd let him know what was going on. She'd gauge his reaction. Because all of these killings most certainly pointed to the husband.

Willie stirred and she looked down at her. Their eyes met and she smiled at the dog before reaching out to touch her head. Willie's bushy tail wagged against the deck at the gentle contact.

Getting a dog had been the best move she'd made when she decided to change her life around. And Willie had turned out to be the *best* dog.

"Ready for bed?" she murmured.

Willie stood off her haunches and led her to the door.

CHAPTER THIRTY-SEVEN

Nina had just gotten the ladies out the door on their assignments when her cell rang. It wasn't the new ringtone she'd given to Quinn's number, and she was disappointed in that. She picked it up, surprised by the caller ID.

"Good morning, Beth."

"Hi, Nina. Am I catching you at a bad time?"

"Not at all." She moved to her office door and closed it, then went back to her desk. "What's going on?"

"Oh, the usual. Trying to muster up some enthusiasm for the Fourth. The kids want to go to the park and stay for the fireworks. I'm not sure I'm up to it. What about you? Do you have something fun planned?"

"Actually, yes. A day at the beach." She hesitated. "You remember Detective Stewart?"

"The one with those killer blue eyes? Of course."

"Well, we've kinda been seeing each other." *Was that the right word to use?* "And I'm spending the day with her and her family."

"Meeting the family? Wow. That's great news. Good for you."

Her tone wasn't quite as excited as her words, however. Beth sounded a little more down than usual. "How are you, Beth?"

There was a long, heavy sigh before she answered. "Oh, I don't know. Nothing feels right in my life. And Brad is like a stranger living in the house with me. Ever since the thing with Jones, he's been acting weird. He hasn't been traveling for his job, yet he might as well be. He's so distant from me. We never talk."

Nina flicked her eyes to the ceiling. *Yeah, because he'd been sleeping with Jones.* She wondered if Brad was still grieving Jones or if he was feeling guilty because they'd been having an affair, and it was eating at him?

"Well, I guess he thought of her as a friend, too," she said diplomatically. "I'm sure her death affected him as well."

"I suppose." Beth paused, as if deciding whether to say more. "I've actually been talking to Josh quite a bit. Several times a week." She paused again. "We…we talk, you know. That's how it should be. We should be able to talk and Brad and I don't. At all. Like I said, he's turned into a stranger."

"How is Josh getting on?"

"He's having a hard time adjusting. I think it's mostly because of the kids. They don't understand it all and I think he's worried about them."

"I imagine so."

"That's really why I'm calling. Josh's older brother, Jonathan—he's the one who started the law firm—has a townhouse over on Mustang Island. It's a vacation place that they offer to clients mostly, I'm told. Anyway, he urged Josh to take some time off and he suggested that Josh invite us down to the beach. Our kids are all near the same ages and he thought that might help them to have that interaction."

"I guess with it being summer and no school, they haven't had much distraction."

"None at all. Brad didn't want to go. In fact, he said no right away. I told him I would go without him then."

Yes, she guessed it would be stressful on Brad's part to be there with Josh, but she said nothing.

"Honestly, I don't care if he goes or not."

"What's going on, Beth?"

"Oh, Nina. I'm just so over my marriage."

"Really? Is it because you think Brad is having an affair?" she asked carefully.

"I was distraught at first, I know. And I'm sorry I dumped all of that on you, Nina."

"You needed someone to talk to."

"I did. But I realized that I'm living with a stranger who I no longer love." Beth blew out a breath. "Oh, Nina. I'll be honest… it's Josh."

Nina frowned. "What about him?"

"I think I'm attracted to him."

"*What?*"

"I know! It's crazy, isn't it?"

Oh my god. Nina grabbed her forehead and covered her eyes. She had no clue as to what to say to that statement.

"That's really why I'm calling. I would love to see you, Nina. We'll be there on Saturday, and we'll stay until Tuesday. I was hoping maybe you could come over on Sunday and we could have a good visit. I've already mentioned it to Josh, and he is fine with you coming. Bring your detective friend too, of course."

"Quinn? Oh, Beth, I don't know. It would be a little awkward, don't you think?"

"How so?"

"Well, I mean, she's investigating Jones's death. Don't you think it might be weird for Josh to have her there?" Of course, Quinn might think it was weird too.

"Oh, Nina, I don't know. I just want things to be *normal*, you know. And if you are there, maybe the big cloud that has Jonesy's name on it won't be as thick."

Nina squeezed the bridge of her nose with her fingers, almost wishing she hadn't answered the phone. She knew she'd go. She didn't feel like she had a choice. But Quinn? She would be hesitant to even mention it to her.

"Okay, Beth. Sure, it would be nice to see you again. And to meet your kids. And Brad," she added. "It's been a long time since your wedding. I'm sure he has no clue who I am."

"Of course he does. Thanks, Nina. I can't wait to see you and visit. I'll call you when we get there on Saturday. We can work out our plans for Sunday then."

"Okay. Great," she said with forced enthusiasm.

"Enjoy your beach day on the Fourth. I can't wait to hear all about the new gal in your life. Talk to you later, Nina."

She placed her phone down and leaned her head back, groaning out loud as she stared at the ceiling. No, she wasn't looking forward to it. No, she didn't want to meet Brad. Good lord, he'd been sleeping with Jones! How was she even going to look him in the eye? And now Beth is attracted to Josh? Good lord! And then Quinn? Would she go? And if she did, it wouldn't be only Josh that it would be awkward for. What about Brad? Quinn had questioned him about Jones's murder. Quinn knew about the affair. Would Brad then assume that Quinn had told her about it too?

Yes. At least it might be fun watching him squirm.

CHAPTER THIRTY-EIGHT

Quinn parked in the lot of the small office building with a large sign declaring it the home of DOWNEY, HINES, AND DOWNEY Attorneys at Law. She got out of her Jeep and smoothed her pants. She'd put on slacks that morning instead of jeans. Since she was going to Josh Downey's office, she thought she'd at least try to dress a little more appropriately. However, the lone dressy blouse she owned was long sleeved and she'd refused to wear it on this hot summer day. So here she was in her khakis and tan leather loafers, with a blue Port Aransas Police Department T-shirt tucked inside and her service weapon in the holster at her hip. She said the same thing now as she'd said to herself earlier while looking into the mirror.

"Fuck it."

With that, she walked confidently to the door and went inside. The reception area was brightly lit, and a young woman sat behind a large desk, tapping away on a keyboard. She looked up with an automatic smile.

"Yes, how may I help you?"

Quinn flashed her badge quickly. "I'm Detective Stewart. I need a word with Josh Downey, please."

"Oh." The woman went back to her keyboard, her hand over the mouse as she clicked several times. "I'm sorry, but I don't show that you have an appointment. Would you like to make one? I can maybe squeeze you in tomorrow."

"No. I need to see him today." She pointed at the phone. "Give him a call, would you?"

"He and Mr. Downey are in a meeting until ten o'clock. I'm sorry."

"Ah. The Downey and Downey part. Brother?"

"Yes. Jonathan."

"I see." She stepped away from the desk and took out her phone, finding Josh Downey's cell number. She smiled at the receptionist as it rang. When it was answered, she smiled broader. "Yes, Mr. Downey. How are you? It's Detective Stewart. You remember me?"

"Of course. I'm assuming this is about Sharon?"

"It is. I'm actually out in your lobby area here. If you could spare a few minutes for me, I have just a couple of things to run by you."

There was a pause, then finally a sigh. "Okay, Detective. You have five minutes."

"Great. Thanks." She pocketed her phone. "He says I have five minutes."

The woman's frown was pronounced as she picked up the phone. "Mr. Downey, I'm sorry to bother you, but—" She nodded quickly. "Yes, of course."

The woman stood then and motioned for Quinn to follow. A pair of heavy-looking doors opened into another room and hallway. The woman's heels clicked on the floor as she walked, and Quinn followed silently behind her. The receptionist came to a closed door and tapped twice before entering. She held it open and stepped aside to allow her in.

"Thank you," Quinn said. The door closed behind her.

Josh Downey and another man were sitting at a massive conference table. They both stood politely when she entered.

Folders and papers were strewn about on the table and a laptop was opened beside Josh. Behind them on the wall was a gigantic wrought-iron clock, and she noted absently that it was twelve minutes after nine.

"Detective Stewart. This is my brother, Jonathan," Josh introduced.

Jonathan appeared to be a year or two older than Josh with his light brown hair showing a trace of gray at his temples. Other than that, he had a youthful appearance. She stepped closer and shook his hand.

"Nice to meet you." She turned to Josh. "Would you prefer to meet in private?"

"No need. Like I said, he's my brother. I don't have any secrets."

"Okay."

Josh pointed to a chair opposite them. "Have a seat, please."

She was surprised at how pleasant and amiable Josh was being. Far different from the last time she'd spoken to him. Of course, that was well over a month ago. Time apparently had healed whatever wounds he'd had.

"I assume you heard on the news that Patrick Engleton had been killed."

Josh nodded. "Frankly, I'm surprised you didn't come looking for me."

"Yes, husbands are always the number one suspect. However, I don't work for CCPD. It's their case, not mine. I did want to run some names by you, though." She held a hand up apologetically. "And I don't mean to upset you with all this, but it appears your wife was seeing others besides Patrick."

Josh looked over at his brother, then back at her. "Yes. I told you that I had thought there were others."

"There were. I'm wondering if you already knew about them. I mean, you hired a private investigator. Was Patrick Engleton the only one they came up with?"

"What are you insinuating?"

"I'm insinuating that if I was able to find these other guys, why didn't your PI find them?"

"Because I was only interested in the guy she was meeting at that gym. I followed her. Sharon had a gym membership, but it wasn't there. She had lapsed going to the gym anyway. But suddenly she took an interest in it. So, I followed her. When she ended up at this place—"

"Island Gym," Quinn supplied.

"Right. I knew something was up. So, I hired a private investigator and told him where she'd gone. I wanted to know who she was meeting there. He gave me the name. Told me where they'd be and when."

She nodded. "Okay. What about Nathan Poole?"

Josh shook his head. "Never heard of him."

"Scotty Fritz? William McDonald?"

Again, he shook his head. "No. Was she…sleeping with them?"

"Assumptions only. Nathan Poole and his wife were killed in their home over the weekend. Scotty Fritz was killed in his home yesterday."

His face registered shock and surprise, not guilt. "The killings are connected to Sharon?" Then his eyes widened. "Wait a minute. You think *I* killed them?"

"Did you?"

Jonathan Downey spoke for the first time. "Detective, I believe your five minutes are up. Unless you are charging my brother with something, we'd like you to leave. Now."

Quinn looked at him briefly, then brought her glance back to Josh. "Did you kill them, Mr. Downey?"

"I did not. I didn't even know they existed. I—"

"That's enough, Josh. You've answered her questions."

Quinn stood then, nodding at the brother, then at Josh. "Thanks for seeing me."

"I did not kill those men," Josh said again. "I know you think I felt no remorse when Sharon was killed. Truth was, I didn't *want* to feel anything. I wanted to hate her. And yes, I was planning to divorce her. But she was the mother of my kids. Her death has disrupted their lives too. I wouldn't do anything to put their well-being in jeopardy."

Quinn arched an eyebrow. "You mean like going to prison for murder?"

"Yes."

She nodded. He either had a hell of a poker face or he was telling the truth. She believed the latter.

"Thanks for your time." She glanced over at Jonathan Downey. "Nice to meet you."

He said nothing as he went to the door and held it open for her. She left without a backward glance, and the door was closed firmly behind her.

CHAPTER THIRTY-NINE

"So, did you meet with Josh?"

Quinn drove them down Park Road 22, the road that would soon dump into the National Seashore. The top was off the Jeep, and she was thrilled to feel the wind on her face. Willie appeared to be enjoying it too as her mouth seemed to be lifted in a smile. Quinn looked relaxed as well, a far cry from the last time she'd seen her. Neither of them had mentioned Quinn's tears. Or the heated kisses and quick make-out session they'd shared in her kitchen.

"I did. And this whole case—it's just classic. Jealousy. Husband finds out wife is cheating on him. Goes off the deep end. Kills the wife, kills the lover." Quinn glanced over at her. "Well, multiple lovers now. But it's perfect. Classic."

"But?"

"But I believe him. I don't think he did it. Now Dee? Yeah, she's convinced it's the husband. She's pulling phone records and tracking his whereabouts during the time of these killings. But he didn't do it."

"So now what?"

"I've got that PI looking into something for me. Remember when I talked to Brad, and he said that Jones was seeing someone before him?"

Nina nodded.

"Well, the way it sounded was, Brad didn't know about these other guys, but he knew about the one guy before him. To me, these other guys were just for sex. Sex with Ingrid. But Brad? I think Jones was really having an affair with him. Like she was emotionally involved with him, not just sexually."

"Really?"

"That's my feeling. And I think prior to Brad, the other guy she was seeing, I think it was emotional too. But she ends that affair and starts one with Brad. The other guys she met online—she's Ingrid, not Jones. Brad was having an affair with Jones, not Ingrid. And I'd guess that was how it was going with this other guy too."

"Wow. That all makes my head spin."

"I know. And it's a long shot that the PI can find someone. She'll be using Jones's phone records, trying to find a number that called frequently then suddenly stopped about six months ago." Quinn held her hand up. "But that's enough talk about that. I'm looking forward to a break today." She smiled at her. "How was your week?"

"It was good. Certainly not as stressful as yours. I did get a call from Beth, though."

"Oh, yeah?"

"Yes. And you won't believe it. She and Brad and their kids are coming here on Saturday to spend a few days with Josh and his kids."

"Oh my god. You're kidding?"

"No. And it gets better. She says she's over her marriage and is attracted to Josh."

"What? You're kidding?"

"I wish I was. And it even gets better than that." She smiled broadly. "She's invited me—and you—to join them on Sunday. Apparently Josh's brother has a townhouse or something on Mustang Island. They're going to stay there."

Quinn laughed. "And she wants *me* to go?"

"I told her…well, I told her that we'd become friends. She insisted I invite you too."

Quinn laughed again. "Can you imagine how awkward *that* would be?"

Nina laughed too. "I know, right? Brad knows that you know about the affair. When he sees us together, he'll assume that you told me so then he'll know that I know too." She laughed again. "He'll be terrified that I'll tell Beth or even Josh. Can you see it?"

"Oh, yes. Vividly. It could be a lot of fun."

Nina raised her eyebrows. "Seriously? You want to go?"

"Sure. It would give me a chance to observe them. Unless you think it would be too uncomfortable."

Nina shook her head. "No. I don't really care if it's uncomfortable for Brad. It won't be for me. Well, other than knowing a secret that I can't tell Beth."

"Then let's go."

She would have never expected Quinn to agree to that, but she was glad she had, because she was not looking forward to going alone. Quinn slowed as they approached the pay station and Nina tried to tame her hair a little. Quinn's short hair had barely moved at all during the drive.

"This has been fun."

"Fun?"

"The Jeep topless," Nina explained.

Quinn winked at her. "Speaking of topless, what kind of swimsuit do you have?"

Nina laughed. "Not topless, I can assure you." She reached into her purse for her wallet. "I have a park pass. No sense paying an entry fee."

"Okay, thanks."

There were two cars in front of them and Quinn was quietly tapping the steering wheel. Nina thought she looked relaxed. "You look like you've been out in the sun."

Quinn nodded. "Yeah. I actually got out on the beach and did some patrolling yesterday. You know, my *real* job."

"How did you get today off?"

"Some of the guys who are on regular patrol volunteer to work holidays for the overtime pay. Besides, I pulled a double yesterday and was out until nine last night."

"And what does patrolling the beach actually mean?"

"Nothing very exciting. Check for parking passes. Make sure those camping know they only have a three-day limit. Make sure people aren't leaving trash out. Making sure dogs are on a leash. Fun things like that."

"And did you spy pretty girls in bikinis?" she teased.

Quinn laughed. "Yeah, there were a few. Unfortunately, most were twenty years younger than me. I felt old."

"You're not old. And you seem to be in great shape."

"Oh yeah? Have you been checking out my shape?"

Nina laughed. "I have. You look great in shorts, and you have a very nice tan. And I'm looking forward to a little downtime today too." She paused. "And looking forward to being with you. I missed you." Her smile faltered a bit. "I am a little nervous, though."

"Why? Afraid of my family?"

"Yes."

"Don't be. They're super nice. If anyone will pester you with questions, it'll be Susie."

"Do you ever bring anyone with you to these family gatherings?"

Quinn shook her head. "No. You'll be the first."

"Really?"

Quinn smiled at her. "Does that scare you?"

Did it? Yes, maybe a little, but only because of what her family's reaction would be. Would they assume their relationship was much farther along than it was? Would they assume that she and Quinn were in a serious relationship?

When Quinn pulled up to the pay window, Nina spotted Joni and smiled at her. "You have to work today, Joni?"

"Hi, Nina. It's not so bad. I get off at two, so Brandon is delaying his grill fest until this afternoon." She took the park pass from Quinn. "Are you just here for the day?"

"Got a family thing," Quinn said. "Over at North Beach."

"I hope they got here early. Lots of folks out already."

"Yesterday, I believe."

Joni handed the card back to Quinn with the white entry pass she was to tape to her windshield. "Well, you girls have fun. Be safe."

"Thanks," Quinn said.

"See you later, Joni."

Quinn pulled away with raised eyebrows. "You come here often, I take it?"

"At least three days a week. Joni works the booth in the mornings. I usually either park at North Beach and walk toward Malaquite, or go to Malaquite and walk farther south. I prefer that, but it's a longer drive and a longer walk, so I only do that if I can get out here by seven."

"You walk the beach every morning?"

"Pretty much. My lone form of exercise, but it's become therapeutic. Or maybe an active form of meditation. I have to set an alarm on my phone, or I'll just keep walking and find myself an hour or more from my car."

"I know what you mean. When I first moved to the island, I walked to the state park boundary, then just kept going and it was so mindless, I found myself all the way at the jetty of North Packery channel. I had a hell of a long walk back."

"Do you and Willie run every morning?"

"Most mornings. I do it for her. I'm not crazy about jogging really." Quinn petted Willie's head, then glanced over at her, reaching out to try to tame her windblown hair. "So, you missed me, huh?"

"I did. Does that surprise you?"

"No. I...I picked up the phone a dozen times to call you the last couple of days."

"Why didn't you?"

"I was embarrassed."

"For?"

"For having a breakdown. And for...you know, the other stuff."

Nina smiled at her, noting a slight blush on Quinn's face. "The other stuff was kinda nice. I hope we get to do that again. Soon."

"Soon, huh?"

Nina laughed at her. "I'm sorry. I'm being too forward." She patted her thigh. "I'll behave." Then she wiggled her eyebrows. "But I've been having delicious dreams of the other stuff. And, you know, some other things too."

"What a coincidence. So have I."

They didn't say anything else, but Quinn still had a smile on her face. So did she and she relaxed, taking a deep breath of the salty air. Quinn turned to the left, down the road that wound through the dunes toward North Beach. There was no parking lot here, not like at the Malaquite camping area, where there were pull-in spots with water and electricity. No, this was all primitive beach camping. Quinn shifted the Jeep into the four-wheel-drive position before hitting the sand. Wooden barricades prevented vehicles from going south toward Malaquite. Quinn turned north, hitting the packed sand, and driving slowly along the surf. Several RVs and campers were parked along the dunes, and other trucks and cars were parked among them, obviously set up for the day with large, colorful umbrellas and rows of lawn chairs.

"Maggie said they were up closer to The Pilings. Not as many people up there."

Nina nodded, but her gaze was on the Gulf as they drove slowly on the beach. The water looked clear and was a pretty aqua green today. Gulls and shorebirds scattered as they came near, then settled down again in their wake. A brown pelican was some twenty yards offshore, seemingly following along with them. Then, quick as lightning, he dove into the surf. He must have missed his fish because he came up again and resumed his hunt.

"There they are." Quinn pointed.

Nina turned her attention to the beach again. As Quinn had predicted, there were fewer campers out this far up the beach. A long silver Airstream sat perpendicular to the beach and a table was set up beside the door. A red and white-checked tablecloth was on the table, its sides flapping in the breeze. On the other side of the table was another camper, this one white and a bit smaller than the Airstream. It was parked parallel to the dunes. A blue tent and two bright yellow ones were erected on the other side of the smaller camper.

"The Airstream belongs to Maggie and Rick. My brother Mike has the other one," Quinn explained.

Nina felt a bout of nervousness hit her as three young boys came running toward the Jeep as soon as Quinn parked.

"Aunt Quinn," they seemed to yell in unison.

"Hey, guys," she said, pausing to hug each of them. "You've been in the water already?"

"Oh, yeah. We got here yesterday," one said.

Quinn opened the back and let Willie jump out. "This is my friend, Nina," she told the boys. "Nina, this is Jeremy, Andrew, and Mark."

"Nice to meet you," she said with a smile.

They didn't appear a bit shy, and the oldest, Mark, came closer. "Are you Aunt Quinn's girlfriend?"

Nina slowly turned her head to Quinn, meeting her gaze. Quinn winked at her.

"Today she is," Quinn answered for her. "Where is everyone?"

"Mom and Aunt Karen went back to town. They forgot something. Dad is in the camper making hamburger patties."

Then the three boys and Willie ran toward the water as quickly as they'd run up to the Jeep. "Shouldn't somebody be supervising them?" Nina asked.

"They can get their feet wet. They all know they can't actually get in the water unless an adult is around. Rules. They all know them. They come camping out here several times a year," Quinn explained.

A horn blew and a large SUV drove up with two smiling women in the front and two young girls in the back. More family, Nina guessed. The door opened and she watched with a bit of envy as Quinn was gathered into a hug. She didn't need to be introduced to know that this was one of her sisters. Envy, yes, because she didn't have this closeness with her family. She didn't really know she'd missed it until that very moment.

CHAPTER FORTY

"How long have you been seeing each other?" Susie asked the second Nina was out of earshot.

Quinn smiled at her sister. "Not long."

"And yet you bring her to a family gathering?" Susie leaned closer. "What constitutes *not long*?"

Quinn shrugged. "We've hung out a few times. Lunch. She's been over for dinner."

Susie linked arms with her and led her away. "Well, I love her. How old is she?"

"She's thirty-two."

"Good. And is it serious?"

"Serious? I wouldn't say that, no. We did kiss, though."

Susie rolled her eyes. "Good lord, Quinn! You're almost forty! You don't have the luxury of dragging out this dating thing. You need to jump right in."

"I just turned thirty-eight so don't push me up to forty already," she said with a laugh. "But you like her, huh?"

"I do. She fits in nicely with the family and she hasn't run screaming from the kids yet. That's a plus." Then Susie leaned closer. "She's cute and she's got a killer body." Then she laughed. "Whatever does she see in you?" she teased.

"She told me *I* had a nice body."

"Oh, you know you do." Susie patted her bare stomach. "I'm jealous. I wouldn't be caught dead in a sports bra out in public." She then touched her own waist. "Maybe I need to take dieting advice from you."

"You're not fat, sis. I told you—get a little exercise and quit eating so many carbs."

Susie waved her hand in the air. "Carbs, carbs, carbs. Keto this, keto that. I like baked potatoes, okay!"

"And sugar, and Cokes, and cookies and bread and—"

Susie covered her mouth with a hand and laughed. "Enough!" Then she motioned behind her. "Here she comes. Now don't screw this up. I think she's a keeper."

Nina came over, holding the two towels she'd gone to the Jeep to get. "I think Willie is nervous. She wanted to get inside."

"Yeah, she likes the kids in smaller doses."

"Where are you two off to?" Susie asked.

"We're going to sneak away where it's quieter," Quinn said.

"Okay. Then I'll keep the kids away, give you two some privacy," she said with a wink. Then she looked at her watch. "The volleyball game starts at one thirty. Don't be late getting back. And the horseshoe tournament will be at three thirty."

"I will definitely be there for that."

"I would think so, considering you've won it the last three years. Oh, and if you come back early, we can get a card game going. I'd love a chance to kick your ass in spades," Susie said with a laugh.

"Yeah, right. When is the last time that happened?"

"I know." Susie turned to Nina. "Don't ever play with her. She's a card shark!" She playfully pushed them away. "Go on. Have fun."

Quinn motioned with her head and Nina nodded, falling into step beside her. Willie walked next to Nina, splashing in and out of the water as she did.

"Card shark, huh?"

"I have a knack for spades, for some reason. I suck at poker, though."

"Well, I like your sister."

"Do you? Good. She likes you too. And she said you were cute and had a killer body."

"Oh yeah? That was nice of her." Nina bumped her shoulder. "Did she ask you if it was serious between us?"

Quinn laughed. "She did. I assume she asked you the same?"

"Yes. She also told me that you were the most honest and reliable person she knew and that I could trust you with my life."

"Is that right? Well, she may be a little biased, don't you think?"

Quinn went up closer to the dunes, out of the way of any vehicles that might be driving the beach. She took one of the towels from Nina and tossed it out. Nina did the same with hers and they sat down. She stretched her legs out and leaned back on her elbows, then lay down fully. Willie climbed on top of her, causing Nina to laugh.

"Get off me, you big lug," she said, pushing Willie to the side.

"Does she sleep with you?"

"She has her own dog bed, and she starts out there, but yeah, she gets into bed with me at some point."

Nina lay down too and rolled to her side, facing her. Quinn leaned up on an elbow, her eyes trained on the exposed white skin of Nina's breast where her swimsuit had pulled away. While she was in her usual beach attire—colorful sports bra and water shorts—Nina was wearing a very enticing suit with a plunging neckline that ended well below her breasts. She was surprised she hadn't drowned earlier when they'd been splashing in the water with the kids. She was certain her mouth had been hanging open as she stared.

"I find you very attractive," she managed to say as she pulled her eyes from Nina's breasts. "I *love* this suit."

Nina smiled a bit knowingly at her. "Is that why I caught you staring at me several times today?"

She felt a blush creep onto her face. "You caught me, huh?"

"I did. And when you weren't looking, I was staring too." Nina did a slow perusal. "You have a really nice body."

Quinn's gaze again dropped to Nina's breasts before finding her eyes. "I'm very, very tempted to kiss you."

"I wish you would. In fact, I think I'd like to do other things too."

Quinn felt her heart beating wildly and she drew in a quick breath. It was at that moment that she realized she was not in control—Nina was. In her old life, she was always the aggressor, the pursuer. And she dictated the pace—always hard and fast. The chase ended in bed and, again, she was in control. And by the next morning, she had most likely forgotten the woman's name.

She looked into Nina's eyes now, seeing desire, yes, but also something else. Affection? She swallowed, trying to push down her sudden nervousness, which made her wonder what it was about Nina that made her nervous. Before she even recognized what she was doing, her fingers were touching Nina's skin, running along the edge of her suit up to her breasts. She saw Nina's eyes darken and heard her sharp intake of breath. Her fingers paused their exploration. She pulled away from Nina's gaze, looking instead to where her fingers rested. Nina's nipple was straining against the suit, and she knew she only had to move an inch to touch it.

She looked back into Nina's eyes, seeing them nearly black now as there was no mistaking her desire. She let out her breath and slowly pulled her hand away.

"I think I want to do other things too," she said quietly.

Nina lay back and groaned. "God, I wish we were alone. Because I'm very aroused."

She lay back too, staring into the cloudless sky. "Would you come home with me tonight?"

She felt Nina roll her head toward her, and she turned too, meeting her gaze. A slow smile formed on both their faces.

"I would love to."

CHAPTER FORTY-ONE

While she had thoroughly enjoyed the outing—and Quinn's family—the afternoon seemed to drag by at an agonizingly slow pace. They'd played more in the water. She'd walked the beach with two of Quinn's nieces to hunt for shells. She'd participated in a volleyball game, and she entered the horseshoe tournament, laying down the ten-dollar entry fee even though she had no clue how to play. What fun that had been. She'd been partnered with Maggie's husband, Rick, and she surprised herself at how quickly she caught on. She and Rick, however, did not come close to winning. As Susie had predicted, Quinn and her brother Mike didn't lose a single game and won the tournament easily. And she'd found herself in a card game with both of Quinn's sisters. Thankfully, she was partnered with Quinn, who as Susie had said, was a shark. They had slaughtered them in two games of spades.

Now, as the sun was setting, a huge fire was lit, and the kids were jostling around it, trying to melt marshmallows for their s'mores. She and Quinn had gone earlier to the campground showers and had cleaned up and changed into clothes. They were now sitting on a towel in the sand, leaning against one another. Willie was lying beside her, not Quinn. She was pleasantly content, yes, but she was also anxious to be alone with Quinn. They had flirted, teased, and not so innocently touched to the point that she was afraid she was going to embarrass herself—and Quinn—by dragging her off somewhere to get some relief. Sitting here touching like they were wasn't helping matters either. Something about Quinn's presence seemed to set her on fire.

Quinn turned to her then, her mouth tickling her ear as she spoke quietly. "Ready to go?"

She nearly moaned and it took all her willpower not to turn her head and find Quinn's mouth with her own. Instead, she closed her eyes, blindly finding Quinn's hand. She squeezed it hard.

"I am most certainly ready," she murmured. She heard Quinn laugh softly and she dared to open her eyes. "I'm ready to get naked with you."

"Then we should definitely go."

Quinn stood and helped her to her feet, although she did not let go of her hand. "We're leaving," she announced. "Unlike the rest of you, I have to work tomorrow."

"It was such a wonderful day. Thank you for allowing me to join you," Nina said to the group.

She was included in the goodbye hugs and Susie even gave her two hugs. "So glad you came today, Nina. I hope we see you again." Susie then turned to Quinn. "In fact, Quinn, why don't we plan a dinner one night next week."

"Let's don't overwhelm her, huh?"

Even the kids came around and hugged her; Nina was certain she'd never once in her life been hugged so much. They walked to the Jeep holding hands, and Willie led the way, apparently anxious to head home too.

CHAPTER FORTY-TWO

The open air of the topless Jeep didn't seem to quell the fire that was simmering between them. They had done enough touching and flirting during the day to qualify as foreplay and if Willie wasn't with them, Quinn would have pulled into one of the many motels they passed and begged for a room. Nina's hand was resting on her thigh as they drove, and her fingers were moving gently across her skin. It was enough of a temptation to make her want to pull over on the side of the road and shove that hand between her thighs.

God, but she was in a heated state, wasn't she? Was Nina feeling the same? Was she about to combust too? Most likely, yes. Their lack of conversation seemed to indicate that neither of them could concentrate on *anything* other than what they were about to do.

When she turned into her neighborhood and waited for the gate to open, Willie moved to stand on the console, her tail wagging. Nina's hand left her thigh to pet Willie, then she placed it back there again. Whether it was her imagination or not, that hand seemed to be a little closer than before. Without even realizing what she was doing, her thighs parted invitingly. She nearly gasped as Nina's hand moved deeper between her legs. She then squeezed her thighs, holding Nina's hand captive.

"I'm going to drive us off the road," she said with an uneven breath.

"Then hurry."

Her entire body was trembling by the time she turned onto her street. She parked in her normal spot and cut the engine. They looked at each other for only a second, then both nearly bolted from the Jeep. Willie ran ahead of them up the stairs, and Quinn fumbled with her keys trying to unlock the door.

Once inside, she didn't bother with lights. They reached for each other simultaneously. Perhaps it had just been too long or maybe her memory was failing her, but she was certain she'd never been this aroused before. Their mouths met in such a fiery kiss, it drew loud moans from both of them. Nina's hands were tugging at her tank, and she separated enough to let Nina pull it over her head. She walked backward down the hallway toward her bedroom, all the while trying to remove Nina's T-shirt.

They didn't make it to the bedroom, however. She simply couldn't wait another second. She pinned Nina against the wall, nearly panting as they frantically kissed, their tongues battling each other for control. She blindly unbuttoned Nina's shorts and quickly shoved the zipper down. Nina's hands, too, made quick work of her shorts. Her hand slid inside Nina's shorts, moving into her wet silkiness, finding her clit throbbing.

Then her knees nearly buckled when Nina's hand found her. Their kisses were wild, hungry, and frenzied, and when Nina's fingers circled her clit she was certain she was going to fall down. She pulled her mouth from Nina, leaning against her for support as they shifted against one another, hands moving in near unison as they stroked each other. She was gasping for breath, as was Nina. It felt like minutes passed, but she knew it was only seconds. Nina cried out then, arching her hips against her hand, causing Quinn's own orgasm to hit with such force she barely avoided biting down on Nina's shoulder to keep from screaming out with pleasure.

They rocked slowly against one another, drawing the sensations out, both moaning as their fingers continued to explore. She finally stilled and Nina did the same. She leaned her forehead against Nina's, sighing contentedly.

"Sorry...but I couldn't wait."

Nina smiled. "I was ready at the front door."

She smiled too. "I was ready in the Jeep."

Nina gave a quiet laugh. "I was ready at the beach."

Quinn took her hand. "How about we try this again? In bed this time."

CHAPTER FORTY-THREE

Nina closed her eyes when Quinn's mouth teased across her breast. She was too sated to even moan anymore.

"Tired?"

She managed only a tiny smile. "As you must be." She opened her eyes. "What time is it anyway?"

Quinn scooted up beside her. "It's about two thirty."

"Good lord. So much for me being worried that it would be awkward."

"Is that what you were worried about?"

She opened her eyes. "Well, first time and all."

Quinn ran her fingers across her nipple. "I was worried too. I was worried I had forgotten how to make love."

She smiled. "Oh, yeah. I had forgotten about your two years of abstinence." She leaned closer and kissed her slowly. "Trust me, you forgot nothing. In fact, I don't think I've ever been quite this gloriously satisfied before."

Quinn smiled against her lips. "Gloriously?"

"Yes. If I tell you something, you promise you won't get a big head?"

Quinn laughed. "Okay. I promise."

"I've never had multiple orgasms before. And you've accomplished that twice in one night."

"Oh, yeah? Well, that is pretty glorious then, isn't it?"

"Maybe I need to try that with you, huh?"

She rolled over and pressed Quinn down, then moved on top of her. Her skin still tasted of the salty air, and she let her tongue trace Quinn's nipple, hearing the other woman moan quietly. She pushed Quinn's thighs apart with her knee, then settled there, still kissing at her breast. At Quinn's urging, she moved lower, her mouth nibbling against her skin, moving across her stomach to the hollow of her thigh. The scent of her, so familiar now, still stirred her. She spread Quinn's thighs wider, moaning as she buried herself in Quinn's wetness, her mouth closing over her clit as she sucked it inside.

Quinn bucked against her, and she held her down, her hands cupping Quinn's hips, holding her to her. As before, Quinn writhed against her mouth, her hands clutching the sheets. Nina closed her eyes, reveling in her task as her tongue stroked Quinn's clit. As Quinn arched up high, she sucked harder, hearing Quinn moan loudly seconds before she called her name.

"God, Nina," Quinn murmured as she lay limply on the bed.

Too spent to go on, she managed to pull herself back up. She curled against Quinn, nearly collapsing as her head rested on Quinn's breast. Quinn's arms went around her, pulling her even closer.

It had been a wonderful day and an even better night. And yes, she was gloriously satisfied. For being new lovers, there hadn't been even a hint of awkwardness between them. They had alternated between serious and playful, a mood that seemed to suit them both. How refreshing that had been.

She was too tired, though, to analyze it further. She simply closed her eyes and went to sleep.

CHAPTER FORTY-FOUR

Quinn slipped her sunglasses on as soon as she walked outside. She yawned absently when she fired up the beach buggy, as the guys called their patrol vehicles. She normally started her shift at seven, especially on holiday weekends. Not today, though. No, the sun was already high and blinding.

She took a sip of the hot coffee she'd brought along in her travel mug. Nina had still been sound asleep, so she'd gathered clean clothes, even using the spare bathroom to shower so she wouldn't wake her. She'd left her a note—a rather sickly-sweet love note—telling her to help herself to anything in the house. And asking if they could have another night together. Of course, she wasn't sure if she was physically able to make it through another night like that.

She smiled as she hit the beach, turning left toward Port A. Physically able? Surely she could muster up the energy. Because, damn, it had been a fun night. Yeah, it had. But she pushed all those delicious memories aside. She needed to work, and people were already on the beach. If she didn't pay attention, she was likely to run over someone while she replayed her night with Nina.

At Beach Access Road 2 she saw Darrell Rogers, one of her guys, heading in the same direction as she was. She radioed him that she was behind him and asked him to wait for her.

"Copy that, boss."

A minute later she pulled up beside him. "Good morning."

"Yeah. Beautiful. Still pretty quiet."

"How was it yesterday?" she asked.

"Fucking crazy. And we had people shooting fireworks, like usual." Then he smiled. "We made the city some money. I issued eleven citations myself just for fireworks."

"Good."

"You working all day?"

"Depends if anything comes up on my case."

"I'm only scheduled to work until two, but I don't mind pulling a double if you need me to."

"We'll see. After your busy day yesterday, don't you want to go home and relax?"

He laughed. "Yesterday was fun. I hit up about six parties where they were grilling. I had fajitas, burgers, hot dogs, and one guy was even grilling pizzas."

She shook her head. "You work too much. You're never going to find a girlfriend that way."

"I meet my share of ladies on the beach, boss."

"Right. And I said a girlfriend." She waved at him. "See you later. I'll let you know when I clock out."

"So does that mean I can pull a double?"

"I'll let you know. But I've got something to do Sunday. You can take my shift for sure then."

"Copy that."

Darrell was twenty-six and had absolutely no desire to do anything other than beach patrol. He was an attractive man with sandy-blond hair and a deep tan. And yes, she'd heard from the others that he'd met lots of women while on his daily patrols. She didn't doubt that. She figured they all had. Oh, well. They did their jobs. That was all she was concerned about.

She spun around in the sand and headed back from where she'd come. She'd cruise to the state park boundary, then she'd retrace and swing by her house. Maybe Nina would still be there.

The ringing of her phone pushed thoughts of Nina aside though. It was Dee. She pulled over next to the dunes and stopped.

"Yeah, Dee. Good morning," she answered.

"Quinn. I hear the surf. You must be on patrol."

"I am."

"God, were you out there yesterday? I heard the beaches were packed."

"Yeah, but I was down on Padre. Playday with the family. You get out?"

"Hell, no. Working three murders doesn't allow for a playday. I did spend yesterday evening with Finn and Rylee, though. Grilled steaks and tried to kill a bottle of scotch. Finn told me you've got her looking for a different guy."

"Yeah, I asked her to check Jones's phone records six months prior to meeting these guys. Specifically, prior to Brad Turner."

"You think there's somebody she missed the first time?"

"I think Jones was having an affair with Brad Turner. A real affair. These other guys she met online—that was just sex. My thought is that maybe before Brad, she was also having an affair with someone. Broke it off."

"And he went nuts and killed her and her lovers?"

Quinn nodded. "Yeah, long shot, I know. But we're running out of suspects."

"Speaking of that, I had put a call in to San Antonio PD regarding William McDonald. Got bad news there. They found his body south of the city, out near Hondo Creek, wherever the hell that is. He'd been shot."

"No knife?"

"No. But he took six shots. If it's the same killer, he's certainly taking pains to make it look like it's not." Dee sighed. "Doesn't matter. McDonald is not our problem, although I did share with them our theory. And you're right. We're running out of suspects. Brad Turner is the only one still alive. Have you warned him about the others?"

"No. He's in Houston. I figured he would be safe there." She frowned. "Although he's coming here this weekend. In fact, I'm supposed to join them."

"What are you talking about?"

"Brad Turner's wife, Beth, is one of the group of ladies who was here with Jones when she was killed. Beth invited Nina—and in turn me—out to a townhouse on Mustang on Sunday. She and Brad and their kids are staying with Josh Downey for a few days."

"Oh, man. How crazy is that?"

"Right. It ought to be interesting."

"And Downey invited them?"

"Yes."

"Kinda interesting, don't you think? I know you don't think he's the killer and everything we've run so far doesn't place him at any of our scenes, but still—"

"I know. It all points to the husband. Which is one reason I'm glad I'm going. I'll get to observe them together."

"Well, I think you should talk to Brad Turner. Let him know about these other killings. If I were him, I wouldn't come anywhere near Corpus. Or at the very least, I'd hire a bodyguard."

"Yeah, I'll talk to him."

"Okay. Well, if anything comes up, I'll let you know. Oh, and we did find the number that called Scotty Fritz that day. Burner phone. No activity other than that one call. Dead end there."

"As meticulous as the killer has been—no evidence, no prints, no sightings—he had to have planned these killings. They are not opportunistic. They're not haphazard."

"Right. I agree. Doesn't help, of course."

"No. But that's why I think it's someone who's had months to plan it all."

"Going back to your assumption that Jones was having an affair with someone prior to Brad Turner?"

"Yes. It's the only thing that makes sense."

Dee laughed. "The only thing that makes sense is the husband, but we won't beat that dead horse."

"You won't?"

"No. Because I interviewed him, and he didn't crack. Doesn't mean I'm not still suspicious of him."

CHAPTER FORTY-FIVE

Nina leaned against the counter, holding a cup of coffee. She yawned deeply, not bothering to cover her mouth. She picked up the note again, reading it once more. She smiled at Quinn's words. So, she'd had a fantastic time, huh? And she wanted to do it again. Tonight.

She took a sip of her coffee, contemplating a quick drive to her house. She'd maybe even take the time for a nap. Then she could pick up something for their dinner. And yes, she could stay the night again.

She moved over to Quinn's desk and found a pen. She flipped Quinn's note over and scribbled her own. She smiled as she wrote, wondering at these feelings she was having—these sweet, giddy feelings that had her thinking like a young girl with fanciful thoughts racing around in her mind. Thoughts like had she ever been so thoroughly loved before? No. Not even close. Thoughts that had her questioning why she and Allison had ever attempted a relationship in the first place. Their sex life positively paled in comparison to last night. And more thoughts, mainly wondering if she was now spoiled for all time after Quinn.

She smiled at that, knowing it was most likely true. Then she flipped the paper over, rereading Quinn's note once again. Quinn wanted a repeat. Quinn wasn't running. This wasn't a one-night stand like she had been famous for in the past. No. Quinn wanted to do it all again.

So she went back to her own note, adding to it as a smile still lingered on her face.

CHAPTER FORTY-SIX

Quinn walked out into her small side yard with Willie. She leaned against one of the house beams, watching her as she sniffed in the grass, looking for the perfect spot to do her business. She had been disappointed that Nina wasn't there, but her flirty note back to her had made her nearly blush. Yes, Nina was coming over and she would bring dinner. And yes, she was up for a repeat of last night's fun.

Yeah, she liked Nina a lot. They had hit it off from the very beginning, which was rare for her. Well, rare now. In her partying days, there were no strangers. She could talk to anyone and drink with anyone. Until those darker days when she'd started to drink more and more at home—alone. There were lots of strangers then. Even so-called friends became strangers. She didn't want to be around anyone, she didn't want to talk to anyone. That seemed like so long ago now.

Her life wasn't dark and dreary anymore. No. It was bright and full of sunshine. And it had sure felt good to be with someone—Nina—and remember every delicious detail of their lovemaking. Her memories of last night weren't fuzzy and dulled by alcohol. Of course, she'd been sober when she and Christie had been together, but her life had still been dark. She hadn't been happy and there had been nothing remarkable about her time with Christie. In fact, she had a hard time remembering the intimacies between them. It was all her fault, not Christie's.

She pushed off the pillar and went out into the yard, taking the ball out of Willie's mouth. The dog danced excitedly around her, and Quinn tossed it down the side and toward the beach. She followed Willie, taking the ball when she brought it back. She tossed it again, a little farther this time.

Yes, her life was bright now and she found she was ready to let someone inside again. She looked up into the sky and smiled. She had already let Nina inside, hadn't she? She was thirty-eight years old and for the first time, she felt like she was falling in love with someone. And she wasn't running from it. It felt too good to run.

Willie dropped the ball at her feet, waiting impatiently for her to throw it again. She picked it up and heaved it onto the sand. Willie spun and darted after it, her tail held high. She didn't know why, but all of a sudden, Quinn felt incredibly alive. The sky was brighter, the puffy clouds whiter, the air fresher. The smile on her face couldn't be broken and she actually laughed out loud with the overwhelming exuberance of it all. It was more intoxicating than any booze she'd ever had. Was all of this because of Nina? Was this sudden onslaught of happiness because she'd been truly intimate with someone? No games, no conquests, no drunken sex. The difference was amazing. And she felt nearly light-headed at the prospect of doing it all over again.

Those feelings stayed with her all afternoon as she showered and tidied the house, waiting on Nina. She'd gotten a text from her saying she would pick up pizza for them and should be there by five. A quick glance at the clock showed it at 4:48. Close enough for her anticipation to grow.

"I've got it bad," she murmured to herself.

And a mere three minutes later, she saw Willie cock her head, then pad into the front of the house. She took a deep, steadying breath, then followed after her. She had the front door open before Nina could knock.

Their eyes locked together, then they both smiled. She finally moved, taking the giant pizza box from Nina. Neither spoke and she wondered if Nina was as nervous as she was. She got her answer when she stood in the kitchen.

"Are you hungry?"

Nina's gaze was smoldering. "How about we put the pizza in the oven, huh?"

"Oh, yeah?"

"Yes."

She turned the oven to warm and put the box inside. Then Nina took her hand and led her back through the house. As before, they only made it as far as the hallway. It was Nina holding her against the wall this time.

"This has been the longest day," Nina said before kissing her possessively.

Quinn felt herself melting right there as Nina's hands moved across her body. Any nervousness she was feeling fled when Nina's tongue met hers and deft fingers unbuttoned her shorts.

CHAPTER FORTY-SEVEN

The pizza box was opened and placed between them on the bed. They were propped up on pillows and Willie was lying patiently at their feet, waiting for a handout. They were both naked, save for the T-shirts they'd slipped on. It was six thirty but even so, the pizza tasted freshly made. Even if it didn't she was positively famished and would have eaten anything. Quinn, too, nearly devoured her first slice.

"Do you know what I like about you?"

Quinn looked at her with an arched eyebrow. "Just one thing?"

Nina smiled at her. "Well, no. Many things. But I love that everything is so informal."

"You mean eating pizza in bed?"

"That, too. But I mean, what we just did, there was no big scene, no drama, no rules." She waved a hand in the air. "Maybe informal isn't the word I'm looking for. It's like last night when there was no awkwardness. Everything felt natural, organic. Nothing was forced. It was—"

"Effortless."

"Yes. Exactly. I don't have to wonder how you're feeling or what you're thinking. I can see it in your eyes, on your face."

"What about with your ex? Allison, I think you said her name was."

Nina picked up another slice of pizza, but she paused before eating. "In hindsight, it's so obvious now that Allison and I should never have been in an intimate relationship. It was the complete opposite. It wasn't natural being with her and it *did* feel forced. And I never felt free to do everything I did with you." She grinned. "Like have sex in the hallway. Allison would never have gone for that."

"What about with Jennifer?"

Nina shook her head. "I don't really want to talk about that. It was just…sex. And I know that sounds so trite, but it's the truth. And it was totally stupid on my part. At first it was like, I'm alone, I'm single, what's the big deal?" She smiled. "And it's not like we got together every night or even once a week. It wasn't like that at all. But I had just ended a relationship. I wasn't going to get into another one. Jennifer was fine with that, and she dated other people." She took a bite of her pizza. "I told you we didn't talk, and we weren't really friends. There was absolutely no emotion involved, which was the main reason it fizzled, and I lost interest."

Quinn bit into another slice of pizza, chewing first before speaking. "And now she's met someone—"

"Yes! I'm off the hook. I don't remember the last time I slept with her. Three or four months, maybe. But I saw her more recently. It was after Jones was killed. Actually, it was the first night I came to your house."

"Oh, yeah?"

"I met her at the bar. She invited me and I was feeling, well, still so disjointed because of Jones. But like I said, we weren't really friends and I needed to talk to someone."

Quinn smiled. "And you picked me. Aren't I lucky?"

"Are you?"

"I think so."

Nina held her gaze. "I like you, Quinn. Sometimes it's hard making new friends. Most times. But it was so easy with you."

Quinn leaned closer and kissed her. "And the other stuff?"

Nina laughed. "I *certainly* enjoyed the other stuff." She took another bite of her pizza. "And when I get my strength back, maybe we could do that again."

"You're going to stay the night? Until morning?"

"I was planning on it. Unless you'd—"

"No, no. I want you to. I've got a short shift tomorrow until noon. Then I thought maybe we could hang out on the beach, cool off in the water. Then I could grill something for dinner. I've got a good chicken recipe with some spicy barbeque sauce. Maybe throw some corn on the cob on the grill too."

Nina was nodding the whole time Quinn was speaking. "Yes. Yes to all. Sounds like fun."

"Good. And are we still meeting Beth on Sunday?"

"She's supposed to call me tomorrow when they get here." She met Quinn's eyes. "Are you *sure* you want to go?"

"Yes. Because I'm dying to see the interaction between Josh and Brad. Aren't you?"

Nina laughed. "Yeah. Is that a bad thing? I mean, Beth is my friend. If this were any other situation, I would feel obligated to tell her."

"I know. And when this case is over, if you still feel that way, then you should tell her."

Nina sighed. "Of course, she's apparently got her own crush on Josh. Do I want to get *that* involved in their lives?"

"Are you sorry I told you?"

"Oh, no. Although I still can't make sense of it. I mean, you should have seen Jones and Beth that weekend. They were as close as ever, laughing and teasing as they always did. You would have thought that Jones should have felt some kind of guilt, wouldn't you?"

Quinn shrugged. "I didn't know her, so I don't know. But yeah, you would think most people would have. Or maybe she was just a hell of an actor."

Nina leaned back and stared at the far wall, seeing them together. "I can still picture them sitting on the floor doing tequila shots. They were so happy. I often wonder if that was Beth's happy place—with Jones. Now that she's shared things about her marriage, I think back to other weekends when we were all together. She never seemed truly happy in her life, and I think that's why she gravitated to Jones like she did. And I think that's the same reason their families got together three or four times a year."

"What about now, though? Jones is gone."

"I don't know. Maybe she's trying to find that connection to her through Josh. She mentioned that she and Josh talk several times a week." She looked at Quinn thoughtfully. "Maybe Josh is trying to find that connection too."

Quinn tore the crust from her pizza and handed it to Willie, who snatched it up. "I didn't tell you, but when I met with Josh, he seemed completely different than he did when I first interviewed him. I attributed it to his anger fading and the shock of it all being not so fresh. But there was something else. He didn't come out and say it, but I think he really hopes we find the guy who did this. He may have been planning to divorce Jones, but I think he still cared for her." She shrugged. "Or maybe I was reading him wrong. Maybe I just wanted to believe that."

"Why?"

Quinn smiled. "I don't know. Restore my faith in mankind?"

Nina smiled too. "Does it need restoring?"

Quinn nodded. "Yeah. Working this case, I told you, it reinforces the reason I wanted out to begin with. All these innocent men—and Nathan Poole's wife—being killed because of what? Jealousy? That seems to be the motive."

"So, you want to just stick to Beach Patrol?"

"I do. It was a bit of a demotion pay-wise, but I wouldn't go back. My piece of mind is worth more than that."

"I'm glad you feel that way. Allison had a super stressful job. I guess she still has the same job, I don't know. But she worked for an oil and gas company out of Houston. Worked from home. She had her laptop out twelve hours a day, easy. She was mentally fried come the weekend, and even then, she worked some. She got paid crazy money, which only made her want to work more so she could get *more* crazy money, which she did. It was like that was all that mattered. Her piece of mind, as you say, never once factored into it."

"Did that help contribute to your breakup?"

"No. She already had that job when I met her." She waved her hand in the air, not wanting to talk about Allison. "What I'm saying is, I'm glad you are the way you are. I like who you are now. From what you've told me…well—"

"You wouldn't have liked me very much." Quinn smiled at her. "We certainly wouldn't have been in bed eating pizza." She paused. "And, you know, other stuff."

Nina laughed. "Speaking of that…"

CHAPTER FORTY-EIGHT

Quinn read through the email that Finley Knight had sent her. Maybe her hunch had been wrong. Finn hadn't found much.

There seemed to be an unusual number of calls to and from Jonathan Downey, the husband's brother. However, the number only slightly decreased after Brad Turner came into the picture. I couldn't find anything else that raised any flags. I've attached the phone records if you want to take a look. I couldn't find any pattern to them. Random. Different times, different days. Let me know if you need something else.

She opened the attachment, but it was as Finn had said—random. Some calls were short, some longer. There was one call that was an oddity. It lasted just shy of an hour. All the others ranged from two or three minutes to ten to fifteen.

"You're frowning," Nina said as she came up behind her.

"Email from the PI didn't really shed any light." She motioned to it. "Take a look."

Nina placed her hands on her shoulders as she read. "The brother?"

"Do you know him?"

"No. In fact, I don't recall Jones ever mentioning him. But Beth did say that it was Jonathan who suggested to Josh that they come down to see him."

She pulled up the attachment again. "Is it odd that they would have spoken this often? Three or four times a week, it seems."

"I would think that would be odd, yes. But it doesn't look like anything had changed. The week before she was killed, they were still calling each other." Nina pointed to the screen. "Jones called him three times. He called her once."

"Yeah. Maybe they were friends. I guess it's not that weird."

"Jones didn't have any brothers. Maybe she thought of him as that."

"Maybe." She closed her laptop. "Let me get that chicken marinating, then we can go down to the beach."

Nina lifted up the T-shirt she was wearing, revealing a bikini top underneath.

Quinn raised her eyebrows. "A bikini?" She swallowed hard. "We can stay in if you want."

Nina laughed. "Sorry to disappoint you, but no bikini." She pointed to her shorts. "Water shorts like you wear. The suit I wore on the Fourth isn't something I often wear."

"No?"

"No." She walked closer. Close enough to touch but they didn't kiss. "I wore it hoping to entice you," she said quietly.

"Was that your plan?"

"It was."

Quinn leaned closer, brushing her lips with hers. "That morning that Willie and I met you on the beach, I was already enticed."

"Really?"

"Uh-huh."

Nina moved fully into her arms, letting their bodies touch finally. The kiss Nina gave her was smoldering, and Quinn knew their playday on the beach was going to be delayed.

CHAPTER FORTY-NINE

Quinn was driving them down the island toward Sea Bird Lane, where they were to meet Beth and the others on Sunday afternoon. Nina wasn't familiar with the area, but Quinn said she knew it. She said the residences were farther back in the dunes with long boardwalks to the beach, unlike where her house was right on the beach. Nina was tired, yes, but in a peaceful and sated sort of way. The long Fourth of July weekend was coming to a close and she supposed she should go to her own house tonight. But god, how wonderful had it been spending these last four days with Quinn. They'd taken long walks on the beach with Willie. They had cooked together. They'd chatted about their childhoods and gotten to know each other better. Last night, Quinn had played the guitar for her on the deck, and she had such a sense of peace and belonging that she'd shivered with it. And she knew then that she was falling in love. Was it too soon to feel this way?

When Quinn turned to glance at her, the sun hit her face and the tiny scar above Quinn's eyebrow was illuminated. She reached over and touched it. Quinn arched that very same eyebrow questioningly.

"The scar. I noticed it that first time I met you. At the hotel. What happened?"

Quinn smiled. "I normally say I was breaking up a drunken brawl and got busted in the head with a pool stick."

She laughed. "And that's not what happened?"

"Nothing that exciting." Quinn touched the scar as if reminding herself that it was still there. "It's faded a lot. I was running beside Bree when she was learning to ride her bike. I tripped and did a faceplant on the road. Landed against the curb and busted my head open."

"Oh, wow. How long ago?"

"Bree was five, so ten years now. She's the oldest of all the kids. I stayed clear of the rest of them when they were learning to ride," Quinn said with a laugh.

"When we were at the beach on the Fourth, that was really the first time I've been around kids like that. It was fun."

"I'm glad you enjoyed it. My family is a big part of my life."

"I think I'm envious, but I really didn't realize that until that day. My family and me—we're far apart not only geographically but emotionally as well." She held her hand up quickly. "And I know three hours to my parents is not that far, it's just..." She shrugged. "It's just such a struggle to try to be close to them."

"Because your mother wishes you'd have a husband and kids?"

She sighed. "Yes. The husband, at least. I told you, I don't think my brothers want kids. My mother probably thinks I'm her last hope to be a grandmother."

"Do you want kids?"

"You mean like get pregnant, give birth and all that?" She nearly shuddered. "Nope." She smiled. "You?"

Quinn laughed. "No way. I like my current arrangement just fine. I get to see the kids when I want and turn them right back over to their parents when I've had enough."

She turned left off the main road, heading toward the Gulf. Nina looked at the colorful houses lining a canal, most of which had a boat near their piers. Expensive houses, she noted. Then Quinn turned again, and she saw Sea Bird Lane. They were close.

"I'm a little nervous," she admitted.

"Afraid you'll slip up and say something to Beth?"

"I know far too much about Jones, yes. And if she pulls me aside and wants to cry on my shoulder about her marriage—or tell me she's lusting after Josh—I may just encourage her to divorce Brad and be done with it," she finished with a laugh.

Quinn pulled to a stop at a cluster of townhouses. "Maybe you should encourage Brad to come clean with her. He must be wallowing in guilt over it all. At least you'd think he'd be."

"Oh, if Beth found out about the affair, it would kill her. She'd be devastated, sure. Humiliated too. But I think it would rip her heart out. Not because of Brad, but because it was Jones, her best friend. That would crush her, and I don't know that she'd get over it."

"Well, as Brad told me on the phone, their marriage isn't any of my business. And it's not. But in your case, you're keeping a secret from a friend. That's tough."

"Yes, it is."

Quinn opened her door, then paused. "If it's uncomfortable, we can always leave. Your call."

Nina met her gaze and smiled. "Thanks. We'll see how it goes."

They got out and walked together. Quinn playfully bumped her shoulder.

"It's been a great four days."

Nina returned the shoulder bump. "Yeah. It has."

CHAPTER FIFTY

"So good to see you!"

Beth's hug was tight, and Nina returned it. "You, too, Beth. You look good," she said honestly. She wasn't sure what she'd been expecting but judging by the last few phone calls between them, she thought Beth would be in a more depressive mood. Perhaps getting away had indeed been good for her. But she had a bit of a dreamy look on her face. Dare she attribute that to Josh? Oh god, what a tangled web it all was.

"It's been nice to be able to relax. And so good to see Josh. I told you we speak on the phone several times a week, but it's so much better to talk in person." Beth actually winked at her, then looked beyond her to where Quinn was standing. "Detective Stewart, glad you could come."

"Hello, Beth," Quinn greeted. "Thanks for inviting me."

"Well, when Nina said the two of you had gotten better acquainted, I was thrilled. I know Jones would have approved. Come in, please. Let me introduce you to my husband."

Nina met Quinn's gaze briefly, noting the smile there. She stood back, anxious to observe Brad's demeanor at the introduction.

"You've met Josh, of course. Brad, this is Detective Stewart. Nina and I met her, well, that night."

Quinn stepped forward, her hand held out in greeting. "Call me Quinn, please."

Oh, if only Nina had dared to whip her phone out for a picture. Brad Turner's face showed a myriad of emotions—shock, disbelief, embarrassment—as his mouth very nearly dropped to the floor. His eyes bounced around the room nervously as he stood, taking Quinn's hand in a brief handshake.

"Nice to meet you," he managed in a shaky voice.

"And you know of Nina, of course."

Nina offered him a brilliant smile as she met his eyes. "Brad. Nice to see you again."

"Yes. Thanks. You too."

Josh came out of the kitchen then, carrying a pitcher of what looked like margaritas. Nina was surprised that his smile seemed genuine when he saw Quinn.

"Detective Stewart, Beth said you would be joining us. Welcome."

"Mr. Downey," Quinn said with a quick nod. "Call me Quinn."

"Sure. And it's Josh." He then turned to her. "Nina. Sharon always spoke so fondly of you. Good to see you."

"Hello, Josh. Thanks for inviting us."

It all seemed a bit surreal as Josh poured his concoction into glasses. Brad sat quietly, avoiding eye contact with everyone. Beth seemed fixated on the margaritas—or was it Josh? She chanced a quick glance at Quinn, who arched an eyebrow sharply in that "what the fuck is happening" kind of look. She nearly laughed and turned away as Quinn smiled too.

"It sure is quiet," she finally said. "Where are the kids?"

"Oh, Julie is staying with us. She's been a godsend," Beth said.

"Julie?" she asked.

"She's our nanny," Josh supplied. He handed her a glass. "Here you go."

"Thanks."

"Julie took them down to the beach. They were going to build sandcastles." Beth then laughed and held up her drink. "Thus, we can partake of adult beverages."

She wondered if Quinn would decline the margarita, but she took a glass too. Unlike the others, though, she noted that Quinn didn't take a drink.

"Oh, that's so good, Josh," Beth exclaimed. "What a wonderful idea to make margaritas."

"I thought it would be appropriate."

"It was Jones's favorite liquor, yes."

"Did you call her Jones too?" Quinn asked Josh.

"No. She was Sharon to me usually. On the weekends that our families got together, she was always Jones, though." Josh glanced at Brad. "You called her Jones too."

"Yes," Brad choked out.

Oh, my. Brad looked on the verge of having a nervous breakdown. She wondered if Beth could tell. Nina took a sip of her drink thinking, yes, it was as awkward as she had feared it would be. Beth, however, didn't seem to notice any tension in the room even though, to her, it was as thick as the winter fog that sometimes settled over the island.

"Josh had the whole weekend catered," Beth said. "Last night's dinner was a wonderful shrimp dish that we served over angel hair pasta. There will be fajitas for dinner tonight, but in the meantime, they sent over a huge charcuterie board." Beth moved to the table. "Come take a look. You won't believe all the stuff they've got on it."

Nina dutifully followed her, as did Quinn.

"Look here." Beth pointed. "Prosciutto, salami, ham, summer sausage. They have cheddar, Swiss, Gouda, and Gruyère. There's brie, Havarti, and cream cheese with hot pepper jelly." Beth reached for an almond. "Four different nuts. Olives. Pickles. Even grapes! Doesn't it look beautiful? I hate to even mess it up."

"Then let me," Quinn said. She skipped over the assorted crackers and grabbed a ham slice and topped it with gouda.

Nina followed suit, choosing a cracker and spreading on a little of the cream cheese.

"How long have you two been seeing each other?" Beth asked.

Nina and Quinn looked at each other, both smiling. "Well, I ran into her on the beach a, well, a few weeks after Jones," Nina said. "And then, uninvited, I went to her house. Twice," she said with a quick laugh.

"And uninvited, I showed up at your office twice," Quinn added.

"But you brought lunch."

"And we had dinner at my place."

"And the beach on the Fourth." She stopped and held Quinn's gaze. "And then..."

Quinn laughed and turned to Beth. "Yeah. So that long."

"Well, Jones would have certainly approved, Nina." Beth turned to Quinn. "Jones was trying to set her up with the receptionist at our hotel."

"She had blue hair and was barely out of high school!"

Josh came over, taking a cube of cheddar and popping it into his mouth. "For all of Sharon's indiscretions, I don't believe she ever slept with a woman. Did she?"

Nina nearly spit out the cracker she'd just eaten, but it was Beth who laughed. "Not that I know of. Do you, Nina?"

Nina stared blankly at Beth. "No. But Jones and I weren't as close as you two. I doubt she would have shared something like that with me."

Josh was studying her, as if trying to tell if she was lying or not. Or worse, maybe he thought that *she* had slept with Jones. Good lord.

"We'll need to recruit one of you to play cards with us. That was a tradition when the four of us got together," Beth said. "We can take turns, of course. I just think in honor of Jones, we should play at least one game."

"Oh, Nina, you should play," Quinn said. "I totally suck at cards."

"We play spades," Beth said. "It's so easy to learn."

Nina slowly turned to Quinn, noting that both of them were trying not to smile. So she sucked at cards? Right. Wasn't it only a few days ago that she'd almost single-handedly beaten Susie and Maggie as Nina was just learning the game?

"No, I don't mind," Quinn said. "I'll go down to the beach and find the kids. I can build a killer sandcastle."

"Really? Well, they would love that," Beth said. "You sure you don't mind if we play a game?"

"Nope. You have fun." Quinn turned to her and winked. "I'll see you in a bit."

Nina touched Quinn's arm as she passed by her. She had a sudden urge to ask her to stay. No, *beg* her to stay. She looked around nervously at the others—Beth, Brad, and Josh. It was Josh who moved first.

"Let's play."

Nina glanced at the door, watching as it closed behind Quinn. With a forced smile, she nodded. "Yes. Let's play."

CHAPTER FIFTY-ONE

Quinn paused about halfway down the long boardwalk across the dunes. She glanced up into the sky, seeing only a few passing clouds. The sun was beating down and she wished she'd worn a tank instead of the T-shirt. She turned toward the townhouse, picturing them inside playing cards. Something had her feeling uneasy. Maybe because she'd left Nina alone with them. Shouldn't matter. She knew neither Brad nor Josh was the killer. Nina should be safe there. With a sigh, she walked on. At the end of the boardwalk, she stepped onto the sand, looking around for a group of kids—five of them—and a nanny. She spotted them at the edge of the packed sand, still damp from high tide.

The kids, ranging in age from maybe five to eight, were digging furiously in the sand, filling buckets and laughing while they did so. Three, she knew, were Beth's kids and two belonged to Josh. The nanny sat in the sand a few feet away, her gaze on the water and not the kids. She walked closer, but none of them paid her any mind.

"Hi," she said, hoping not to startle them. It was the nanny who glanced sharply at her.

"Yes?" the young woman asked hesitantly.

"I'm Quinn." She pointed back toward the townhouse. "My friend Nina and I came to visit Josh and Beth. They've got a card game going so I thought I'd join you."

"Oh." Obvious relief crossed the woman's face and she smiled. "I'm Julie."

She nodded, then pointed to the kids. "Building a sandcastle or just digging."

Julie laughed. "Mostly just digging."

"Well, I can help. I'm pretty good with sandcastles."

One of the kids looked up at her—a boy. "I want to build a sea dragon."

She squatted down to his level. "What's a sea dragon?"

The little boy shrugged. "Something big and ugly."

"Does it blow fire out of its mouth?"

The boy actually rolled his eyes. "Not in the water, silly."

"Okay then. Let's build a sea dragon." Before she could get started though, her cell rang. She ruffled the boy's head. "Be right back."

She walked away before looking at her phone. It was Dee. "Hey. What's up?"

"Got some news, Quinn. Don't know that it'll help us, but I wanted to pass it on."

"That's great." She walked farther away from the kids, back toward the boardwalk. "What did you find?"

"I'll start with what San Antonio PD found. They've got a car on camera that was seen three times driving on the street where McDonald lived. Doesn't belong to any of the neighbors. It's a residential area so not a through street. Couldn't get a plate number, though. Dark-gray Mercedes."

"Doing surveillance maybe?"

"Right. So we went back through the security feeds that we got from Nathan Poole's street. Not a lot. I think four houses had cameras. Anyway, we got a glimpse of a dark-gray Mercedes there too. It was on that Thursday before the killings. No plate."

"What about Scotty Fritz? Hernandez said he saw a dark vehicle drive away."

"Yes, but he couldn't tell make or model. No security cameras there."

"Well, I guess that's something, but without getting a shot of the license plate—"

"Doesn't help us much. But you'll be happy to know that Josh Downey does not own a Mercedes. He drives a rather conservative Lexus and his wife drove a BMW."

She smiled. "So, you're going to strike him off your list finally?"

"I guess. If anything else comes up, I'll let you know. Enjoy the rest of your Sunday."

"Thanks, Dee."

It was news, yes, but did it help them? And a Mercedes? If their killer drove a Mercedes, he wasn't just your average Joe meeting women online. Could this be the man Jones had been having an affair with before she and Brad started theirs?

She tilted her head thoughtfully, still staring along the boardwalk. If he drove a Mercedes, that suggested he was a successful man of some sort. Not normally the type of person to commit multiple murders because of jealousy. She blew out her breath with a bit of frustration. She was about to go back to the beach when a car pulled up near the townhouse, driving slowly. A dark, nearly black car. Was it a Mercedes? She couldn't tell from here. She hurried back to Julie and the kids.

"Listen, I need to run up there real quick. I'll be right back. Please keep the kids here, okay."

Julie had a questioning look on her face, but she nodded. "Okay, sure. I'll attempt the sea dragon without you."

CHAPTER FIFTY-TWO

Nina accepted another margarita from Josh before they started their second game. She and Beth were partners and they had beaten Josh and Brad handily. She wasn't going to gloat, though, because it was obvious that Brad was distracted. Even Beth commented on his lack of concentration.

"When Jones and I partnered up, we rarely beat you guys. I don't know if it's because Nina is so much better or if you're way off today, Brad."

He nearly slammed his cards down. "This is just so weird. We're acting like Jones is just missing or something. Like she might come back."

Nina stiffened, her gaze going to first Josh, then Beth. It was Josh who spoke.

"Should we all stop living because she's gone? Sharon got mixed up with the wrong guy apparently. I know Beth has told you about her affairs. Told you that I was going to file for divorce. I may not have loved her like I once did, but she was the mother of my kids. I miss her for their sake, not necessarily mine."

"I miss her too," Beth said. "She was my best friend. But should we not ever talk about her? Should we act like she never existed?"

Nina stared at Brad Turner, his eyes darting around the room nervously. Good lord, was he about to confess to the affair? She *so* did not want to be there for that. He stood quickly, nearly knocking his chair over. Oh, god...he *was* going to confess. She hung her head down, wondering if she could escape to the bathroom or something.

* * *

Quinn moved along the boardwalk, not seeing the dark car from where she was. She relaxed, wondering if she was jumping at shadows. But as she got closer, she spotted the car parked on the other side of the townhouse.

She stared in disbelief at the dark-gray Mercedes. She pulled out her phone, going purposefully toward her Jeep. Dee answered after three rings.

"Yeah, it's me. Can you run a plate?"

"What is it, Quinn?"

She opened her Jeep and bent down, unlocking the box under her front seat. "You won't believe this, but you know I'm at Josh Downey's townhouse."

"Oh, that's right. You got invited to dinner or something."

"Yeah. I'm outside and a dark-gray Mercedes just pulled up. Can you run the plate?"

"Sure. What is it?"

She squinted, making sure she was reading it correctly. "Bravo-delta-mike-eight-zero-one-nine," she said distinctly.

"Okay, hang on a sec."

She opened the box and took out her weapon and hip holster, quickly attaching it at her waist. The car wasn't a coincidence. She could feel that in her gut.

"Jesus Christ," Dee muttered. "Plates come back to Jonathan Downey."

"The brother." She lifted her eyes up to the townhouse. "Nina's in there," she murmured as she ran toward it.

CHAPTER FIFTY-THREE

Nina turned when the door opened, as did everyone else. She expected Quinn. But it was a man. Josh didn't seem surprised to see him, although Beth had a frown on her face. She could see the resemblance and assumed this was Josh's brother.

"I didn't think you would be coming by," Josh said.

"Yes. I have some things to discuss with you." His tone seemed very clipped, very businesslike. His gaze slid to Brad. "With both of you."

Nina felt her skin crawl at the evil look in his eyes. She barely had the thought registered when he pulled out a gun that had been hidden behind his back. Beth gave a sharp gasp and backed away. Josh's eyes widened.

"Jonathan? What the hell are you doing?"

"What am I doing?" he nearly yelled. "I'll tell you what I'm doing. I'm eliminating all of Sharon's lovers. That's what I'm doing." He turned toward Brad. "You're the last one left, Mr. Turner."

"Oh, dear god," she whispered under her breath. This couldn't be happening.

Beth seemed oblivious to the threat. She turned to Brad. "What in the world is he talking about?"

Brad was nearly hyperventilating. "I...I don't...I don't know what—"

"I *loved* her!"

Josh stepped forward. "Jonathan, what the hell is wrong with you? Put the gun down!"

Jonathan turned the gun on Josh. "She was *mine*! Always mine! Not yours!" He turned the gun back toward Brad. "Then he came along. *He* took her from me."

Beth gasped. "*What?*"

"You didn't know?" Jonathan waved the gun in the air. "He and Sharon had been seeing each other for six months or more. Yes. And she called it off with me. Said she had feelings for *him*."

Beth turned accusing eyes to Brad. "*What? You and Jones?*"

Josh too seemed shocked as he stared at Brad. "Is this true?"

Brad held his hands up. "No! I don't know what he's talking about! I—"

Beth's eyes turned nearly feral. "You bastard! How *could* you?"

Nina grabbed Beth's arm when she would have run toward him. "Don't."

Beth tried to jerk away, but Josh stepped forward. "What the hell are you talking about? Are you saying you and Sharon...and then Brad and Sharon—"

"Yes. We were in love! Then this guy comes along, and she called it off with me!"

Josh held his hands up, his voice nearly soft. "Oh, Jonathan, please say you didn't kill her."

"Of course I killed her!" he yelled. "She had all these...all these men! She now had Brad. She didn't need me anymore! She didn't *want* me anymore! Yes, I killed her! And I killed them!"

Oh my god. Nina could barely take a breath, let alone think clearly. What the hell was happening? She kept a tight grip on Beth's arm. She didn't know if it was to prevent her from pummeling Brad or for her own comfort.

Jonathan swung his gun toward Brad then. His voice was calmer now. "I loved her. None of you could have given her what I could have."

Brad held his hands up defensively. "I loved her too. It wasn't just you. I loved her too."

Beth sobbed beside her, and Nina pulled her closer, praying that Quinn would come back. She wondered if she could pull her phone out of her pocket without him noticing. Could she try to call Quinn? Dare she try?

"You didn't *love* her!" Jonathan shot back. "You just wanted to fuck her! Just like all the others! You didn't care about her! You just wanted to *fuck* her!"

Josh stepped closer again. "Stop it! Put the goddamn gun down!"

"Or what, Josh? You never deserved her."

Jonathan fired, knocking Josh backward. Beth screamed and Nina simply took her to the ground, pulling her with her as she crawled behind the sofa. There were three more shots and she saw Brad's body slam back against the table, knocking off their margaritas and the cards as he crashed against it.

Beth screamed, a loud, pitiful shriek as she stared at Brad. Nina closed her eyes as she squeezed Beth tightly, silently begging for Quinn to come as Jonathan walked toward them. They were the only witnesses. Would he kill them too? She felt her body trembling head to toe, and she forced her eyes open. She nearly whimpered from fear as he pointed his gun at them.

Then the door burst open, and Nina saw Quinn standing there. She looked so powerful, so in control, she could finally take a breath. Everything seemed to happen in slow motion.

Jonathan swung his gun around, firing twice at Quinn. Quinn fell to the ground and rolled. She came up shooting. Two, three, four shots and Jonathan stumbled backward, his gun falling to the floor as he landed against the large bay windows overlooking the Gulf. He slumped down to the floor and was still, leaving a blood smear against the glass.

"Nina?" Quinn yelled urgently.

"I'm okay," she managed.

Quinn pulled her up, holding her in a tight hug. "You're okay? You sure?"

"Yeah." Nina clung to her. "I was fucking scared, I don't mind saying." She attempted a small smile. "You were right on time, not a second to spare."

Quinn squeezed her tighter, then pushed her away. "Take care of Beth," she said quietly.

Nina nodded, watching as Quinn went first to Brad, then to Josh. She was shocked to hear Quinn talking. She pulled Beth up, trying to shield her from Brad's body.

"Let's go outside," she suggested, but Beth resisted.

"No," she said in a strangled voice.

Beth moved beside Brad's body, taking only a cursory glance at him. Then she went to where Quinn was. Nina followed. Quinn was on her phone, requesting an ambulance. She stared at Josh, surprised to find his eyes open.

Beth knelt down beside him, touching his face.

"I'm okay," he said hoarsely. "What about the kids?"

"They were still out on the beach," Quinn said. She got up and hurried to the kitchen, coming back with a towel. She pressed it to his shoulder to try to stop the bleeding. "Julie was going to build a sea dragon."

Josh smiled. "Hayden's request, no doubt."

Nina stood by helplessly, her gaze going between them and Jonathan, who lay in a bloody heap, and then to Brad, who was sprawled beside the table. She noted absently that some of the cards had sprayed down on top of him. Fittingly, the ace of spades was lying on his chest. She turned away from it.

When she looked back, Quinn was staring at her, her eyes compassionate.

"You okay?"

Nina swallowed and nodded. Was she okay? She didn't really know. Beth was still kneeling beside Josh, but she saw her glance toward Brad, her husband. She was obviously in shock.

Her eyes were nearly blank, as if she wasn't really there. And maybe she wasn't.

Nina then heard sirens approaching, and that sound alone made it all real. She took a shaky breath, then turned, stumbling out the door. She needed some air. She needed some sunshine and blue skies.

And god, she needed Quinn.

CHAPTER FIFTY-FOUR

Quinn leaned against the deck railing, doing something she hadn't done in two years—drinking bourbon straight, two ice cubes, no Coke. It was as smooth as she remembered, yet it was different. It didn't have the same hold on her. She didn't need it like she once thought she did. Perhaps it was only habit that she poured it now.

Willie was leaning against her leg, and she reached down to touch her head. It was dark over the Gulf, but the sound of the surf had a calming effect on her. She turned and glanced inside the house. The lights were out, and she knew Nina was asleep.

It had been a long, hectic afternoon, maybe more so for Nina. Dee had come, wanting a statement from both Nina and Beth. Beth had been too shook up to say much of anything coherent. Nina had seemed calm as she'd recounted all that Jonathan Downey had said to them. Nina seemed calm, yes, but she could see the slight twitch of her fingers as the spoke. She could see the anguish in her eyes as the disbelief of what had happened still lingered.

Thank god Julie was there to take care of the kids because Beth was in no shape to. Julie had taken Josh's car back to his house with all five kids. All five of them were crying, though she wasn't sure how much they'd been told. After Dee had finished with Beth, she had had Officer Ramos take Beth to the hospital in Corpus to be with Josh, as that was what she'd wanted. Beth had still been in a dreamlike state, still in shock no doubt.

And even though Nina had wanted to stay, she had given Nina the key to her Jeep and sent her here. She had been another three hours at the scene, going over everything with Dee to make sure they could close their cases.

Quinn blew out her breath. Since she had been the one to shoot and kill Jonathan Downey, Sergeant Fields had come down to take her statement. Even though theirs wasn't a large department, her actions still were going to warrant a visit or two with a shrink.

She wasn't sure how she was feeling, really. She had never shot another person before, let alone kill them. She thought she should feel something—remorse, regret. Something. Yet all she seemed to see was young Scotty Fritz's face as the blood drained from him despite her best efforts to stop it. Anger was what she was feeling, not remorse. And she supposed it would be a good thing to speak to a professional about it.

She swirled the last of the bourbon in her glass, hearing the ice clank the sides. She drank it down, and then, with one more look toward the Gulf, she went into the house.

Nina had already been in bed when she'd gotten home. There were streaks of tears on her cheeks and her eyes were puffy from crying. She had clung to her tightly, more tears falling as she'd held her. Quinn didn't know what to say to her, so she said nothing. After a few minutes, Nina lay down again.

"Have you heard from anyone? How is Josh?"

Quinn shook her head. "No."

"I should call Beth. She probably needs—"

"In the morning, Nina. I would guess that she's going to stay at the hospital with Josh tonight."

Nina had accepted that and had squeezed her hand. "Okay. In the morning."

"Yeah. We'll go see them."

She moved quietly through the house now, Willie at her heels. She paused before opening her bedroom door. The case was over. Sharon Jones Downey's murder was solved. And six men had died in the process. Josh was damn lucky to be alive. She wondered if Jonathan had intentionally spared him, them being brothers and all. But from how Nina had described the scene, Jonathan had simply been eaten up with jealousy, and consequences be damned.

That consequence, of course, was his own death. At her hands.

She took a deep breath, then let it out slowly, finally opening the door to her bedroom. The lamp was still on, but Nina was asleep, curled on her side and clutching Quinn's pillow to her. She smiled as she watched her, feeling a sense of contentment at the sight.

Amazing how Jones's death had brought them together. After Christie, she hadn't thought she'd ever want to settle down with someone again. She was satisfied with her life as it was. But now? Now she knew how empty it had been. Nina brightened her world somehow, chasing out the darkness that she hadn't realized was still there.

Nina now would need her to chase the darkness away.

And she would.

CHAPTER FIFTY-FIVE

Nina watched as Quinn and Josh set off on a beach walk, Willie walking along with them. It was an unusually pleasant day for late August with temperatures only in the low nineties. She heard the door open, and she turned, seeing Beth come out with two margarita glasses.

"Try this. It's perfect."

Beth had changed a lot in the last two months, and Nina knew she played a huge role in that. It was at her insistence that Beth had seen a therapist, first in Houston and now here. She hadn't been surprised that Beth had wanted to sell her home—she wanted absolutely no reminders of Brad, she'd said. She was surprised, however, when Beth announced that she and the kids were moving in with Josh.

She took a sip of the margarita and nodded. "Yes. Very good."

Beth joined her against the railing, her gaze on the water. "It's so relaxing here."

"Yes, it is."

Beth smiled at her. "When are you moving in?"

Nina laughed. "I own a house. What would I do with it?"

"Sell it. You're here most of the time anyway."

"True. But we haven't talked about it. We're taking things slow."

"Whatever for?"

She sighed. "I'm not sure, really. I think we're both afraid it's too good to be true."

"Are you in love with her?"

"Yes," she said without hesitation.

"Have you told her?"

"No," she said also without hesitation. "And neither has she."

"Ah. Afraid to be the first one to say it." Beth nodded. "I get it."

Nina smiled at her. "You and Josh?"

Beth blushed. "We had sex." Then she laughed. "I was terrified. I mean, after Jones, I'm...well, I'm *so* not Jones. I thought he'd be disappointed."

"But?" she prompted.

"But it was wonderful and everything I had imagined it would be and he was so sweet and so very different than...than Brad." She held her hand up. "I don't want to talk about him. I do enough of that with Dr. Hancher."

"You look really good, Beth. I'm so glad you're seeing her."

"I feel good. Actually, I feel better about myself now than I ever have. When we were kids, I was always in Jones's shadow. I was always second. I got married young, had kids, didn't have a job. I was a drab old housewife at twenty-five. That's how I thought of myself. That's how Brad treated me. That's who I was in my mind. And then we'd get together with Josh and Jones three or four times a year, and there I was, in her shadow again. The differences between us were glaring, but she was still my best friend."

"Why, Beth? Why was she still your best friend?"

Beth shrugged. "It just carried over from childhood, I guess. We had nothing in common anymore. And I think back now, and all our visits were nothing more than reminiscing about the past."

Nina nodded. "Yes. That's what our girls' weekends had evolved into too. We never shared much about our current lives. We had two or three days together and we talked about the past and we slipped into those same roles."

"I know," Beth said. "And Dr. Hancher said that we were afraid to talk about our current lives because it would reinforce how much we had all grown apart. We were afraid to let go of the past for fear—"

"Yes! Exactly," Nina said. "I told Quinn that we had all changed so much since we were kids that there was nothing binding us anymore. Nothing except our past. Our childhood."

"Yes."

"It feels good to say that out loud. If any of us met as adults—"

"We wouldn't be friends," Beth finished.

Nina put an arm around Beth's shoulders. "We can start again, Beth. You and me. It doesn't all have to be about the past. It doesn't have to be about Jones."

"Thank you, Nina. I'd like that."

They both leaned on the railing, facing the Gulf, holding their glasses out. A brown pelican flew by, and Nina watched its progress until it was out of sight.

"How much do you know about Jones?"

Nina turned to her. "What do you mean?"

"About her affairs. About these men."

Nina blew out her breath. "More than I want to know."

"I always had her up on this pedestal. I had no idea how troubled she must have been. Emotionally. What do you think caused it? Why would she want to have all these affairs?"

"I guess it goes back to her childhood. She felt inferior. So, sleeping with the senior class was her way of convincing herself that she wasn't."

Beth gave a quick laugh. "I bet Jones slept with every single guy in high school at one time or another." She touched Nina's arm. "Josh knows nothing about all that. Actually, we don't talk about Jones anymore. Or Brad. We did at first, of course. Cleared the air."

"That's good. You're getting to know each other on your own terms. No need to bring them into it."

"No. But we can't totally ignore them. The kids, you know."

"How are they getting on?"

"Moving them here was the best thing. And they're all going to grief counseling, so that's been helpful. They're all so close in age, we're going to homeschool them this year."

"Really?"

"Yes. I think my kids especially need that. They've had a big change in their lives not only with Brad but the move too." Beth smiled. "I always wanted to be a teacher. That was my major in college, but then I met Brad and...well, I got married instead."

"I think you'll do great."

Beth downed her drink. "Enough of that. Let's get a refill and go down to the beach and find them."

Nina nodded, then let her gaze travel along the sand, wondering how far Quinn and Josh had gone. She saw Willie before she saw them. They were a good way down, seemingly having a serious discussion.

CHAPTER FIFTY-SIX

"I need to thank you for not arresting me way back at the beginning of this. I know you thought I did it."

Quinn shook her head. "I *never* thought you did it. Well, not after we got your security feed, and I checked your phone records. I mean, you were the obvious choice. Jealous husband." She shook her head again. "But no, I never really thought you did it."

"That other detective—"

"Dee Woodard."

"Right. She grilled me. She was like a bulldog."

"Yeah. She was convinced you were the killer."

They walked on in silence for a while, then Josh stopped. "I never suspected that Sharon and Jonathan were having an affair. It never once even crossed my mind. I mean, there were no signs at all."

"Maybe you weren't looking for them."

"Maybe not."

They walked on again.

"Are you selling the townhouse?" she asked after a while.

"Oh, yeah. It's already on the market. It was owned by Jonathan, not the firm. But he wasn't married and had no kids. I was his only beneficiary." Josh shoved his hands in the pockets of his shorts and stopped walking. "Going to sell everything. Jonathan's house in Corpus. My house." He met her gaze. "Going to start over."

"With Beth?"

He smiled. "It's crazy, isn't it? Beth and I just bonded over this whole ordeal. I realize that what I had with Sharon was... she was a beautiful, striking woman. And that was what I was attracted to. Not *her*. Not what was underneath all of that. Beth is the complete opposite. What you see is what you get. She's steady. She's true. She's honest. After what I had, it's so refreshing."

"Good. I'm happy for you."

Josh stared at her, his head tilted thoughtfully. "Do you think Sharon had affairs all along?"

"Oh, hell, I'm not the one to ask that." Quinn shrugged. "But I don't know. From what everything Nina has told me about high school and college..." She shrugged again. "Well, not my place to say."

"Yeah, I don't know anything about that. She never talked about her home life. Never talked about her parents. When we met, it was like she had no past. Like there was nothing for her to share." He smiled. "I should have known something was up then."

"Does it matter now?"

He sighed. "I don't suppose it does." He looked at the surf for a moment, then back at her. "It's been a traumatic summer, to say the least. It seems like it's dragged on, yet it's all a big blur sometimes. The kids have adjusted better than I thought, and I think it's because, for the last eight months or so, Sharon wasn't really with us. I told you that when we talked. She stopped interacting with us. Like she just checked out. Having Beth and her kids here helps too."

"It's none of my business, but did you ever suspect she and Brad were having an affair?"

Josh laughed. "No. Never. Brad was too normal. Too simple." Then his smile faded. "Of course, I don't guess I even knew her anymore. Maybe he was her type."

"Do you and Beth talk about it?"

"No. Not anymore. When everything came to light, we talked about it. And we cried. And we got pissed. But neither of us want that to be the reason we're trying to make a new life together. We don't want them in it."

"Understandable."

"I hope Nina will be Beth's friend. She doesn't know anyone else in Corpus."

Quinn nodded. "I'm sure she will."

He met her gaze and smiled. "I'd like us all to be friends. We kinda invited ourselves out today and—"

"I'm glad Beth called. So is Nina."

"How is she? I know it must have been as terrifying to her as anyone that day."

"Yes. But she's good. We've talked through it." She didn't tell him that Nina sometimes woke during the night from a bad dream, sometimes crying out, sometimes clutching Quinn in a near-death grip.

She glanced at her watch. "We should head back. I'll get those steaks on the grill."

He nodded. "Thanks, Quinn. For the talk."

"Sure." She gave a quick whistle, Willie came running back to her, and they made their way back to her house. She smiled when she saw Nina and Beth walking toward them. Willie saw them too as her tail started wagging. "Okay, girl. Go get Nina."

She met Nina's eyes across the sand. Something about the way she was looking at her made her breath catch. Then Willie ran back toward her, breaking the spell.

"There you are," Beth said as they got closer. She held up her glass. "The margaritas are great. We've started without you."

Nina smiled at her and offered her glass. "Want to share?"

"I'll just have a sip."

The four of them and Willie walked back. Beth was chatting, but Quinn wasn't listening to her. Her eyes were on Nina instead.

CHAPTER FIFTY-SEVEN

Nina snuggled closer to Quinn, her eyes still closed. She felt Quinn's lips nuzzling her neck and she sighed. The murmured words she spoke were out before she could stop them.

"I love you."

Quinn paused, and Nina swore she heard a sharp intake of breath. She closed her eyes tighter, wondering how she could have let the words slip out. She'd been so careful. But Quinn's lovemaking tonight had been so slow, so sure, so deliberate that she was in such a relaxed and dreamy state, she couldn't keep them in any longer.

"God, Nina," Quinn whispered.

She was about to say she was sorry, but she didn't. Instead, she opened her eyes, finding Quinn watching her.

"I love you too." The look in Quinn's eyes, the misting of tears she saw, made her own eyes dampen. They said nothing else. Quinn kissed her then, a kiss meant to convey all that she was feeling. Nina pulled her closer, holding her tightly. They stayed like that for long, quiet moments…just being close.

"I've been afraid to tell you," Nina admitted.

"Me too."

She pulled away a little, again looking into Quinn's eyes. "Is it too soon?"

Quinn smiled. "Does love have a timeline?"

Nina rolled onto her back. "I'm blissfully happy." Then she smiled. "I don't think I've ever said that before—blissfully happy."

Quinn came up beside her, their shoulders touching as she lay back too. "Can I steal it? I feel blissfully happy too."

Nina turned her head to look at her. "It's scary to think that, if not for Jones, we wouldn't have met."

"No? Maybe we would have met on the beach."

Nina shook her head. "I don't think so. I'd seen you before, you and Willie, but I never would have gone up to talk to you." She reached out to touch Quinn's cheek. "Jones was always trying to set me up with someone. This time included. The blue-haired girl at the reception desk."

"Not your type."

She smiled. "Not at all." She rolled closer and kissed her. "*You* are my type."

"Yeah?"

"Yes. You did save me and all, you know." It was something they'd not talked about—Quinn saving her. Not really. "He had his gun pointed at us. Me and Beth. If you—" She swallowed. "If you had been just a few seconds later, well…"

"But I wasn't. If I'd been a little quicker, maybe Josh wouldn't have gotten shot. Maybe Brad would still be alive."

Nina's eyes widened. "Oh my god, you're feeling guilty? Oh, Quinn, no." She sat up. "Don't. You're my hero. You saved my life."

Quinn's expression changed. "Is that why you think you love me?"

Yes, she saw the doubt now in Quinn's eyes. So maybe it had been too soon to say the words. Quinn's vulnerability was showing—a product of her past. Deep down, she didn't think she was worthy of receiving love like this. Her penance for the sins of her younger years.

"I started feeling things for you long before we even kissed. It was that first night, when we were in the rocking chairs in the dark, not speaking. Just rocking quietly together. I felt so at peace being with you. I felt safe." Nina leaned closer and kissed her softly. "So no, you saving my life has nothing to do with me falling in love with you." She stared into Quinn's eyes. "But it's a nice added bonus."

Quinn finally relaxed and smiled. Nina could see the relief in her eyes as she spoke.

"I've only ever told one woman that I loved her—Christie." Quinn held her gaze. "But I didn't mean it. I never really felt it. I didn't know what love felt like. What it was supposed to feel like. I just knew it wasn't her."

"But you know now?" Nina asked gently.

"I think so. Do you believe me?"

"That you're in love with me? Yes. I've known it for weeks now, Quinn. The way you make love to me, the way you look at me. Yes. We can hide things with words sometimes, but you can't hide your eyes."

"Windows to the soul and all that stuff, huh?"

Nina smiled. "Yes."

Quinn took her hand, then squeezed it tightly. "I *do* love you, Nina. I feel it deep inside when I look at you, when you look at me. I feel like the luckiest person alive."

"Me, too."

Quinn seemed to exhale, and she closed her eyes. When she opened them, there was no uncertainty there at all. In fact, she completely changed the subject.

"Dee invited us for steaks on Saturday. Well, it's at Finn's place. Finn and Rylee. She said we'd love them."

Nina nodded. "Okay. I'll look forward to meeting them."

"And then Susie invited us over for dinner again. She wants a rematch in cards."

Nina laughed. "Really? After we beat their ass so bad the last time?"

"I know."

"I would love to. Susie and I get along great."

"You like my family, right?"

"I love your family."

"Good." She grinned. "I kinda promised them a party here at the beach for Labor Day."

"Oh, yeah?"

"Yeah. All of them. And the kids."

"I'm game."

"Willie will want to hide in our bedroom."

Nina smiled at her. *Our bedroom.* Yes, it had become theirs, hadn't it. Oh, they stayed at her house sometimes, but it wasn't the same. This felt like home now. She met Quinn's eyes, and she seemed to know the direction of her thoughts.

"Is it too soon?"

Nina smiled again. "For?"

"To talk about living together."

"We kinda already are."

Quinn nodded. "Yeah. Kinda. But I thought maybe we could make it official."

Nina looked into the crystal-blue eyes that she knew so well now. Love was looking back at her. She moved closer and kissed her.

"Okay."

Quinn smiled. "That's it?"

Nina laughed. "What? Should we have a big discussion about it? I've already stolen two of your drawers. I keep clothes here. It feels more like home to me than my place. So, if you want to make it official, I'll put my house up for sale." She kissed her again. "Okay?"

"We could do like Josh and Beth and sell both houses and get something new. Something that is ours."

"Jones is not haunting this house like I'm sure she was at Josh's. They needed something new. We don't, Quinn. The only hold Jones has over us is that she brought us together. And I'm so thankful I found you."

"Well, I'm still gonna think that we would have run into each other on the beach one day. I'm not going to give Jones all the credit."

Nina smiled and snuggled closer to her. "Now, I must get some sleep. I haven't beaten Lisa to the office in weeks. I'm shooting for tomorrow."

Quinn reached over and turned the lamp off. "And my shift starts at daybreak. I'm so glad to be back on beach patrol."

Nina closed her eyes. "You're not allowed to watch pretty girls in bikinis any longer. You'll have to make do with me."

"Why would I look at them when I've got the most beautiful woman in the world right here?"

Nina smiled. "Thank you."

"I love you."

Her eyes opened for a moment, then closed again contentedly. "I love you."

Bella Books, Inc.
Happy Endings Live Here
P.O. Box 10543
Tallahassee, FL 32302
Phone: (850) 576-2370
www.BellaBooks.com

More Titles from Bella Books

Hunter's Revenge – Gerri Hill
978-1-64247-447-3 | 276 pgs | paperback: $18.95 | eBook: $9.99
Tori Hunter is back! Don't miss this final chapter in the acclaimed Tori Hunter series.

Integrity – E. J. Noyes
978-1-64247-465-7 | 228 pgs | paperback: $19.95 | eBook: $9.99
It was supposed to be an ordinary workday...

The Order – TJ O'Shea
978-1-64247-378-0 | 396 pgs | paperback: $19.95 | eBook: $9.99
For two women the battle between new love and old loyalty may prove more dangerous than the war they're trying to survive.

Under the Stars with You – Jaime Clevenger
978-1-64247-439-8 | 302 pgs | paperback: $19.95 | eBook: $9.99
Sometimes believing in love is the first step. And sometimes it's all about trusting the stars.

The Missing Piece – Kat Jackson
978-1-64247-445-9 | 250 pgs | paperback: $18.95 | eBook: $9.99
Renee's world collides with possibility and the past, setting off a tidal wave of changes she could have never predicted.

An Acquired Taste – Cheri Ritz
978-1-64247-462-6 | 206 pgs | paperback: $17.95 | eBook: $9.99
Can Elle and Ashley stand the heat in the *Celebrity Cook Off* kitchen?

Printed in the USA
CPSIA information can be obtained
at www.ICGtesting.com
JSHW021011170824
68256JS00002B/3